IN SUNLIGHT
OR IN SHADOW

Cape Cod Morning

IN SUNLIGHT OR IN SHADOW

STORIES INSPIRED BY THE PAINTINGS OF
EDWARD HOPPER

EDITED BY
LAWRENCE BLOCK

PEGASUS BOOKS
NEW YORK LONDON

IN SUNLIGHT OR IN SHADOW

Pegasus Books Ltd.
148 W 37th Street, 13th Floor
New York, NY 10018

First Pegasus Books cloth edition December 2016

Interior design by Maria Fernandez

Frontispiece: *Cape Cod Morning*, 1950. Oil on canvas;
34 ⅛ × 40 ¼ in. (86.7 x 102.3 cm)
Gift of the Sara Roby Foundation, Smithsonian American Art Museum.
Credit: Smithsonian American Art Museum, Washington, DC/Art Resource, NY

Library of Congress Cataloging-in-Publication Data is available.

ISBN: 978-1-68177-245-5

10 9 8 7 6 5 4 3 2 1

Printed in the United States of America
Distributed by W. W. Norton & Company

CONTENTS

FOREWORD
BEFORE WE BEGIN . . .

E dward Hopper was born in Upper Nyack, New York, on July 22, 1882, and died in his studio near Washington Square in New York City on May 15, 1967. The life that filled those years is an interesting one, but it's not up to me to recount it here; for that I'd steer you to *Edward Hopper: An Intimate Biography*, by Gail Levin.

(Gail, who also edited Hopper's catalogue *raisonné*, is one of our contributors. Her offering, *The Preacher Collects*, renders as fiction an extraordinary little-known episode toward the end of the artist's life, of which she has firsthand knowledge.)

But I digress, and probably not for the last time. Let me say a little about how the idea for this volume came about, and why such an illustrious list of contributors signed on for it.

Over the years I've written a lot about writing, and about the generation of ideas, so you'd think I'd be able to tell you the source of this particular idea. But I can't. It was just there, premise and title and all, and without overthinking it I put together an A-list of the writers I'd most like to invite to the party.

Almost all of them said they'd love to come.

Not out of friendship (although they're all friends of mine). Not for lack of other things to do, or because they hungered for the pittance I was able to offer. The attraction was Edward Hopper. They all loved and responded to his work, and in a very writerly way.

A strong positive response to Hopper's paintings is by no means uncommon, in America and throughout the world. But I've come to believe that it's singularly strong among readers and writers, that Hopper's work resonates profoundly with those of us who care deeply for stories. Whether we delight in being told them or in telling them ourselves, we tend to be Edward Hopper fans.

And it's not because of the stories his paintings tell.

Hopper was dismayed on those occasions when his work was dismissed as illustration. No less so than any Abstract Expressionist, his concern was with shape and color and light, not with meaning or narrative.

Hopper was neither an illustrator nor a narrative painter. His paintings don't tell stories. What they do is suggest—powerfully, irresistibly—that there are stories within them, waiting to be told. He shows us a moment in time, arrayed on a canvas; there's clearly a past and a future, but it's our task to find it for ourselves.

Our contributors have done just that, and I'm gobsmacked by what they've provided. Thematic anthologies tend to generate stories that have rather too much in common with one another, and it's often advisable to dip into them from time to time rather than read one story after another.

But that's not the case here. These stories are in various genres, or no genre at all. Some of them spring directly from the canvas, making a story to fit the chosen painting. Others rebound at an oblique angle from the canvas, relating the story it somehow triggered. As far as I can make out, these stories have only two common denominators—their individual excellence and their source in Edward Hopper.

I think you'll enjoy them. And, while you're at it, you'll get to look at some pretty pictures.

Including "Cape Cod Morning," our frontispiece painting, for which you'll note there is no corresponding story. And thereby hangs—or doesn't hang—a tale.

"Cape Cod Morning" was the selection of a prominent writer and Hopper enthusiast who accepted an invitation to the anthology and subsequently found himself unable to deliver a story. These things happen, and no blame attaches when they do.

But it left us with a painting. We'd already chased down the requisite permission for "Cape Cod Morning," and had tucked the high-res jpeg in the folder of Our Man at Pegasus—who pointed out, helpfully enough, that it seemed to be unaccompanied by a story.

I recounted the circumstances of our having it in hand. "Fine," said Our Man. "It's a beautiful painting, and we can use it as a frontispiece."

"Ah," I said. "But there's no story to go with it."

"So? Let them write their own."

And so, Gentle Reader, we've provided you with an eighteenth painting, and isn't it a compelling one? Have a look at it, take it in. There's a story in it, don't you think? A story just waiting to be told . . .

Feel free to tell it. But, um, don't tell it to me. I'm outta here.

But not without jotting down a few words of thanks. To Edward Hopper, of course, and to the book's contributors; without his paintings and their stories, all we'd have is some blank pages and a title.

To Shannah Ehrhart Clarke, who chased down and secured the artwork and the requisite permission to use it, and who performed this thankless task efficiently, resourcefully, and with unquenchable good humor.

To Danny Baror, my agent and friend, whose faith in and enthusiasm for this project never wavered.

To Claiborne Hancock of Pegasus Books, who was quick to see the book's potential, and who—with Iris Blasi and Maria Fernandez—has been its passionate supporter throughout.

And, finally, to my wife, Lynne, who has been *my* passionate supporter for thirty-some years, and who knows just when to say, "You know, you've been at that computer forever. You must be exhausted. Why don't you walk over to the Whitney and look at some pictures?"

—Lawrence Block

MEGAN ABBOTT *is the Edgar award-winning author of eight novels,* *including* Dare Me, The Fever *and her latest,* You Will Know Me. *Her* *stories have appeared in collections including* Detroit Noir, Best American Mystery Stories of 2015, *and* Mississippi Noir. *She is also the author of* The Street Was Mine, *a study of hardboiled fiction and film noir. She lives in* *Queens, NY.*

The Girlie Show, 1941

GIRLIE SHOW

BY MEGAN ABBOTT

S he went udders out."

"No pasties even?"

"Like a pair of traffic lights."

Pauline hears them on the porch. Bud is telling her husband about a trip to New York City a few years ago. Going to the Casino de Paree.

Her husband says almost nothing, smoking cigarette after cigarette and making sure Bud always has a Blatz in hand from the metal cooler beside him.

"Nipples like strawberries," Bud is saying. "But she never took off her g-string. And she never spread her legs."

"That right?"

"Maybe you've seen things I ain't."

"Can't say I know what you mean," her husband says, flicking a match onto the lawn.

"Uh-huh."

After, her husband comes inside, cheeks like dark flames.

The next day, she finds him in the kitchen, working, feet on the table.

It's the first time he's taken his sketch pad out in four months. Lately, he's started giving Pauline black looks when she came home from work at the ad agency, especially the time she wore the new beaver hat the man from Schmitt's Fine Furs had given her for all her hard work.

But now, he is sketching frantically, and she doesn't say a word or stand too close. They've been married fourteen years and she knows all his frets and stops, wood warps and sweet spots.

"But it's so cold," she says. It's been so long since he's asked her she almost thinks it might be some kind of joke.

He needs a model.

"Stand by the stove," he says, rolling his shirtsleeves above his elbows. That angry vein in his forearm.

She moves over to the cookstove, its frill of heat.

The memory comes back to her, nearly fifteen years before. The coldest January she'd known. Cuddling up to the potbelly stove at the train station, she felt something pressing against her back. Turning, she saw a man behind her, hands deep in his coat pockets, red-cheeked.

She could smell Sen-Sen on his breath and the Macassar oil he used in his hair.

She was startled, but he was so handsome and she was twenty-seven, the only girl from her town without a husband.

They were married three months later.

My masher, she used to call him, affectionately, a very long time ago.

Sketch pad on his knees, he waits as Pauline pulls loose her housedress, unrolls her stockings.

The last is her underdrawers, which shiver to her feet.

"You'll see all the things I don't want you to see," she whispers, throatily. She doesn't know where this voice comes from.

Wifely duties, married intimacies have never been easy for her. Everything came as a great shock on her wedding night, even though she'd read

4

Ideal Marriage: Physiology and Technique, the book given to her by her maid of honor, who'd already been married eighteen months and, as she whispered over creamed coffee at the luncheonette, was now as "looser than a wagon tire" down there.

Pauline hadn't gotten as far in the book as she should have, or her Latin wasn't good enough, because it turned out the thing her new husband liked to do most was more than two hundred pages in, and the movements required, and the sounds he made, she could not find in the book at all.

The parts she liked were the accidental moments, often things she felt almost by accident while he was moving her, hands on her shoulders so rough she had marks like blue petals, and they recalled certain private moments when the subway train braked suddenly, coming to a long, shuddery stop.

Everything is off now, dress, stockings, slip, brassiere, step-ins, and she is standing on the kitchen stool. She wonders if a very tall man might be able to see her through the pane above the kitchen curtains.

"Turn to your right."

She can feel the gooseflesh rise, the veins behind her knees like tickling spiders now.

She is forty-two and no one has asked her to take off her clothes in a long time. (*How about lunch*, Mr. Schmitt said every time he called now. *I'd love to see that beaver on you.*)

As she turns, she lifts her breasts, which she's always been proud of. No puling babies have ever hung from them and they have never *fallen like a pair of yeast cakes*, as some of the other women she knew confided. Once, Mrs. Bertrand, the head of the switchboard at the office, asked if she could touch Pauline's breasts, *just to remind myself.*

Catching a glimpse of herself in the chrome toaster, she smiles a little, but only to herself.

He makes her take many different poses, her arms high and twined like Marlene Dietrich, her legs apart, a boxer's stance. Hand on hip, like a department store model, and knees bent; hands on hips, like a momma saying *kootchie koo* to a baby in a stroller.

"What is this for?" she finally asks, her back aching, her body tingling head to toe. "Am I dancer or something?"

"You're not anything," he says, coolly. "But the painting will be called the 'Irish Venus.'"

She used to pose for him the first few years they were married, but only for his pay-work. She posed as an aproned housewife (*Romance dies at the sight of dishpan hands!*), a bathing beauty (*Ten more pounds changed my life. A skinny girl hasn't a chance!*), a June bride, a beer hall girl in lederhosen. Eventually, once she started bringing in regular pay at the ad agency, where she drew herself all day (rows and rows of women's shoes, or men's hats, or children's pajamas), he suggested he start hiring girls from the art school, but she resisted.

"Don't be so jealous," he would say.

"It's the only time we spend together," Pauline insisted, gently.

But then one time, she came home late from work, soon after her promotion.

The canvas on his easel was torn in half and he was gone to McCrory's till four. When he finally returned, knocking over the milk bottles on the front step, he did some nasty things under their covers that she was required to be part of. She had to go to a doctor the next day and have some stiches put inside. Pushing through the train turnstile made her cry in pain.

He swore he didn't remember any of it, but the following week, he hired a girl from the art school. She had buck teeth, but he said it worked out because she always kept her mouth shut.

That night, he sketches her until nearly two.

When she comes out of the bathroom after washing her teeth, she sees him asleep on the bed, his shoes still on. Most nights, he sleeps on the sunporch.

She unlaces his shoes and removes them quietly, along with his socks.

At some point in the night, he must have taken off his trousers because just before the pink of dawn she feels his bare leg against her back.

"Honey," she whispers.

He moves closer to her in the bed, the mattress springs making embarrassing sounds. She turns slowly so she is facing him, but he turns away. She can feel it, even though her eyes are closed.

The next night, he asks her to do it again. He's ready to move onto paint. He has everything ready by the time she gets home, paints mixed and a newly stretched canvas on the easel.

Her legs still ache from the night before, and from working all day, but she feels some excitement in her chest, like a pair of gypsy moths dancing.

She warms coffee on the stove and slides the stool back into place, under the fly-specked tungsten lamp hanging from the ceiling.

He sketches her for hours that night, her body aching, feet numb in her work heels, the smell of turpentine and linseed oil so strong in the air.

He is so caught up, a furrow from his browline to chin.

He has caught fire.

"Can you just move that way?" he says, paint-streaked thumb jabbing.

It is even colder tonight, the sixth night in a row since he began painting. She's burned her hip once and her thigh twice on the cookstove as she swiveled, teetering on her heels, the stool squeaking.

The first time, her fingers fly to her mouth like a little girl in a cartoon, or one of those women on the calendars that hang at Al's Garage, the ones whose skirts are always flying up, flashing garters like black arrows.

He looks at her from over the top of the easel but doesn't say anything.

Late, late, her body aching, he suggests they end the session with a glass of Old Schenley's. Pauline isn't much of a drinker, but she thinks it might help with the pain.

He takes her feet and puts them on his lap. At first she doesn't know what he's doing, but then he reaches for an ice cube and rests it on her thigh, the two angry burns like open mouths.

Even later, in bed that night, she feels something. His fingers touching the grooves of the burn, fingers cold from the icy pitcher on the bedside table. And then the fingers trace circles that go wider and wider toward her inner thigh, to the center of things. She feels her lips part, a breath. The fingers move closer and closer, so slow.

In that moment, a picture flashes through her head, out of nowhere and it makes no sense: a sloe-eyed woman the next lane over at the bowling alley years ago, arm outstretched to hand Pauline a bright red ball, the woman's long fingers dipping into its holes. *I warmed it up for you.*

The next day, she leaves work early, a sneaking smile on her face. *Won't he be happy,* she thinks. *We can start early. We can work all evening.*

When she walks into the kitchen, just after four, she finds a box on the dropleaf table. Her smile grows wider as she lifts the cardboard top and parts the tissue inside. It is a pair of green slippers with tiny gold heels. Pressing one up to her face, it almost feels like satin, though she knows it can't be. The card inside describes the color as *absinthe.*

They are two sizes too small, but she won't say a word.

"You," she says, when he comes home, kissing his cheek, "you." She has made him his favorite beef stew with plenty of Worcestershire.

He gives her a strange look, so she points down to her feet, tapping her heels together like Dorothy.

There's a catch of surprise on his face. Maybe he'd wanted to spring them on her after she took her clothes off, she thinks, blushing to herself.

He wants to stop early that night. He keeps looking at her in the slippers. Eventually, he asks her to put her work shoes back on.

"The arch is better," he says. "That's what I'm saying."

He tries for a while, but it's not working.

He says the red is wrong. That he has to mix again, or go to the store tomorrow, or could she bring home a vermillion from work.

Then, he pulls on his flannel jacket and says he's ducking out with the boys to "talk business," which means shooting craps behind the butcher shop.

Before he leaves, he covers the canvas with the same old shabby muslin he always uses. She's never been allowed to look, not until it's done.

But his sketchbook is right there on the kitchen table. There's nothing covering it and she's never heard any rules about that. So she lifts its cover and takes a peek at the first sketch, a blaze of color from the special Dixon pencils he made her steal from the office.

It's a woman on a dark stage, spotlight illuminating her. In the band pit beneath, a cadaverous drummer sits, facing away. Facing toward her are the charcoaled heads of several men in the front row, heads tilted up hungrily, like baby birds.

She is nude, save the narrowest, flimsiest blue fabric, far too narrow to be called panty briefs.

She is nude, and parading her nudity, nut-brown bob shimmering, a cream-pink body, breasts fulsome and high, arms lifted, almost like a bird, wings spread, a long blue fabric swinging behind her. The legs and feet aren't done yet, but she can see the charcoal lines, the legs curved, strong, a faint skein of stretched skin along the left hip.

Head tilted, the face has an expression Pauline recognizes but cannot name.

"My, but that's something," she whispers to herself. "I look like a queen or something."

She's not a fool. She knows this must all be about Bud's story, the dancer he saw with nipples like strawberries. Maybe she should be bothered by it, like her mother might have, or the Bible punchers back home. At one time, it might have made her sad. But it doesn't now.

It makes her start thinking of things she hasn't thought of in a long time. Like when she was a seven or eight, looking for her father's shoeshine brush in his chifforobe. On tiptoes, she reached inside the top drawer and felt the cool gloss of a photograph. Yanking the drawer further, it fluttered to the floor, a tinted image of a young woman wrapped around a long-necked swan, nude except for long curling red hair that reached her perfect white toes. It was the first time she'd ever seen a dirty picture and the first time she found out about certain things on a woman's body, a grown woman. That flame of red between her legs.

Her mother found her looking at it and whipped her with boar bristle brush for what seemed like the longest time.

She hasn't thought about that picture in a long time, had put it in a chifforobe in the back of her head, and shut the drawer.

The following day, on her lunch hour, she stops at the department store with the sumptuous window displays. Mostly, she buys her things at the Woolworth's, with its corn cures and girdle supporter displays. But sometimes, especially at the holidays, she peeks in here to look at the sumptuous glass cases, especially the cosmetics department where the walls are pink damask and they sell perfumes in colored bottles and powder puffs like snowballs.

As she walks through the aisles, the cases like shimmering jewel boxes, she thinks of the woman in her husband's sketch, the proud lift of her jaw, those legs like calla lilies though a thousand times as strong.

The salesgirl behind the counter beckons her, holding the tiniest rose-colored bottle in her palm.

"It makes time disappear," she says, rubbing it into Pauline's hands, making stroking circles until her hands feel like warm silk, like she imagined the soft inside of a fur muff might feel.

Moments later, in the fourth-floor ladies room, behind one of the wooden stall doors, Pauline wriggles and squirms until she can slide her dress down a bit.

Slowly, she dabs the lotion over her collar bone, chest, her breasts—running her hand beneath them, dotting her nipples. The smell is suddenly too much, making her dizzy. She has to sit down and count to one hundred before she goes back to work.

Late, very late, the sky black as pitch out the kitchen window, he stops working for a moment and looks at her over the top of the canvas.

"How would you do it?" he asks, abruptly.

She lets her arms fall, resting them. "Do what?"

"If men were to see you like that," he says, his voice tightening suddenly, like a screw. "Would you really stand like that? Would you really show them? Like that?"

She knows these are not questions, and she knows better not to answer.

Without saying anything, she steps off the stool and takes two beer cans out of the refrigerator and punches them open.

They both drink them greedily, and then Pauline gets on the stool again. The smell of the afternoon's perfume is strong and she has never been happier.

In the morning, she finds him sitting at the kitchen table, Bromo-Seltzer before him, and a dark look in his eye.

The easel is in the center of the kitchen, and he's staring at it.

"Something's wrong," he said. "I didn't see it until just now."

"Wrong?" she says.

"The painting," he says, eyes fixed on it. "She's all wrong."

There is no posing that night, or the next.

Saturday, he goes to play cards at the veterans' hall, but he's home before midnight.

She finds him on the sunporch, strewing his sketches all over the floor. They are, mostly, details: a half dozen of her legs, the soft bulge of calf muscles from every summer of her youth spent milking Holsteins at the dairy down the road.

"Met a guy tonight," he says, without looking up. "A new fella works in the city. Said he saw you having lunch with a fella this week at the Barrowman Hotel in the city. Said it looked pretty cozy."

"I told you about that," she says, trying to keep her voice even. "That was for work. He's our new printer."

In one clean move, he backhands her, a crack like a ball bat.

"You keep a cold bed, my girl," he says after, catching his breath. "And you never once made a good Sunday roast."

The next day, there are carnations.

He's working on the painting again but says he no longer needs her. There's a girl coming from the art school, and she only costs two bits an hour.

That Monday, just after dawn, she steps into the kitchen, eyes fixed on the easel, ghostlike with its tattered coverlet.

She prowls across the tiles and without pause, lifts the cover, tossing it to the floor.

At first, she thinks something's gone horribly wrong. Grabbing for the kitchen matches, the dawn-dark space, she lights one and holds it up to the canvas.

What is this, she thinks.

It's nothing like the sketch at all. Yes, it's a woman, naked, a stage. The pose is the same, but different. Everything is different. The feel is different.

In place of her chestnut bob is a long hennaed mane, stiff as a wig. The cream pink body is chalkier, and the feet and legs look nothing like the sketches. They're narrow, spindlier, the hips bruised looking. On the feet are ankle-strap pumps with Cuban heels, electric-blue to match the woman's scarf.

Instead of her large but firm breasts, of which she is so proud, these jut out like little ledges, small and conical, the nipples garishly red, like the pointed hats of circus clowns.

The face, though. The face is what she can't stop looking at. From a distance, it's almost like a smudge. When she looks closer, the features look harder, the lips painted a hard red, the cheeks rouged, also like a circus clown.

"I lost my wallet," he says when he comes home that night.

The lining of his left pocket hangs loose, like a comic strip rummy.

"Where have you been?" she asks, the spaghetti noodles mushed cold in the pan. "Where were you all day and all night?"

"Looking for work. Met with the guy who owns the Alibi Lounge. Says maybe I could paint a mural on the back wall."

"Is that where you lost it?" she asks. "Your wallet."

"No," he says, and tells her it was probably walking home along the train tracks. "Like some kind of hobo."

There's an edge in his voice that shuts her up. He pours a glass of milk and drinks it over the sink. When he passes behind her, there's a smell on him she doesn't like. It's not booze.

He's stepping out of a smoke shop when she sees him. She can't guess what he's doing in the city during the day, especially without his portfolio.

She's returning from the printer and needs to get back to the office, but instead she follows him as he heads west.

It's hard to keep track of him, the crowds thick and the blare of car horns, barking newsboys.

The theater is one of the small ones, red brick and smoked windows.

Nipples like strawberries. But she never took off her g-string. And she never spread her legs. That's what she'd heard Bud say to her husband. Then adding, insinuatingly, *Maybe you've seen things I ain't.*

She isn't thinking at all until he slips inside.

A five-foot-tall poster shrieks at her: *Direct from the West: Rondell Bros's Burlesque! A MusiGAL Revue Feat. the Shanghai Pearl! Concha, the Snake Girl! Continuous Shows Daily!*

And beneath it, a banner: *Tuesdays: The Irish Venus Ascends!*

There is a drawing of a red-haired beauty emerging from the half-shell.

Standing in the alley, out of the crush, she smokes two cigarettes and thinks.

There's a tall man lingering by the box office. He may be looking at her.

Pauline turns away from him just as he calls out to her: *Hey, good-lookin'.*

"Got a light?" a female voice sounds out, and Pauline turns to see a woman walking toward her from the far end of the alley, the backstage door. Something about the way her body moves, her pale arm outstretched, her narrow legs and bright blue shoes, is familiar.

"Do I know you?" Pauline finds herself saying.

The woman pushes her up hat brim with one painted finger, and leans into Pauline's struck match.

The deep red hair, so brassy in the painting, looks so vivid in person. And the face, far from a charcoal smudge, is lively, bright.

"The Irish Venus?" Pauline asks.

The woman grins. "You can call me Mae."

The tall man loitering by the box office is now at the foot of the alley. He's looking at both of them.

"That man," Pauline says.

Mae nods. "He's a bad baby, that one. Grabbed my heater one night so hard I had bruises for two weeks."

She starts walking toward him. "I see you, Mr. McGrew," she shouts, cupping her hand over mouth. "Keep it in your trousers. I call Wade, you won't even have a tongue left to flap."

The man's face goes white and he scuttles away quickly, like a crab. "Who's Wade?"

Mae beckons her to the mouth of the alley and points to a pair of dice on the ground. Or were they pearl collar studs?

Peering down, Pauline gets a better look. She remembers seeing something like this at a boxing match. The pale middleweight, his mouth like a red fountain, teeth scattering across the ring.

Mae kneels closer. One of these, she sees now, is a molar.

"Keeps a pair of pliers in his sock garter," Mae says.

Pauline wonders where she has found herself.

The man returns to the foot of the alley.

"Wade!" Mae calls out into the open theater door. "Wade, Bingo Boy is back."

Pauline looks at Mae.

"Maybe," Mae says, "you should come inside."

The backstage smells strongly of smoke, old coffee, and the tang of sauerkraut.

"Greta makes her own every cold day," Mae says, winking. "You can take the Kraut out of Yorkville, but you can't take the Kraut out of her."

Pauline can barely hear her over the kick drum and caterwauls on the other side of the tall curtains, brocade so smoothed by time it looks like it would disintegrate between her fingers.

Quickly, they maneuver past a row of streaked mirror stalls, netted garments drying over radiators, coffee cups stacked, stained makeup towels, the ghostly remains of painted faces, scattered across folding chairs.

In one alcove, a girl in a golden kimono is slathering something from a bottle all over a naked six-foot blonde, transforming her in seconds from ruddy and veined to satin-skinned.

In another, Pauline sees two long-legged girls with matching brittle blonde waves straightening the green feathers on their costumes.

"Mae's mama's come to take her back to Kansas," one of them mutters, eyeing Pauline. "Get religion back in her cooch."

Pauline starts to say something, but Mae tugs her arm, moving them past. "Don't feed the parrots. You could catch trench mouth just by looking at those two."

They arrive at a tiny private dressing room with two mirror stalls, the air so heavy with powder, Pan-Cake, and perfume, Pauline can barely breathe.

"Come on," Mae says, beckoning her to a stool. "Cleo got bit by her snake again, so I'm solo today."

Once she's seated, Pauline begins to breathe again, and she wonders what she's doing here. A trombone wails from the stage and suddenly she's worried she might cry. Clenching her hands at her side, she steels herself from it. Refuses it.

Meanwhile, Mae is watching her and probably figuring everything out.

In the softer light of the bulbed mirrors, her hair is even more striking, specked with gold. And when she bends down to slide off her spectator pumps, creased with street soot, Pauline can't help but notice her legs, like stretched satin.

"So. You followed your old man."

Pauline doesn't say anything, her eyes snagging on something, a pair of slippers on the floor beside Mae. They are still sitting in their box. Pauline knows what they will look like before she reaches down to push the paper aside. Absinthe green.

"Ah," Mae says, following Pauline's gaze to the slippers. "That's the one, huh?"

Pauline nods.

"He's a regular Romeo. Gave me those, too," she says, nodding her head toward a large, heart-shaped candy box perched on the edge of the next dressing table.

Pauline nods again, picking up the candy box and looking at it. She wonders at the absence of something inside her. She no longer wants to cry. Something else is happening.

"For what it's worth," Mae is saying, "he didn't get anywhere."

"It's fine," Pauline says, distractedly stroking the heart of the candy box.

"He moved on to Cleo. She's used to snakes."

Pauline fingers the candy box heart and can't make any words come, the boom-szzz-boom of the drums hovering in her ear.

Mae looks at her, twisting her lips a little, then turns to her mirror and begins painting her face. Taking a pot of rouge, blueish-red, she dips a finger in and begins swirling it on her cheeks, conflagrating them.

"Hey," she says, pointing one red-tipped finger at the candy box, "can you pluck me one? I'm famished."

Pauline sets the box on her lap. *Madame Cou's Crème Bon-Bons.* The inside is lined in coral satin and when she opens it, she sees a dozen confections, gleaming globes of brilliant pink, glossy white, gold-leafed and fairy sprinkled.

"You too," Mae says, "you first, honey."

One tap of the tooth, and they give themselves away.

Gleaming maraschino jam, tongue-curling cream, nougat like sea foam, nose-tingling liqueurs of almond, bitter orange, soft apricot.

Huddled close, grinning like two schoolgirls at church, they eat two apiece, then two more. Pauline has never tasted anything like them.

"When I was seven, another girl caught me stealing a box of divinities from the Five and Dime," Pauline says. She's never told anyone this ever. "She promised if I shared she wouldn't rat me out."

Pauline thought of it now, the freckled girl with two skinned knees. They hid behind the leg display in the hosiery section and ate the whole box, stuffing the wrappers in bedroom slippers. The cardboard legs above them, all those candies, it was sugar and magic.

Mae licks her index finger and thumb, smiling. "Trouble shared is trouble halved."

Pauline grins.

"Have another candy," Mae says, holding her box out. "Or something."

The sweetness is making her drunk, is making her forget everything. Maybe it's the rums and liqueurs in the candy, or maybe it's just Mae, her curved white legs draped across Pauline's lap now, her head back, laughing. Her mouth as red and luscious as one of those cherried confections.

"Mae," Pauline says, "will you help me do something?"

Mae looks at her and says, "Sure."

"You might get in trouble."

"Haven't you heard?"

They both laugh.

"Have another candy," Mae says. "Or something."

Taking everything off is easy. Easier than in the kitchen with him watching.

She should feel cold, her dress whorled at her feet, but she doesn't

Mae unrolls her stockings for her, Pauline's foot propped on the dressing table.

"Now, the first trick I ever learned," Mae says, dipping two fingers back in the red rouge pot. Leaning forward, she daubs both Pauline's nipples. "They love this."

Pauline swallows her candy.

"Aren't you cute?" Mae says, swirling the rouge now, swirling them into tiny roses. "Squirming like a mink."

It feels warm and sweet, like the candies, which maybe were sitting under the lights too long.

Mae points to the pocked mirror, a cold cream thumbprint in the corner.

Cradling her daubed breasts under her hands, Pauline looks at herself and smiles.

The costume is only a delicate patch of sequined peacock-blue netting between her legs. It covers her, barely.

"I'd've lined the flap with plush for you," Mae whispers, making sure the sequins lay flat, "if we had more time."

Pauline looks down at Mae's red-maned head, her fingers arranging things along Pauline's hips, between her legs.

For a second, unaccountably, she can't breathe.

"And you'll need this if you wanna stay out of the paddy wagon," Mae is saying, draping a peacock feathered cape over Pauline's shoulders, tying it under her neck.

"I'm using to doing it much colder," Pauline says.

Mae just looks up her, slowly smiling, and winks.

They stand in the cool dark of the stage wings, the music so loud Pauline's feet are vibrating in the absinthe-green slippers.

Mae's head is ducked behind the masking curtains.

"Is he still there?" Pauline asks.

Mae nods. "I talked to the fellas in the pit. They'll give you fifteen seconds of pure cooch. Any longer, the manager's likely to wake up from his nap and give you the hook."

"Okay," she says, though she has no idea what Mae means. All she knows is her whole body is tight and tense, a spring ready to spring.

"You're already peeled like an egg, so just parade like a Ziegfeld Girl, got it?"

Pauline nods.

"Swivel the hips a few times, a flutter kick or two. And keep this on," Mae whispers, draping the cape more tightly around Pauline's shuddering shoulders, "or the cops'll ticket you twelve dollars."

Pauline steps onto the stage, which is no bigger than a boxing ring.

Taking a few steps, she has never felt more naked.

"Go on, gorgeous," hisses Mae from the wings.

The lights are hotter than she ever imagined, and through the smoky brume she can't seem any of the *ghouls*, which is what Mae calls them (*the ghouls just wanna see pink*).

Suddenly, the music kicks up and the spot lands on her and she sees herself.

Before she knows it, she's moving, her thighs brushing against each other, her feathers tickling her neck, arms, hips.

As the horns slur, she stalks her space, loosening the cape's ribbons, her breasts leading.

Her body is sparkling, her nipples red as American Beauties.

Her chin is high and she has never felt like this, her skin hot and magnificent.

Wolf whistles scream out, a few jeers, some keen laughter and raucous joy.

Her eyes adjusting, she can see the men, mostly smudges, but they're there.

There he is, she thinks. And yes, he's there, front row, beside the lantern-jawed pit drummer in shirtsleeves, just like in the painting.

Red-faced, eyes wide, he's calling her name, first loudly, then more so. *Pauline, what are you—*

On his feet now.

Pauline!

The trombone slides forward like a slingshot, and she pivots, shimmies to beat the band, and makes one last turn across the stage, the cape unloosed, flying behind her now, like peacock wings aflight.

Her eyes shuttle past a man in front doing things under his sack of candy, showing her what he's doing, showing himself to her, a fleshy bundle from his open pants.

Nearly to the wings, she watches serenely, a cool smile on her face, as her husband grabs for the man, tearing his shirt collar.

In seconds, a large man in shirtsleeves charges them both, lifting her husband up like a handkerchief. Crumpling him.

Wade, she thinks. *Oh, dear.*

Just as she reaches the curtain edge, the music giddying up to its end, she turns and offers one last shimmy, one kick, and strides into the wings.

Pauline, her body still warm and lit, walks through the wings, passing the six-foot blonde as she glides onto stage, a Viking headdress on, tassels dancing.

"Wade's going what-for," one of the green-feather girls is saying, pushing open the exit door into the alley. "C'mon for a free show."

Walking over, Pauline peeks above the girl's pale head and watches her husband take a roundhouse punch to the jaw from the man in shirtsleeves.

For a moment, looking at her husband's small, angry face, she feels sorry for him.

"Pauline," he cries out, spotting her. "Pauline, what have you done to me?"

But she's already drifted away from the door, plucking one of the girl's tail feathers as she does.

Slowly, slippers clicking, she walks backstage, toward the pink glow of Mae's dressing room.

The door is halfway open, and she sees a long, freshly powdered arm dangling, hears that soft, flame-haired thing calling her name.

Stepping inside, Pauline shuts the door behind her.

JILL D. BLOCK, *whose first story appeared in* Ellery Queen's Mystery Magazine, *is an author and a lawyer living in New York City. She vaguely recalls having taken an art history class in college during which she may have seen a slide of an Edward Hopper painting in the brief time after the lights were turned off and before she fell asleep.*

Summer Evening, 1947

THE STORY OF CAROLINE

BY JILL D. BLOCK

HANNAH

Once I decided it was finally time to look, it really wasn't so hard to find her. After so much anticipation, having prepared myself for the frustrations and disappointments, the false leads, dead ends and wasted money that I assumed were inevitable, it actually took me less than a month. Massachusetts' open adoption laws helped, and I made some lucky guesses. And then Google and Facebook helped bring it home.

The hard part was figuring out how I was going to get close to her, close enough to look into her eyes, to hear her voice. I wasn't looking for a big emotional reunion. I certainly didn't want or expect to forge a relationship at this late date. I didn't even intend to let her know who

I am. This isn't about her, and I'm not here to answer her questions. I mean, if she was so interested in knowing who I am, she could have looked for me, right?

That sounds like I am mad at her for having given me away. But I'm not. All I really mean is that I don't assume she has any interest in knowing what became of me. And that's OK. Look, I'm almost forty years old. I get it. I learned a long time ago that you can't blame someone for not loving you.

She was sixteen when she had me. So pretty much wherever I ended up was going to be better than with her, right? And it was fine. The people who raised me, my parents, were perfectly nice, well-meaning people. They were older, in their forties, when they got me, and they took me into their home and made me a part of their family. Well, sort of. Looking back, it seems like once they got me they couldn't quite remember why they'd bothered. Let's just say, there was not a lot of love in that house. They raised me, gave me shelter, food and clothes and an education. I know exactly what they did for me, and I appreciate it. Lots of kids grow up with a lot less than I had. But now I need to see what I missed.

GRACE

She sat at the kitchen table and listened to him breathing in the next room. She took a sip of coffee. Cold. She should be in there with him. She should be cherishing this time, spending these final days with him, these final moments. She knew that there would come a day, soon, when she wouldn't remember what kept her paralyzed in here, in this room, when she could have been by his side, and she would be left with nothing but regret.

Missy and Jane had decided when he came home from the hospital that he should be down here, in the family room, and not in the bedroom upstairs. They'd come roaring in like a storm, waving cell phones and Starbucks cups, throwing open the windows, unpacking groceries, rearranging furniture, directing the guys who delivered the bed, acting like they own the place. Like they live here. Like this was their problem to solve. When she brought him home, they sat with him, sometimes together, sometimes taking turns, holding his hand, smoothing his hair, speaking softly to him, kissing his forehead. And then, blinking back their tears, telling her they'd be back soon, they got in their cars and they left.

That was two days ago. Since then, she'd mostly sat here, at the kitchen table, drinking coffee and listening to him breathe. Aside from the feedings every few hours, when she busied herself with detached efficiency, mixing and measuring, chirping and clucking like an idiotic bird, asking him questions she knew he wouldn't answer, she couldn't bear to be in the room with him.

The one-sided conversations don't really bother her. She is used to it. He hasn't been able to speak for more than two years, not since the last big surgery. He'd tried in the beginning. He would say something, and she would guess, trying to understand what he was saying. She had about as much success as she would have had having a conversation with the cat. They sometimes laughed about it, back when it still felt like they were in this together.

Eventually, they stopped trying. After repeating himself three or four times, and shaking his head no to each of her guesses, he'd dismiss her with a wave of his hand, never mind, and turn back to the newspaper. That was when she felt most like she was failing him. If their bond was really so deep, shouldn't his words be able to reach her?

If it was important enough, he would write her a note. The house was filled with his notebooks, their spirals crushed, and the pencils he used, sharpened with a knife. What would she do with the notebooks when he was gone? She wondered if the girls would want them. They probably imagined that they would find them full of poetic declarations of love, essays on the singular joy he'd known being their father. In fact, they were mostly reminders of things she needed to pick up at the store. Q-tips and kitty litter.

There had been fewer and fewer notes the last few months before he'd gone into the hospital. He responded to her questions with a thumbs up or down, the occasional shrug (which she took to mean "I don't know" or "I don't care," depending on her mood), raised eyebrows ("really?") or a smile. There hadn't been many smiles lately.

Jose had told her he would come every day, that he would bathe him, and change the bed. He told her he had put a box of medications in the refrigerator that she could administer as needed, and he stuck a note to the door with a magnet. He left her with a stack of pamphlets, and said that he would arrange for a volunteer to come by every few days.

HANNAH

My plan had been to show up at the gallery where she worked. I figured I would recognize her from her Facebook pictures, and I could just say I was new in town, act confused and ask for directions or something. I would be gone before she noticed if anything I said didn't make sense. And I swear that would have been good enough for me. But after I went by for the fourth time and didn't find her there, I gave in and asked for her by name. It is amazing how much people are willing to tell you about other people's private shit. They told me that she'd retired quite suddenly to care for her sick husband. His cancer was back. He was in the hospital but he'd be going home since there was nothing more that they could do for him.

Plan B came to me right away. I signed up for a five-day training course to become a hospice volunteer. Yeah, I know. False pretenses. But it really does sound worse than it is. I mean, it isn't like I am going to do anything. I'll go in, get a good look, talk with her for two minutes, and then sit with the husband for an hour or two while she goes out and gets her hair done, or whatever it is you can't do while your husband is dying. And then I'll tell the fine folks at Pioneer Valley Hospice that it turns out I can't do it. I am very sorry but it is just too sad, that I am not cut out for this. And then we can all get on with our lives.

GRACE

She had just made a pot of coffee when she heard the car in the driveway. The volunteer. She took a quick look around and tried to assess the impression she was about to give. It was a good thing that Jose came in the mornings; otherwise she might be sitting here in her nightgown. She took a deep breath and opened the door with a smile.

"Hi. You must be the volunteer. Thank you so much for coming. I'm Grace. Richard is in the next room. He's the, well, you know. Anyway, please come in. I am not exactly sure how this works. I've never done this before. I mean of course I haven't. So you tell me—what do we do? Am I supposed to leave?"

"Hi. I'm Hannah. I, umm . . . actually, I've never done this before either. This is my first time, too."

"Then I guess we will figure it out together, won't we? Come on in."

Richard was sleeping when they looked in on him, so they went back to the kitchen.

"I just made coffee. Would you like some?"

"Sure. I mean, yes, please. Thank you. But I'm supposed to be here to help you. Did you have anything that you need me to do? I can run some errands if you want. Or I can stay here with—I mean, if you wanted to go out or something."

"No, no. Not today. Let's just sit for a little while. If you don't mind. I can use the company."

They took their coffee to the table and sat down.

"This is a really beautiful house. Have you lived in Northampton for a long time?"

"We moved to the area when we first got married. We've been in this house about thirteen years. Since right after our youngest went away to school."

"Oh, you have kids?"

"Two girls. Women, I suppose. Missy and Jane. They are probably about your age. A little younger maybe."

"Do they live around here?"

"Missy's in Connecticut, Hartford. And Jane is in Stockbridge. Not too far. It's about an hour for each of them, in opposite directions. That picture is of Missy and John from a few years ago. When they were in Hawaii. And those are their boys, Willie and Matt. And that is Jane, with Kathryn and the baby. Jane is the one with the earrings. Richard took that picture at the airport when they came home with Madison. They were both just here for a couple of days, Missy and Janie, when we brought him home. Richard. When Richard came home. And they'll be back on Thursday for dinner. It's my wedding anniversary."

"Oh, that's nice. I mean that you'll all be together. How long have you been married?"

"Thirty-eight years. Hard to believe we made it this far."

"Thirty-eight years? How can that be? I'm sorry. I just meant, wow. You must have been very young."

"Yes. We certainly were young."

"When did—how did you meet?"

"Meet? Who knows. I've always known Richard, for as long as I've known my own name. He lived down the street from me, and our parents were friends. We were what they used to call high school sweethearts."

They sat in silence.

"Let's go in and see if he's up and I can introduce you. I don't know what they may have told you about him. He can't speak, and I feed him through a GI tube. Come on. Richard? Hi, honey. This is Hannah. She is going to come by every few days. Right, Hannah? I think that is what Jose told me. She is just going to keep us company. Do you want me to turn on the TV? Maybe I can find a baseball game. Or the news? Here, let me—"

He shook his head no.

"OK, honey. Are you too warm in here? Let me just fix—OK, OK, I'm sorry. I'll stop. It's fine. Hannah's going to go now. And then I will come in and give you your supper. OK?"

Grace walked her to the door.

"I can come back tomorrow if you'd like. Unless you think that's too much."

"Tomorrow is fine. God knows, we're not going anywhere. I'm sorry. That sounded terrible. I only meant—"

"No, no. It's fine. It sounded fine. Really. Can I bring you anything? I can stop at the store if you need anything."

"No. I don't think—actually, do you know what I'd really like? I am absolutely craving McDonald's french fries and a milkshake. Could you do that? But you have to promise not to tell anyone. I honestly never eat food like that. Here, let me give you some money. Vanilla. You don't mind, do you?"

HANNAH

Just be normal. Get in, put on your seat belt. Turn, wave, start the car and drive. It doesn't matter where. Just drive.

What the fuck just happened? I just met my mother. I just had coffee with my mother. For the first time in thirty-nine years, I just hung out with my mother. Who married her high school sweetheart. What does that even mean? She grows up with Richard. He's her boyfriend. She gets pregnant, and she gives me away. And then she marries him? And has two more kids with him? And then they spend the next thirty-eight years together?

It doesn't make sense.

Richard is my father. Or maybe he's not. Maybe there was another boy, who snuck in between before and after, and stuck around just long enough to get her pregnant? I honestly never even thought about the father. It never occurred to me to look for him, or even to wonder who he was. He didn't exist in the life I imagined for the mother. For my mother. For Grace.

And what about those sisters? Or maybe they are still just my half-sisters. Missy with the square-jawed husband and the exotic vacation. Jane the lesbian. I have a gay sister. A gay sister with a Chinese baby. How totally cool. How totally clichéd. Shit. I just become the loser sister.

GRACE

Jose asked her on Wednesday if she's noticed that Richard was sleeping more. He doesn't seem to be in pain. But in just the four days that he's been home, they could both see that he was fading. She finally had the nerve to ask Jose how long he thought it would be. The social worker at the hospital had said that hospice was for people not expected to live more than six months, but she hadn't wanted to know anything more than that. Today, Jose said it could be days or weeks, but probably no more than a week or two. He told her that he wished the hospitals would release terminal patients to hospice sooner, so that there would be more time at home, better time. She didn't know what she wished.

When Hannah arrived, they piled both orders of fries onto a plate, and they opened all of the ketchup packets into a pool for dipping at the edge of the plate. They didn't speak until the last french fry was gone.

"It's going to be soon. Jose told me today. Do you know Jose? The nurse? Days, he said. Or maybe a week or two."

"Oh, I'm so sorry."

"I will have to tell the girls tomorrow. This is going to be hard for them. They aren't really prepared for this. They haven't had many difficult days."

"And you? Are you prepared for it?"

"Well, I have had my share of hard days if that's what you mean. I thought the hardest ones were behind me. Stupid, I know. When we got married, Richard promised that from that day forward we'd get through our hardest days together. That I would never again have to suffer alone."

"Again?"

"It's a long story. Let's first clean this up and I'll go check on Richard."

"Why don't I make us some coffee?"

"I got pregnant. It was the summer before my senior year. Richard had just graduated, and was going to be coming out this way, to Amherst. We were from Danvers, so he was going to be more than two hours away. Anyway, I just couldn't tell him. I was afraid it would ruin his life. That I would ruin his life. Eventually, I told my mother, and she told his mother, and they came up with a plan. Just before Thanksgiving, they sent me to this place in Dorchester. St. Mary's Home for Unwed Mothers. Can you believe it? It sounds like something out of a gothic novel. The story was that I had gone to Chicago to help a sick aunt, and that is what we told everyone. Including Richard."

"And people believed it?"

"They did or they didn't. It didn't matter. You have to remember, it was 1967, and there weren't a lot of options. Every year there were one or two girls at school who just disappeared, for a few months or forever. And we didn't talk about it. It just wasn't nice."

"I'm sorry. I interrupted you. You were saying you went to St. Mary's?"

"St. Mary's. It was wonderful and terrible. I had never been a part of a group of girls like that. Every night was like a slumber party. But we were also bored to tears, and so ashamed, and absolutely terrified of childbirth. Whenever a girl had her baby, she didn't come back. So we never heard from anyone what it was really like.

"We talked endlessly about what we would do—would we keep our baby, or give it up? We all had boy's and girl's names picked out, and we imagined what our lives would be like if we decided to take our babies home. My names were Thomas and Caroline. What we didn't know was that there was nothing to decide. The decision was already made for us. Our babies were gone before we even had them. I had a little girl. Caroline. They never even let me hold her."

"Oh, Grace, I am so sorry. That's terrible."

"Yes. It was terrible. I was absolutely devastated. But it was like I was in shock. My parents came to get me, and we all seemed to agree that we wouldn't speak of it again. I went back home to finish my senior year.

"I honestly didn't think I would ever tell him. I figured he would probably break up with me when he came home for the summer. I had been so awful to him, and he couldn't understand why. I didn't answer any of his letters until I was back home, and even then, I would only write a few lines, mostly about the weather and my classes at school. It was awful keeping a secret from him. If I'd had any guts at all, I would have broken up with him, instead of just waiting for him to do it."

"How did he send you letters? I mean, where did he send them? Didn't he think you were in Chicago?"

"I really did have an aunt in Chicago. My mother's sister. She was in on it, too. She mailed his letters to our house, and I read them all when I got home. Funny. It all seems so silly now, the trouble we went to."

"So he came home?"

"Yes. For the summer. I was still finishing up the school year when he came home. I had managed to catch up and was able to graduate with my class. We went to my senior prom together, just like everyone expected we would. He couldn't understand what was wrong with me. Why I wasn't happy. And I honestly didn't know. There had been a little problem, and it had been taken care of. It was over. No one got hurt. Life went on. Except that I hated myself.

"I will never forget when I finally told him. It was the hottest day of the summer. We'd spent the day down on Nantasket Beach and then we went to Paragon Park. We ate fried clams, and rode on the roller coaster, and after that we went to the movies. I think we saw *The Thomas Crown Affair*. Was that the one with Steve McQueen?"

"Oh, yeah. I guess so. There was a remake a few years ago. With Rene Russo, I think."

"Anyway, it had been a perfect day. Except that every time I opened my mouth I was afraid of what I might say. So I barely said a word. When Richard took me home, he asked me for what must have been the twentieth time that day what was the matter."

"I still remember it like it was yesterday. We were standing on my porch. It was still hot, even close to midnight. All the lights in the house were off, but I knew that my mother was awake upstairs, waiting up for me. Maybe even listening from her bedroom window. I didn't have a curfew anymore, but even after everything that had happened, she still wouldn't go to sleep until I got home and turned off the porch light."

"So you told him? About the baby?"

"About Caroline, yes. I couldn't look at him. I looked down and just started talking. I told him about missing my period, and feeling sick in the mornings. That was before he even left for school. I told him about how scared I was when I finally had to tell my parents, and how my father cried. And how the next day our mothers sat down together, with a pot of coffee and a telephone book, and figured out what we were going to do. I told him about St. Mary's, and the other girls, and how I hated being away from home. I told him how much I'd missed him, and how scared I'd been. I told him about when Caroline was born, and how they took her away from me. And that I'd never held her. Or said that I was sorry. Or told her goodbye. I told him that I hated myself. And that I would never forgive myself."

"And then what happened?"

"He kneeled down, took my hand, and asked me to marry him. He said that if he'd known about Caroline at the time, we would have gotten married, and she would be with us. And that just because Caroline was living with another family instead of with us, that didn't change anything."

"And you said yes."

"And I said yes. We were married a year later. We didn't want to wait, but our mothers were afraid of what people would think if we didn't have a proper engagement. Silly."

"Wow. And then you lived happily ever after."

"Happily ever after. Until death do us part. Speaking of which, I've got to feed him. And you should go. I didn't mean to keep you here all afternoon."

"Would you like me to come back tomorrow? I can stop at the store if you need anything. For your dinner?"

"Please come tomorrow. That would be very nice."

"And do you need me to pick up anything?"

"No. Missy said she's bringing anything we— Oh, you know what? What about Taco Bell? Maybe you can get us some of those Super Nachos they have at Taco Bell?"

HANNAH

I have a mother who sneaks junk food. And a father who is dying. And two sisters. And a niece and two nephews. I have a family. And they have no idea who I am. I am in this thing way too deep. Now what do I do?

GRACE

"I wasn't sure you'd come back after yesterday. I apologize for dumping all of that on you. I honestly hadn't even thought about it in a long time."

Grace rinsed the plate and put it in the dishwasher.

"Oh, don't apologize. It was an amazing story. Richard sounds like a really wonderful man."

"I have been very lucky . As a family, we've been very lucky, even with Richard's illness. I expect I will have to remind Missy and Jane of that. Coffee?"

"Yes, please. Do they know about Caroline?"

"Of course. I decided a long time ago that I wasn't keeping any more secrets. Caroline was their favorite story when they were little. Here you go."

"Thanks. Did you ever look for her?"

"Oh no. I couldn't do that. It wouldn't be right. I can't undo what I did to her. I wish I could, but I can't."

"But she doesn't know that. I mean, how could she know?"

"When she wants to find me, she will. I think she'll see that I'm actually pretty easy to find. But I've been talking too much. I just want to listen for a while. Tell me about yourself. Do you live around here?"

"Oh. OK. Well, I'm actually sort of between situations right now. I mean, I'm here for the summer. I am staying at a friend's place in Holyoke. Sort of housesitting while she's away. I had an apartment and a job and a boyfriend in Providence, but it seems I may have run away from home. I'm going to be forty in March, and I think I might be going through some kind of mid-life thing."

"Ah, yes. I do remember forty getting my attention. Are you from Providence originally?"

"I was born in Massachusetts, but I grew up in Cranston."

"Is your family still in Rhode Island?"

"Actually, no. Not really. They, umm, my parents actually passed away."

"Oh, I am very sorry to hear that."

"That's OK. I mean, they were older. I was adopted."

"Oh."

"I'm sorry. I didn't mean for that to come out like that. It just felt awkward not saying so after yesterday."

"Yesterday. Right. How old did you say you are?"

"I'll be forty in a few months."

"You said March?"

"Hmm, yeah."

"And you were born in—?"

"In Massachusetts. Grace?"

Silence.

"I'm so sorry, Grace. I didn't mean to—"

"Are you—?"

"I think so. Yes. I mean, yes."

"You're Caroline?"

"I guess I am."

"Was that a car? Oh, Jesus. OK, Missy's here."

"Hi, Mom. Here, take this. I made a lasagna; we can just heat it up when we're ready. Jane is bringing a salad and I told her to pick up a bottle of wine. Wine's OK, right? I spoke to her right before I left the house. She should be here any minute. Oh, hi. I'm sorry. I didn't even see you. I'm Missy. I mean, who says we can't have wine? How's Daddy?"

"Hi. I'm Hannah. I'm the—"

"He's OK. He's been sleeping a lot today. Come on, let's go in. He was looking forward to seeing you."

Hannah sat back down. Even though Missy was speaking softly, in that gentle singsong reserved for babies and sick people, Hannah could hear every word.

"How are you feeling, Daddy? Are you comfortable? Here, let me fix the pillow a second. There, that's better, isn't it? John and the boys send their love. We are all going to be here on Sunday, OK? Would you like that? Oh my god, you wouldn't believe the traffic I hit on 91. Near Springfield? There must have been an accident or something but whatever it was, I was so far back I didn't see a thing. Mom, who was that woman?"

"That's Hannah. She's a hospice volunteer. She's been helping me out. Running some errands for me."

Hannah waited for her response, but there was none.

"Go ahead. Sit here. I'll let you talk to Daddy."

She came back into the kitchen and sat down.

"That's Missy. It can sometimes be hard to get a word in."

"She seems very nice. But I should go. And let you—"

"Please don't go. Stay. You can meet Janie, and have dinner with us. I would like that."

"OK. Are you sure? If you want me to."

They listened to Missy speaking softly to Richard in the next room.

"Would you like me to read to you Daddy? I just got that new Prey book, by John Sandford? I can't remember what it's called. Something Prey, no doubt. Wait, I'll be right back."

Missy came into the kitchen and took a book from her bag.

"I thought I might read to him for a little while. I got the new John Sandford book. *Phantom Prey*, that's it. Wait, let me just put the lasagna in the oven. Where is Jane? I thought she'd be here by now."

They listened as she started reading to him in the next room.

"'Something wrong here, a cold whisper of evil. The house was a modernist relic, glass and stone and redwood—'"

"He knows. Richard. He heard us."

"He heard us?"

"He knows who you are."

"How do you know? I mean, what makes you think so?"

"You hear Missy reading, right? Just listen. You can hear every word. For days, I sat here and listened to him breathe. It didn't occur to me that he could hear us in here. But of course he can. Just now, when I told Missy who you are? He made a face."

"He made a face?"

"He raised his eyebrows, like he was saying 'oh, really?' Like he was saying 'Come on, Grace. I thought you said you were done keeping secrets.'"

"Grace, I'm so sorry. I feel like I am making a terrible mess here. I shouldn't have done this. Any of this. I never meant to—"

"Honey. It's OK. It's really OK."

A car pulled into the driveway.

"There's Jane."

"Oh, Mommy. Is he OK? I had the most terrible dream last night. I was driving here and no matter how long I drove, I kept not getting any closer. In the dream, I mean. I was so afraid he would die before I got here, and I drove for hours and hours but the GPS just kept saying that I was still 42 minutes away. Why 42 minutes? Isn't that weird? Anyway, when I woke up this morning I knew that it was just a dream but then once I was driving here I started to think, what if it's true? What if it was some kind of a premonition or something? I was crying so bad I had to pull over. I was so afraid I would get here and he'd be dead. And then I thought that if I didn't keep driving I would never get here and then it really would be true."

"Honey, stop crying. Come here and give me those bags. He's—"

"Jesus, Jane. What is your fucking problem? He's OK. I was just reading to him until you came busting in like a lunatic."

Jane pushed past Missy and went into the family room.

"You'll have to excuse my sister. She's unstable."

"Missy, be nice. She's just upset."

"So, Hannah. I'm sorry, it is Hannah, right?"

"That's right."

"You do volunteer work for hospice? That's very generous of you. I am sure it has been a big help to my mom."

"Oh, well, it's really not so much. There are nurses who come who can actually do things to really help. They call what I do respite care. I've just been coming by to give your mother a break if she needs it."

"My family and I really appreciate your help. But I'm sure you must have better things you could be doing, so—"

"Missy, I asked Hannah to stay for dinner."

'You asked— Oh. OK, sure, that'll be— That's fine. There's plenty of food."

"I'm going to give your father his dinner now. Why don't you girls set the table? I will ask Jane to come in and help."

Hannah and Missy could hear Grace and Jane talking while they set the table.

"Wait, who is she?"

"I told you. She's been coming by to help, and to keep me company."

"And now she's such a good friend that she's joining us for a family dinner? After two days?"

"It's been three days and yes, she's become that good a friend. I need you to give your father and me some privacy. So stop acting like a brat and go in and introduce yourself properly. You are embarrassing me."

Jane came into the kitchen and walked to the counter where she had put down her bags. Missy and Hannah watched her open a bottle of wine. Jane brought it to the table where she poured three glasses and sat down. Missy raised her glass in a silent toast, and they drank.

Missy took her cell phone from her bag. Jane straightened and re-straightened the pamphlets still on the table where Jose had left them days before. Hannah looked at her hands. Each of them strained to hear what Grace was whispering to Richard, but it was just below audible.

Grace appeared in the doorway.

"Can you come in here? Your father and I want to talk to you."

Missy and Jane got up.

"Hannah. You, too. Please."

The four women stood around Richard's bed, Jane and Missy on one side, Grace and Hannah on the other. Richard's and Hannah's eyes met for the first time. Richard smiled, and turned to Grace and nodded.

"Missy and Jane. You remember the story of Caroline . . ."

ROBERT OLEN BUTLER *has published sixteen novels and six volumes of short stories, one of which,* A Good Scent from a Strange Mountain, *won the Pulitzer Prize in Fiction. He has also published a widely influential volume of his lectures on the creative process,* From Where You Dream. *His latest novel is* Perfume River, *about the baby boomer generation and how it has been permanently affected by its war in Vietnam. His previous three novels comprise the commencement, for Otto Penzler's Mysterious Press, of a historical/espionage/thriller series set during the First World War. Butler teaches creative writing at Florida State University in Tallahassee, Florida.*

Soir Bleu, 1914

SOIR BLEU

BY ROBERT OLEN BUTLER

While I've been distracted, the clown has taken a seat at our veranda table in absolute silence. But of course. He is, after all, Pierrot, and beneath the makeup, a mime.

Damnable distraction. Before I knew the clown was there, Colonel Leclerc, sitting at my right hand, was leering at Solange, who returned from a freshening inside the hotel and stopped to vamp for him. I could not bear to see her play at being the woman she once was. I'd rescued that woman from the Place Pigalle and made her my model. I'd redeemed her nakedness with my art. But Leclerc would rather buy her than one of my paintings. Instead of a Vachon, he would have the artist's erstwhile whore.

All this flared through my limbs, so I forced my eyes to go beyond her, out to the Esterel Mountains and the twilight that has begun to transform the cerulean blue of afternoon into the Prussian blue of incipient night. I thought: *This present shade is on my fingertips even now. I have come to*

Nice to paint, not just to hawk. She is a whore no longer. She is exalted.
She is my Muse. My necessary Muse. She knows that.

With this I looked from the Esterels back to Solange. At her *toilette*
she'd painted her cheeks and her mouth afresh. Heavily. Luridly. She'd
created a nakedly impassioned face. But she immediately shot me her
eyes. I know the nuance of her looks. I have painted them. This look was
to say: *I will snare him for you. He will buy your paintings. He will have*
me only through you.

This is what she told me. All of this in the briefest of glances. She
returned her attention at once to the colonel, and they continued.

So I lowered my face and looked across the table.

And he was there.

He did not startle me. I had already taken my seat in the theater. I had
already begun to watch a scene from the *Commedia*. Colonel Leclerc and
Solange—as *Il Capitano* and *Columbina*—were so absorbed in each other
they did not even notice Pierrot's entrance. They still haven't.

Now we look at each other, Pierrot and I. He is painted as if by
a child using Delacroix's palette, his hairless head and face done in
zinc white, his outsized lips and his arched brows and the tears of
the cuckold falling from his eyes done in vermilion. This is the living
portrait of the tormented clown painted on the canvas of the actor's
face. The theaters are near this hotel, along the Avenue de la Gare. He
has, no doubt, come straight from a performance. Perhaps he too is
hawking, for his troupe.

His eyes are deep in darkened sockets. But that is the actor, not the
clown. Perhaps he is old. Perhaps he just did not have the strength tonight
to remove his makeup. Not till he can drink for a time.

Those eyes in shadow are impossible to read.

But we stare at each other for a long moment and then he mimes with
two fingers the drawing of a cigarette to his lips and, with a flourish of
his other hand, mimes the striking of a match and the lighting up, and
then the blowing of a perfect smoke ring, which I fancy I can actually
see. He angles his head. I cannot see his eyes well enough but I imagine
he has just winked.

I understand.

From my inside pocket I pull my pack of Gitanes, but with a crooked smile Pierrot flips his chin and unfurls his right hand. He has conjured a lit cigarette. He puts it in his mouth and he drags deep and blows a real smoke ring, which dilates toward me.

I look to Leclerc.

He is still enrapt with Solange.

The ring of smoke drifts beneath his gaze and dissolves without his noticing.

I return to Pierrot and we smoke together for a time, long enough to twice mingle plumes above the table. Between the first and the second, Solange sits down to my left. I do not need to look at her or at the colonel to feel their gaze still linked together.

And then Leclerc addresses me. "Monsieur Vachon. I offer my apologies to you and to Mademoiselle. I am weary and will retire. I will come in the morning to choose a painting."

I turn my face to him.

He is looking past me.

"But of course," I say.

He rises.

He goes.

I watch his wide, muscled back move away, rendered in Napoleonic blue.

I turn to Solange.

She smiles. "He will buy," she says.

I cannot help but hear the ambiguity. Still, I overcome this. After all, she has fallen deeply in love with my genius. She has fallen in love with the image of herself I've made for her. I have revealed the true colors of her flesh, in sunlight and shadow, in sleep and in passion. Beneath the garish colors she has used to paint the ardent face she presents to Leclerc, only I know the true flush of her cheeks, the raw sienna and yellow ochre and cadmium red of it. We have come to understand, Solange and I, that in the deepest sense she no longer exists except by my hand.

She has been looking only at me since Leclerc left. I glance at Pierrot and he is staring at me as well, unwaveringly, solemn-faced. I look back to Solange and I unfurl my hand in the clown's direction, as he did in his bit of legerdemain.

She follows the gesture.

She registers nothing. Indifference. Not even this incongruous figure can shake her from her intentions. I think: *She has her mind on the tin-pot soldier.*

I am tired of this. I do not wish to drink my wine and smoke my cigarettes while trying to read her mind.

"Go up now," I say to her. "I will drink a while longer. Wait for me."

She begins to push back in the chair.

"Be wary," I say, employing my own ambiguity: wary of him; wary of me.

She pats my forearm. Then she rises.

I turn my attention to Pierrot as Solange moves behind me and away. His eyes are in shadow but his head is painted against the night; he does not seem to follow her passing. But after she is quite gone, he nods at me. As if: *Well done.*

I lean a little toward him.

He arches his brows and leans toward me.

"She does what I tell her," I say.

He lifts his shoulders at this, lifts his face, pushes his lower lip upward, inverting the faint smile of his vast clown lips, turning it into a skeptical frown. He metronomes his head back and forth, as if weighing the possibility that I am correct, but his frown and the measured movement of his head clearly convey that he thinks I am wrong.

I let this pass. He is a clown. I am to laugh this off.

I do. Though the laugh sounds as forced as it feels.

But it satisfies Pierrot. His face descends. A smile blooms, a bright, large smile. He is good, this actor. I must be wrong about his being old. His face is wonderfully flexible.

Now I realize why he captivates me. Why I am ready to laugh at him, even if he contradicts me. I say, "I've seen you in a pantomime."

His eyes widen and he cocks his head.

"Perhaps not you the actor," I say. "I've seen your character."

He furrows his brow, nods contemplatively.

"It was long ago," I say. "I was a boy."

I pause with another realization. This is, in fact, a difficult memory. A place I should not go.

But something presses me on. "How old?" I ask this question of myself, lowering my voice, trying to visualize the boy I was.

Pierrot shrugs and flares his hands as if I am asking him.

I have been prompted to remember by this simple image of childhood before me—the face of a clown—even as the adult in me wishes to stop. There is someone sitting at my side in the memory.

Pierrot has begun to beam, canting his head, now to one side, now to the other and back again, encouraging me.

I have computed my age, but I need say no more. I do not have to go on. Still, I do. Resolved, though, to remain focused on the pantomime itself.

"I was twelve," I say. "In Valvins."

I pause. Pierrot has resumed his pose of rapt attention.

I study him as he studies me.

Perhaps I was right about this man's age. Could he possibly be the same actor? He need only be in his fifties. Unlikely things do happen.

I say, "The theater in Valvins. I saw Paul Margueritte's *Pierrot the Murderer of his Wife*. He himself played Pierrot."

I watch the actor across the table, looking for him to give me a sign that it is he. A lift of the brow, perhaps. A nod. Something. But he is once again a portrait in oils, unmoving against the darkening blue of the night.

"He was brilliant," I say, baiting him with praise, and I wait again.

"Do you know the play?" I ask, with a wink.

He hints at a smile.

"Do you know him? Monsieur Margueritte?"

This Pierrot lifts a forefinger and tick-tocks it, as if to say *You have found me out, but do not speak of that.*

"I understand," I say.

The lifted finger stops and the hand flows into an upcurving gesture for me to continue. Then that hand falls and plumes upward again but this time with the other hand rising in concert: He wants to hear it all.

So I begin now to describe Paul Margueritte's protean performance, perhaps to the man himself as if he were someone else. But I can hardly hear my own voice. I am transported to that stuffy suburban Paris theater on a late summer night three decades ago, and Pierrot, in white surtout and white kerchief, acts out his crime, terrible but seemingly perfect, unsolved. The stage flats, tightly defining an undertaker's parlor, are black. On one of them is an oversized funeral poster announcing the lying in state of Columbina, Pierrot's wife; on another is her portrait, the poor dead woman. In the retelling of the murder, Pierrot plays both himself and his wife. No. More than that. Even as a boy I am dazzled by these people inside people. Paul Margueritte the writer creates the pantomime in which Paul Margueritte the actor plays Pierrot who in turn plays himself, and plays his wife as well, in a re-enactment of an event in which the clown becomes a murderer and his wife becomes his victim.

At first, alone, Pierrot agonizes over why he must kill her. She has robbed him. She has neglected him. Worse. She has gone to a man and lain with him. She has betrayed Pierrot, has made a cuckold of him. Then he considers how to kill her. Perhaps a rope for strangling, but the face he will provoke, with bugging eyes and gaping mouth and flailing tongue, is too awful. A knife for slashing, but all the blood. Blood and blood. Poison brings convulsions and vomiting. A gun brings the police. And in the fervor of his planning, Pierrot trips and hurts his foot. He rips off his shoe and rubs at his bare foot and he begins to laugh, in spite of the pain he is trying to alleviate. He can't help tickling himself. He rubs and laughs and he rubs and laughs. A desperate laugh. Then he knows what to do.

"The next was masterful," I say to the clown across the table. "*You* were masterful." And in my mind I see Margueritte portray, with absolute clarity, both Pierrot and his wife in bed together, embodying now one and now the other, as the clown binds his wife to the headboard and strips off her stockings and tickles her bare feet and she laughs and cries out and laughs and cries until, in a wild undulating spasm, she dies from the agony of unremitting reflex hilarity.

Though all the laughter and the cries are mimed—are utterly silent— the murder scene clamors terribly in the head of my twelve-year-old self. But as soon as Columbina is dead, my head now, as an adult, fills with something else.

I feared it. I ignored it. And now it is upon me.

I have not listened to myself speaking to the Pierrot of this veranda in Nice, but I hear myself suddenly fall silent with him. And in that theater in Valvins, as Columbina dies, I enter another pantomime beside me.

I turn my head to look at my father.

His muscled bulk. His drunkard's bloated red nose. His vast, pocked red nose. But a smart man, for all that. A dealer in bonds. Even a refined man. My father frightens me and he enchants me. His black wool suit, his long roll collar faced with black satin. His absolute attention on the stage. His fierce attention. He has brought me many times to the theater.

He senses me looking at him.

The crowd around us gasps and laughs. The pantomime on stage continues, but my father turns to look at me. Our eyes meet. I do not understand the look, but it is as ferocious as his gaze at Pierrot a moment ago.

I look away.

That night at the theater is the last time I will ever see my father.

The next day my mother is dead, her neck snapped.

And he has vanished.

I struggle against all this now. I widen my eyes, trying to return to the scene before me. The veranda of the Hotel Splendide in Nice. Chinese lanterns. The just-vanished twilight in Prussian blue. A clown. A frowning clown. I feel my own mouth widening to him, forcing a smile, as if I were myself a clown trying to distract a frightened child.

And Pierrot speaks.

"You must go to her," he says. His voice is a deeply rasping, jagged thing. A voice ravaged by disease or injury or long use. I think: He was once a stage actor. *He has somehow lost his instrument and become a mime from necessity.*

He flexes at the shoulders. Impatient with my delay.

"Be wary," he says. "You must go."

His vermilion mouth arches upward into a vast frown.

I understand. My chest clenches. I've been a fool all along.

I jump up. I am pressing past the other diners, men in evening clothes, women with shoulders bare, and I am through the veranda doors and walking briskly across the marble floor of the lobby, trying not to run, trying to contain myself. My face. My face feels stretched tight. Frozen in a mime's pose. I think: *Do they know, those lounging in chairs between the Corinthian columns, holding their drinks, pausing their conversations,*

*turning their eyes to me? Can they read my furious silence? Did Sol-
ange and Leclerc meet here, brazenly? Did she put her arm publicly
in his?*

I stride faster, turning beside the front desk into the passage to the
cast-iron door of the electric elevator. But the carriage is not there. I
veer to the carpeted stairway and hurry now, mounting the stairs one
floor and then another, two steps at a time, and I am strong and I am
quick and I am light as the flames that flare in my chest and behind
my eyes, and I emerge from the staircase into the hallway to our rooms.

I rush down the corridor, but as I near our door I slow abruptly. If she
is unfaithful I do not want to alert her. I will find her out. I slow to a
stop. Only a few more steps to go. But I wait. I am panting. My hands are
trembling. I need to be calm.

And then I am. I draw the key from my pocket. I am now as calm, as
coldly deliberate as I was enflamed a few moments ago.

I step to the door.

I turn my head and draw it close to listen.

I hear nothing inside.

I lean to the keyhole beneath the knob. My hand is as steady as if I am
holding my brush and I have taken up a bit of paint and I am about to
make the first touch of the day.

I slip the key gently, quietly into the hole. I grasp the knob with my
other hand. I take a deep breath, and I turn key and knob together. I push
open the door. Softly.

Our parlor is empty. My easel stands before the window. The door to
our bedroom is ajar and the crack is lit with the urinary yellow of electric
light. From within, Solange laughs lightly, and there follows a rustling of
clothes and the grunting of a man.

I cross to the bedroom, a great, blue stillness expanding within me. I
push open the door.

It is true.

They stand at the foot of the bed, Leclerc enfolding Solange in his arms,
leaning into her, and she is bent backward, about to tip and fall upon the
bed, her hands splayed white against his bastard blue back. He is kissing
her on the lips, but she has seen me in her periphery and her eyes cut to

me and widen and there is a stopping in her and he senses that and also stops, and for a moment they pose there as if for my brush.

Then she fists her hands and makes a show of beating on his back and they break apart and struggle upright. Leclerc turns to me, and he straightens into military erectness.

I think for a moment I will have to fight him.

But suddenly he blinks and then he shivers, as if a winter chill has come over him. He says, "It is a lie. She has seduced me."

He clicks his heels and marches toward me and past me and out of the bedroom and away.

Solange is posing again. I could never hope to capture—even with my estimable art—the complexity of expression on her face as she seeks a lie and plans an escape and fears for her life and rues her cuckolding passions, stymied here but fulfilled half a dozen times before, betrayals that she sees me recognizing now, in retrospect.

The room is hot and she is beautiful and she is my Muse and I hesitate. But suddenly a shoulder-wide column of achingly frigid air descends upon me, and all my passion for Solange—the unified passion of body and creative spirit—freezes and shatters, and I cross the room quickly, so quickly her face does not even change, her eyes do not even widen, and my hands are upon her throat and I watch them clamp hard upon her and I squeeze and squeeze, and as I take away her life, I ponder first the shade of blue stained upon my fingers and then her wide-mouthed soundless cry.

Finally she is dead.

I let her go and she falls upon the bed.

And I am filled with a smell.

Greasepaint and Gitanes.

I turn.

Pierrot is standing barely an arm's length before me. His face is solemn.

He nods once and raises his right hand and it pauses at the base of his throat, and he grasps something, and now his hand is rising and the whiteness is rising with it. More. It is his skin, his flesh rising, and the bones of his neck are emerging and now the chin of a skull, and higher his hand goes, passing upward, and the skull's teeth appear and the bones of cheek and lip and now a fleshy nose emerges, preserved in this skull, and in one final stroke he rips off the rest of the clown's face and all is gray bone and empty eye sockets. All but the nose, which remains uncorrupted by the grave. A drunkard's bloated red nose. A vast, pocked red nose.

As skulls are apt to do, it is smiling.

I cannot share the smile.

"Father," I say. "What have we done?"

Previously a television director, union organizer, theater technician, and law student, **LEE CHILD** *was fired and on the dole when he hatched a harebrained scheme to write a bestselling novel, thus saving his family from ruin.* Killing Floor *went on to win worldwide acclaim.* Night School, *the 21st Reacher novel, is due November 2016. The hero of his series, Jack Reacher, besides being fictional, is a kindhearted soul who allows Lee lots of spare time for reading, listening to music, and watching Yankees and Aston Villa games.*

Lee was born in England but now lives in New York City and leaves the island of Manhattan only when required to by forces beyond his control. Visit Lee online at www.LeeChild.com for more information about the novels, short stories, and the movies Jack Reacher *and* Jack Reacher: Never Go Back *starring Tom Cruise. Lee can also be found on Facebook. com/LeeChildOfficial, Twitter.com/LeeChildReacher and YouTube.com/ leechildjackreacher.*

Hotel Lobby, 1943

THE TRUTH ABOUT WHAT HAPPENED

BY **LEE CHILD**

I came out of my deposition feeling pretty good about it. My answers were brief and concise. My control was good. I said nothing I shouldn't have said. I used an old trick someone taught me long ago, which was to count to three in my head before replying to a question. Name? One, two, three, Albert Anthony Jackson. The trick mitigates against hasty and unwise responses. Because it gives you time to think. It drives them crazy, but there's nothing they can do about it. The oath doesn't say "the truth, the whole truth, and nothing but the truth, all within three seconds of opposing counsel shutting his yap." Try it. One day it will save your ass. Because unwise responses are tempting at times. As in my case that morning. The committee chairman had a clear agenda. The very first substantive question out of his mouth was, "Why aren't you in the armed services?" As if I was a coward, or a moral degenerate of some kind. To take my credibility away, I supposed, if necessary, if the deposition ever came to light.

"I have a wooden leg," I said.

Which was true. Not from Pearl Harbor or anything. Not that I discourage the assumption. Truthfully I was run over by a Model T Ford in the state of Mississippi. A narrow wooden wheel, a hard tire, a splintered shin, a rural doctor miles from anywhere. He took the easy way out by taking the leg off below the knee. No big deal. Except the army didn't want me. Or the navy. But they wanted everyone else. Which meant by the summer of 1942 the FBI was hurting for recruits. The leg didn't worry them. Maple, like a baseball bat. Not that they asked. They gave me training, and then a badge and a gun, and then they sent me out in the world.

So a year later I was armed, at least, if not in the service. But even then the guy gave no ground. He said, "I'm sorry to hear about your misfortune," disapprovingly, accusingly, as if I had been careless, or long premeditated a plan to avoid the draft. But after that we got along fine. He stuck mainly to procedural questions about the investigation, and one, two, three, I answered them all, and I was out of the room by a quarter to twelve. Feeling pretty good, as I said, until Vanderbilt grabbed me in the corridor and told me I had to go do another one.

"Another what?" I said.

"Deposition," he said. "Although not really. No oath. No bullshit. Strictly off the record, for our own files."

I said, "Do we really want our files to be different than their files?"

"The decision has been made," Vanderbilt said. "They want the truth to be recorded somewhere."

He took me to a different room, where we waited for twenty minutes, and then a stenographer came in, ready to take notes. She was an ample, hard-bodied thing. Maybe thirty. Brassy blonde hair. I figured she would look good in a bathing suit. She didn't want to talk. Then Slaughter came in. Vanderbilt's boss. He claimed to be related to Enos Slaughter of the St. Louis Cardinals, but no one believed him.

We all sat down, and Slaughter waited until the hardbody had her pencil poised, and then he said, "OK, tell us the story."

I said, "All of it?"

"For our own internal purposes."

"It was Mr. Hopper's idea," I said.

Always better to get the blame in early.

"This is not a witch-hunt," Slaughter said. "Start at the beginning. Your name. For posterity."

One, two, three.

"Albert Anthony Jackson," I said.

"Position?"

"I'm an FBI special agent temporarily detached for the duration."

"To where?"

"Where we are right now," I said.

"Which is what?"

"The project," I said.

"State its name, for the record."

"The Development of Materials Group."

"Its new name."

"Are we even allowed to say it?"

"Relax, Jackson, will you?" Slaughter said. "You're among friends. You're not under oath. You don't have to sign anything. All we want is an oral history."

"Why?"

"We won't be flavor of the month forever. Sooner or later they'll turn on us."

"Why would they?"

Vanderbilt said, "Because we're going to win this thing for them. And they don't like to share the spotlight."

"I see," I said.

"So we better have our own version ready."

Slaughter said, "State the name of the project."

I said, "The Manhattan Project."

"Your duties?"

"Security."

"Successful?"

"So far."

"What did Mr. Hopper ask you to do?"

"He didn't, at first," I said. "It started out routine. They needed another facility built. In Tennessee. A lot of concrete. A lot of specialist engineering. The budget was two hundred million dollars. They needed a man in charge. My job was to run the vetting process."

"Tell us what that involves."

"We look for embarrassing things in their personal lives, and suspicious things in their politics."

"Why?"

"We don't want them to be blackmailed for secrets, and we sure as hell don't want them to give secrets away for free."

"Who were you investigating on this occasion?"

"A man named Sherman Bryon. He was a structural engineer. An old guy, but he could still get things done. The idea was to make him a colonel in the army and put him to work. If he came up clean."

"And did he?"

"At first he was fine. I got a look at him, at a meeting about something else entirely. Concrete ships, as a matter of fact. I like to get a look at a guy first. From a distance, when he doesn't know. Tall guy, well dressed, silver hair, silver mustache. Old, but erect. Probably very well spoken. That kind of guy. Patrician, they call it. There was nothing on paper. He voted against FDR all three times, but we like that, officially. No leftist sympathies. Considered to be a seal of approval. No financial worries. No professional scandals. None of his structures ever fell down."

"But?"

"Next step was to talk to his friends. Or listen to them, actually. To what they say, and what they don't."

"And what did you hear?"

"Not much, initially. Those type of people are very discreet. Very proper. They talked to me like they would talk to the mailman. They were polite, and I was left in no doubt I worked for a solid and useful organization, but they weren't about to share confidences."

"How do you get around a thing like that?"

"We tell part of the truth. But not all of it. I hinted there was a top-secret project. War work. National security. Concrete ships, I hinted, absolutely vital. I told them these days sharing confidences was a patriotic duty."

"And?"

"They loosened up some. They like the guy. And respect him. Business-wise he's a straight shooter. He pays his bills. He treats his people well. He's very successful in a high-end niche."

"All good, then."

"There was something they weren't saying. I had to push."

"And?"

"Old Sherman is married. But there are stories about a piece on the side. Apparently he's been seen with her."

"Did you classify that as a blackmail risk?"

"I went to see Mr. Hopper," I said.

"Who is, for posterity?"

"My boss. Director of Security. It was a big decision. Mr. Hopper especially liked the part about being a success in a high-end niche. He was thinking about making him a brigadier general, not a colonel. He was the exact type of guy we needed. To pass on him would be a big step to take."

"Did Mr. Hopper think blackmail was likely?"

"Not really. But where do you draw the line?"

"Did you advise Mr. Hopper one way or the other?"

"I said we should get more information. I said we shouldn't take a big step based on rumor alone."

"Did Mr. Hopper listen to your advice?"

"Maybe. He's not a stuck-up guy. He's got time for us all. Or maybe he agreed with me anyhow. Or maybe he's getting gun-shy about going to meetings and putting a wrench in their gears. Maybe he wanted to put it off. But whichever, he said he wanted more information."

"How did you go about getting it?"

"There was nothing I could do for the first three days. Old Sherman wasn't seeing either one of his women. He was stuck in a concrete boat conference. I mean, do you think they could possibly work?"

"Do I?" Slaughter said. "Concrete boats?"

"Sounds like a dumb idea to me."

"I'm not a nautical expert."

"It's not like steel plate. They'd have to mold it real thick."

"Can we stay on the subject?"

LEE CHILD

"Sorry. The guy was in the boat conference. He was working hard. He wasn't spending the day between the sheets. But Mr. Hopper wanted to see it with his own eyes. He really liked the guy. Liked him for the job, I mean. He wanted no doubt about it. So we had to wait."

"How long?"

"We spread a little grease around. Hotels, mostly. We got a call from a clerk that old Sherman had booked a room for Friday night. A double. The names given were him and his wife. Which no one believed. Why book a hotel? They have a house. So Mr. Hopper made a plan."

"Which was?"

"First we went to look at the hotel. Mr. Hopper wanted to do it in the lobby. He felt the bedroom was wrong, for that type of guy. So we measured it up. There were gray velvet armchairs, three on one side and two on the other. There was a reception hutch, all heavy carved oak. There was a curtained doorway to the breakfast room. Mr. Hopper figured out how he wanted to do it. There was a window. To the right of the door. A person on tiptoe could see in from the street. Which was good, except it wasn't really. He couldn't spend hours peering in at the window. Not out there on the sidewalk. Passersby would tell a cop. He would have to time it just right. He couldn't see a way around it."

"How did he solve the problem?"

"He didn't. I suggested I take over from the reception clerk for a couple of days. Like an undercover role. I figured I wouldn't have much to do. I figured I could hide behind the lampshade most of the time. No one would be looking at me. So I figured I could flash the outside neon when the time came for Mr. Hopper to take a peek. The switch is right there."

"Your idea was you would alert him as they were checking in together?"

"We figured it would work two separate ways. He would get the visual he wanted, and I would see the girlfriend signing in as the wife, up close and personal. Mr. Hopper wasn't happy, because he liked the guy, as I said, but he had to draw the line somewhere. This project is a big deal."

"Did the plan work?"

"No," I said. "It really was his wife. She showed me her driver's license. Kind of automatically. I guess she travels with him a lot. To all those secure conferences about concrete boats. So she does it without thinking. The name was right and the photograph was right."

"So what did you do?"

"Nothing. I played at being a hotel clerk. Then the phone rang and it was Mr. Hopper in a booth across the street. Urgent. We had a tip the other woman was on her way to the same hotel. Right then. Mr. Hopper told me to stand by. I was to get old Sherman to come downstairs. Which I figured wouldn't be a problem. He wouldn't want me to send her up. Not with his wife in the room."

"Did the woman arrive?"

"It was like something in a motion picture. One of those screwball comedies. I heard the elevator moving. It was between me and the breakfast room. The gate opens and out steps old Sherman. He's carrying his wife's fur wrap. She steps out right behind him. In a blue dress, carrying a magazine. Half of me is thinking like an agent, and half of me is thinking, come on, pal, get the hell out of here before it's too late. But the wife sits down in a chair, right in front of me. She starts reading her magazine. Old Sherman just stands there, two steps from the elevator. By this point I'm hiding behind the lampshade. Then the other woman walks in. Fur coat, fur hat, a red dress. An older woman. Sherman's age. She bends down and kisses the wife on the cheek and then walks over and does the same thing to Sherman. I'm thinking, what have we got here? Three in a bed? That would be worse."

"What happened next?"

"The other woman sat down, and the wife kept on reading. The other woman looked up and said something to Sherman. Polite conversation ensued. I flashed the neon and I saw Mr. Hopper look in the window. He saw it all. He remembers all the details. The painting on the wall, of a mountain lake. But he couldn't make sense of what was happening. He didn't know what the scene was about."

"What did he do?"

"He stood down, and waited on the sidewalk. Old Sherman left with his wife. The other woman stayed behind and asked me to call her a taxi. I took the initiative and showed her my badge, and I gave her the same spiel I gave his friends. National security, and all that. I asked her some questions."

"And?"

"She's old Sherman's mother-in-law. Younger than him by two years, but that's how the cookie crumbles. Old Sherman is very happy with his child bride. She's very happy with him. The mother-in-law is happy with them both. She's visiting for a month and he's showing her around. She thinks he's sweet to take the time. We think he's doing it to please his wife. And she's worth pleasing. Especially for an old guy. They were in the hotel not their house because they had an early train. So panic over. Plenty of men marry younger women. No law against it. Mr. Hopper passed him fit for the job, and he's out there in Tennessee already, making a start."

Slaughter paused a beat, and then he said, "OK, I think we have what we need. Thanks, Jackson."

So for the second time that day I came out of a deposition feeling pretty good about it. I had said nothing I didn't want to say. Some of the truth was recorded. Everyone was happy. We won it for them in the end. Then they turned on us. But old Sherman Bryon was dead by then, so it didn't matter.

NICHOLAS CHRISTOPHER *is the author of seventeen books: six novels—* The Soloist, Veronica, A Trip to the Stars, Franklin Flyer, The Bestiary, *and* Tiger Rag; *nine books of poetry, most recently,* On Jupiter Place *and* Crossing the Equator: New & Selected Poems; *a nonfiction book,* Somewhere in the Night: Film Noir & the American City; *and* The True Adventures of Nicolò Zen, *a novel for children. He also edited two poetry anthologies,* Under 35 *and* Walk on the Wild Side. *His books have been widely translated and published abroad. He lives in New York City.*

He writes: "Edward Hopper lived and worked in a fourth-floor studio at 3 Washington Square North from 1913 to 1967. I live a couple of blocks from his brownstone and pass it nearly every day. I see the light outside his windows that illuminates so many of his canvases, the red brick and mansard roofs that were among his touchstones, and the neighborhood buildings (including my own) that appear in the paintings, often rearranged geographically to suit his composition. It's always made his work that much more special for me."

Rooms by the Sea, 1951

ROOMS BY THE SEA

BY **NICHOLAS CHRISTOPHER**

1

There were two doors into this house. The first, in a small unfurnished room, opened directly onto the sea. It could only be entered from the water. When it was left wide open on a sunny day, the light slanting into the room illuminated half of the near wall on a diagonal. As the sun descended to the horizon, the wall could be read like a sundial: its illuminated half shrinking until the entire wall had darkened.

The second door, in a foyer on the other side of the house, opened onto a rough path that wound through a forest and ended in an obscure park at the city limits. The fountain in that park, centered by stone mermaids that spout water, had been dry for months. The buildings that lined the city streets were red and brown. The sun ate into their brick, sending up puffs of dust. At dusk their blue windows turned amber. On the fire escapes women were smoking and reading, gazing up occasionally at the river of bruised clouds that flowed to sea. One of them, a redhead, was reading a slim memoir entitled *Rooms by the Sea*, written a century ago. The author, Claudine Rementeria, was married to a Basque shipping magnate who had immigrated to America. She herself was Basque, and shortly before her untimely death at thirty, she wrote the book in their native language, Euskera, in order to please her husband. Aside from a small private printing at the time—of which only a few copies have survived—her book hadn't been translated and published in English until recently. The redhead, Carmen Ronson, the thirty-year-old great-granddaughter of Claudine Rementeria, owned both the English translation and one of the extant Euskera copies.

Carmen arrived at the house today at nine o'clock. She emerged from the forest and strolled down the path, a cigarette between her fingers and both editions of *Rooms by the Sea* under her arm. She took a key from under a stone at the end of the path, unlocked the door, and entered the house. She was wearing a green dress, a green silk scarf imprinted with tridents, green shoes, and a blue suede hat with a peacock feather in the band. Her lipstick was coral, to match her fingernail polish. In the black-and-white photograph that comprised the frontispiece of Claudine Rementeria's memoir, she was wearing the same hat.

Carmen walked down a long corridor with a dozen narrow white doors that had been salvaged from the *Sabina*, an ocean liner shipwrecked in the Bay of Biscay. She passed through the room with the door open to the sea, and sat down on a red sofa in the adjoining room, which had a window opened to the water, but no door. She removed the hat and scarf and unclipped the barrette that held up her wavy hair. She was tall, with fair but unfreckled skin, a fine delicate face, and strong hands. Her hazy blue eyes matched the curtains fluttering in the breeze.

She opened her two books side by side on a low table, along with the Euskera-English dictionary she kept at the house. Though she had studied Euskera, and spent two summers in Basque country, she read slowly, mouthing the words and translating haltingly, under her breath. *There are two doors into this house . . .* The smells from the kitchen, many rooms away, wafted to her. Shallots frying, tilefish filets sizzling on the grill, biscuits in the oven.

2

The cook had caught the fish that morning, casting his line from the door onto the sea, his legs dangling over the sill, the wavelets licking at the soles of his sandals. His name was Solomon Fabius. For many years, he worked for Carmen's mother, Calleta. When she died and left the house to her daughter, Fabius remained. He promised Calleta he would give Carmen the copies of *Rooms by the Sea*. A Spaniard born in Senegal, he spoke French, Senegalese, and Euskera as well as Spanish. Though he had settled in America, he got by in rudimentary English. He claimed that he already spoke enough languages. With Calleta he mostly conversed in Euskera, which was one reason she had hired him. Other members of the household, including Carmen and her father, Klaus, rarely understood what they were saying. Klaus Ronson was a Danish doctor who had met Calleta in Venice and married her two months later. He died when Carmen was six, the year after Fabius arrived at the house. Each year on Klaus's birthday Calleta drank the same champagne they had shared the night he proposed to her in Rome. She toasted him and said he was the only man she had ever loved and ever would love. After her husband's death, she and Fabius spoke exclusively in Euskera.

Fabius had gone to Spain as a young man and studied his craft at the finest culinary institutes in Barcelona and Madrid. He worked as a chef at two five-star hotels: the Sultana in Bilbao and the Atlantis in Sevilla. His specialty was Basque cuisine. It was at the Atlantis, after a six-course meal, that Juan Azarola, a powerful lawyer from an old Basque family, told Fabius how impressed he was with his cooking. Azarola practiced law in Cádiz, fifty miles to the south, and ate at many Basque restaurants; but even in the Pyrenees he had seldom enjoyed dishes as original and distinctive as Fabius's. Azarola said he had a wealthy cousin in America who was looking for a chef. Whatever Fabius's salary at the Atlantis, Azarola went on, she was willing to quadruple it. His work permit, visa, living quarters, and medical needs would all be taken care of, and he would receive a pension, in the currency of his choice, deposited in any bank in the world. Was he interested in such private employment? Taken aback, and only half-believing all this, Fabius said he had to think it over. Azarola replied that he would like an answer in twenty-four hours, before he left Sevilla. Fabius made his own inquiries, with his boss, the hotel manager, and the law firm that represented the hotel. Azarola's credentials were impeccable. The offer was solid. Fabius accepted it, and never looked back. Over the past twenty-five years he had become a very rich man himself. He had not yet informed Carmen, but he intended to retire soon and return to Spain.

Fabius was a broad-shouldered, barrel-chested man. Even at sixty-eight, his muscular arms, large flat hands, and long neck combined to make him look taller than he was. He wore the white smock and pants, but not the hat, of a chef; instead, a red fez with a gold tassel sat atop his thatch of curly white hair. His quarters, down countless corridors, were in a room so far from the room with the door onto the sea that no one else could find their way to them. It was just as well, because his one condition upon accepting the job was that his quarters be completely private, without exception, at all times.

3

The house had other unique—to Carmen, alarming—properties. For example, the fact that, each year, without human assistance, it acquired another room. This began the year of Fabius's arrival, a few months before Klaus Ronson contracted lung cancer. Calleta Ronson dismissed the coincidence. And she never doubted that rooms could appear suddenly, as if they had risen from the sea. She said such things happened all the time, defying conventional laws of physics, but usually went unnoticed. Carmen, age six, asked her for examples that *did* get noticed.

"There are salamanders with two heads and one heart," Calleta replied, "and waterfalls in the Brazilian highlands that flow upward."

"You've seen these things?" Carmen asked.

"Of course. How else would I know? Take such marvels as a sign of good luck—a divine blessing, even."

Carmen understood that, for her mother, the fact something was inexplicable made it all the more real and powerful. As Carmen got older, she grew accustomed to her mother's circular logic and flights of fancy.

But even Calleta was unsettled when it became clear that this process was not going to end, that there was no telling how many rooms the house would end up with. After seven years, she contacted the architects she and her husband had commissioned and explained the situation. They didn't believe her. So when they came out to the house with the original blueprints and did a walk-through, they were stunned to find seven extra rooms, well constructed and freshly painted. At first, the architects were convinced she was playing a trick on them, that she had had the rooms built by real contractors in real time. But tricked them to what end? Especially when they were charging her four hundred dollars an hour. They returned unannounced two years later, thinking they would surprise her, and instead found two new rooms. One architect got lost roaming the house, tripped in a dark room, and broke his arm. The other, a right-wing Spaniard whose father had served under Franco, angrily told his partner that this was what they got for doing business with Basques. Then he burned the blueprints on the front lawn as a form of exorcism. His parting shot to Calleta was that she needed an exorcist, not an architect. The next day he suffered a massive heart attack.

4

A month ago, on a humid afternoon, Carmen had a boating accident. She had taken out the small sailboat that once belonged to her mother. She learned to navigate it as a child and had never suffered any mishaps. But on this occasion, a rogue wave rose up suddenly from a calm sea and swept over the deck. She wasn't knocked down or injured, she didn't lose consciousness, the boat didn't capsize, but for a long moment, suspended within the wave as if she were suspended in time, she was terrified it would carry her overboard. Instead, the wave rolled on into the mist, the sea grew calm again, and she steered back to shore.

Ever since that day, Carmen was certain the number of rooms in the house began multiplying at a faster pace, not annually but monthly. Whenever she tried to count them, she came up with a different number. Though externally the house appeared unchanged from the time of its construction thirty years earlier, internally it seemed to grow larger whenever she set out to explore it. Finally, she was convinced she could not find her way around her own house. It had become too enormous a construct in her mind. The rooms and corridors were no longer just multiplying, they were also expanding, contracting, and shifting position. The overall layout had become elastic. She could set off down the same corridor on successive days and find that it branched into four bedrooms one day and two bedrooms the next. Or that it stretched to a dead end, where there was a locked closet.

The rooms were bedrooms and sitting rooms. Their walls were painted white, their ceilings blue. The bedrooms were furnished identically: a bed, a bureau, and a night table. The sitting rooms all had a desk with a green glass lamp and an easy chair. On each desk was a blue notebook and a fountain pen. The beds were neatly made and the notebooks were blank.

Only Fabius, in his unseen quarters, and—until recently—Carmen slept in the house. Her bedroom and studio were the only rooms on the small second floor, a self-contained unit in a kind of watchtower. It was accessible by a spiral staircase and had a 360° view: three windows overlooked the sea, the fourth faced the forest.

Carmen didn't know why Fabius had a clearer knowledge of the house than anyone else. Not only could he walk to and from his quarters with ease, he could also travel between other rooms more quickly. When she asked him about this, he first pretended not to understand the question. When she reframed it in her imperfect French, he evaded it by replying that the house was a lucky house, "just as your mother always said." Carmen realized he wasn't going to tell her anything more.

5

Though Fabius had been around for most of her life, Carmen knew surprisingly little about him. His childhood, his schooling, his life in Senegal—it was all opaque. He never talked about his history in any of his several languages. Carmen was certain that her mother knew more, much more, but only once had Calleta shared some of this knowledge, an abbreviated story of Fabius's origins.

She told Carmen that Fabius's father was a Spanish missionary who married a Frenchwoman, the widow of an engineer, whom he talked down from committing suicide. She had walked into the square of a jungle village—mangy dogs sleeping in patches of shade, chickens pecking at the dust—and pressed a pistol to her heart. The barrel was cool against her chest. Sweat gathered in the small of her back. The cook's father tossed aside the pamphlets he had been offering passersby. The pamphlets were titled *Salvation Is Your Compass* and *Set Sail Across a Sea of Light*. He clasped his hands and dropped to his knees before the widow. Startled, but without blinking or saying a word, she lowered the pistol. She stared at him as he rose up, took the pistol, and uncocked it. Then he led her out of the sun, to a moldy bench beneath an ironwood tree where she collapsed, bursting into tears. He sat beside her, neither of them saying a word for four hours until she told him that her daughter, her only child, had drowned in a flood during the rainy season. A week later, she married the missionary, and nine months after that gave birth to the infant who would grow up to be the cook in this house. She gave him the name Solomon, and cradling him, told his father that the child would live a hundred years or more.

Carmen knew for herself that Fabius's only close relatives were two sisters, seventy-year-old twins, one a retired science teacher in Marseilles, the other a nightclub owner in Dakar. He kept a photograph of the sisters, taken when they were twenty, on a shelf in the kitchen. They are wearing white dresses and sharing an umbrella in the hot sun. Caletta said Fabius had never been married, and he had no friends Carmen was aware of. Though a servant, he had also been a resident of the house for twenty-five years, with the run of the place. Except for the two weeks each year that he visited one of his sisters, he rarely left the property. He did go out on the water in his ocean kayak, rowing many miles from shore, and no matter the weather or the season, he took long swims twice daily. He received deliveries of groceries and supplies twice a week, by way of a private water service. He always had a chessboard on the kitchen counter. While he cooked, he played out famous games recorded in chess books. Alekhine, Capablanca, Morphy.

Carmen's relationship with Fabius was deceptively simple. Below the surface, it was a tangle of complications. They conversed in French, the language they had in common. They discussed the meals he was preparing, and because they both liked to sail, the science of currents and winds. That was as personal as he got. Carmen had always been curious about her mother's relationship with Fabius. Caletta had been at ease with him from the first, when a water taxi deposited him at the door open to the sea and he greeted her in Euskera. For a time, Carmen suspected their relationship was sexual. However, after her father's death, Carmen realized the intensity of Caletta's faithfulness to her late husband. She never had an evening out with another man, much less a romantic entanglement. While maintaining her boundaries—he cooked and served every meal and never sat at the dinner table with the family—she treated him less as a servant than a kind of artist-in-residence. They played chess and worked together in the vegetable garden. For Carmen, the oddest aspect of all this was the very fact of Fabius's presence. His predecessor was a housekeeper who was also an above-average cook. While Caletta liked a good meal, she often went whole days fueling herself with tea, cheese, and an apple. But while visiting Basque country with her husband on their extended honeymoon, she developed a passion, both cultural and culinary, for the cuisine and its hearty intricacies, the soups and stews in iron crocks that simmered for days in brick ovens. The same sort of oven she had built for Fabius, to his specifications.

When Carmen asked her mother how they could know Fabius so little after so many years, Calleta replied without hesitation, "I know all I need to. I prefer people who remain within their own mysteries. Who don't betray their true selves. The first months Fabius was here, I waited for him to open up and talk about himself. Then I saw he was never going to do that. And it struck me that that was all I needed to know about him. I respected it. If you pry with him, Carmen, he'll step back. He'll disappear."

6

Carmen had only seen Fabius reveal strong emotions once: at her mother's funeral. He had described her mother's death to Carmen. Two days before, during Calleta's morning swim, it was Fabius, at the kitchen window, who recognized how much trouble she was in, even before she did. A hundred yards from shore, she thought she was cramping up, but in fact she was experiencing a minor stroke. It nearly froze her right side. The pain was excruciating. On land, she might have survived long enough to receive medical attention, but not out there. She was trying to right herself with her left arm, to keep her head above the waves. Fabius said he ran through the house, into the room with the door open onto the sea, kicked off his shoes, and dived in. He was a strong swimmer, but he couldn't cover that distance, against the current, before she went under. Swimming sidestroke, he pulled her in, lifting her to the threshold of the open door and climbing the short ladder there himself. He gave her mouth-to-mouth, pressing on her chest to get the water out of her lungs, to get her heart beating, but it was too late. He wept over her body, and he wept at the funeral, and he wept with Carmen, who had flown home in time to toss her mother's ashes into the sea. He was solicitous of Carmen all that week. But then he stopped talking altogether. Already taciturn, he withdrew into an unbending silence. He asked Carmen if, for a while, she would put all her requests and instructions in writing, and he would reply in kind. She agreed without resentment, though she herself was in mourning. She guessed that the only reason he had remained at the house to cook for her was out of loyalty to her mother.

The one time Carmen's curiosity got the best of her, she broke the one absolute rule of the house, laid down to her by her mother, and after dinner tried to follow Fabius to his quarters from the kitchen. After walking quietly down two short corridors, she could no longer hear his footfalls, and she found herself in a large pitch-black room with cold stone walls. It was only by feeling her way along three of the walls that she found a door which opened onto a corridor she had never seen before, just wide enough for her to pass through. With several twists and turns, it led to a storeroom off the kitchen.

She would never try to follow him again.

7

After Carmen's accident, weariness, then fear, began eating away at her. She couldn't sleep. She visited two doctors, both of whom said she was in perfect health. They gave her sleeping pills and told her to quit smoking. She thought of going abroad. She had studied drawing and painting in Austria and Italy, and been happy there. Until her mother died, Carmen had never thought of returning to live in her childhood home. But now it was her house, and in the short time she lived there she painted the so-called "ocean canvases" that would make her famous. She was also trying to sketch a large house that she saw clearly in her mind's eye, but could never capture with her pencil. She felt it was central to her next painting. She kept drawing and erasing—altering the slope of the roof, the number of windows, the size of the porches and doors—determined to fix the dimensions and fill in the details.

The sleeping pills didn't work, and she couldn't bear another night of staring into the darkness, so she rented an apartment in the city. A brownstone on a quiet street with shade trees. She slept well there every night since, only returning to her house to paint by day. She ate lunch in the room that opened onto the sea, but had Fabius pack her supper in a basket that she took back to her apartment at dusk. She didn't say why she had adopted this regimen and was not surprised that he made no comment.

She continued reading Claudine Rementeria's *Rooms by the Sea*. She had nearly finished the English version, but was finding the Euskera edition harder to get through now. She couldn't afford to put that much energy into it. Claudine wrote a great deal about her marriage, the books and music shared with her husband, and the births of their son, the future father of Calleta Rementeria. She also wrote in passing about the sprawling Victorian house she lived in. Carmen realized that its foundation would have included the site of the current house, but was five times as large. The four-story house was constructed of pale gray limestone transported from Indiana. The trim was oak, the roof slate. Mostly she mentioned the details of the interior in passing, a backdrop to the life of the family. People were born, died, fell ill, fell in love, ate and drank, gazed at the stars from the solarium and at night, from their beds, listened to the soft rhythms of the surf. Members of the family—men, women, and children—spent a great deal of time swimming and fishing and taking long hikes along the shore. It was a fairly new house, well built, airy and light. And constantly expanding, Carmen noted with a chill. It seemed the Rementerias were inveterate renovators, adding new wings, knocking down walls, redesigning rooms, upgrading fixtures.

Calleta had once told Carmen that, incredibly enough, no photograph, painting, sketch, or other visual rendering of the house existed. A fire in the library had destroyed the family photograph albums, financial records, and a filing cabinet that contained the house's blueprints and construction drawings. Calleta had searched in vain for duplicates of the blueprints in the county clerk's archives.

One afternoon Carmen found a murky photograph tucked between pages 178 and 179 of the Euskera edition. It was the house. The entire Rementeria family was lined up before it on a snowy Christmas morning. Between the falling snow and the fading of the photograph, she could barely make out their faces. The most distinctive features of the house were a pair of turrets with 360-degree windows, a broad widow's walk, and a pair of right whales carved into the limestone, flanking the front door.

So the surviving, definitive image of the house was that photograph, augmented by a series of brief, fractured descriptions scattered throughout *Rooms by the Sea*.

There were also the images in Carmen's sketchbook, for this was the same house she had been trying to draw.

8

Claudine began her last chapter recounting, as fact, the Basque legend that they were descended from the inhabitants of the lost continent of Atlantis. That Atlantis was destroyed by a mysterious cataclysm, an earthquake or volcanic eruption, and sank to the bottom of the Atlantic. That its last king was Gades, who founded and gave his name to the ancient city of Cádiz, on the southern coast of Spain. Atlantis's few survivors washed up there. They made their way north and settled high in the Pyrenees, as far from the sea as possible. She added to the story her own twist: that several survivors who had come closest to drowning were transformed into amphibious beings and forced to remain behind. To survive, they needed to remain close to the sea. They became fishermen and built houses on stilts along the coast. They had to spend at least eight hours a day in the sea, either swimming on the beach, or far from shore, off their boats.

Claudine's husband, like his father and grandfather before him, had inherited the vast fishing fleet—two dozen ships by the time he was running the company—that had been assembled by his great-grandfather, himself descended from generations of sailors on fishing boats whose earliest ancestors were humble fishermen, those same survivors of Atlantis who settled by the sea.

9

Several weeks after she tried to follow him, Fabius served Carmen lunch at the long dining room table. He had prepared a more elaborate meal than usual, all seafood: monkfish soup, seaweed salad, octopus ceviche, and squid stuffed with crab and scallops. While she ate and drank a glass of wine, Carmen was reading *Rooms by the Sea*. Comparing the two editions, she realized that at least three pages of the last chapter had been cut in the English translation.

She was so immersed, going back and forth between the books and flipping through her dictionary, that she didn't notice Fabius had brought out a dish of apricots stuffed with goat cheese, another wineglass, and the bottle of wine. He was standing on the other side of the table watching her. She was startled to see him in a double-breasted blue suit with a blue shirt and pale blue tie, rather than his customary whites.

"Thank you," she said. "This was delicious."

"May I sit?"

He had surprised her again, not because he wanted to join her for the first time ever, but because he had asked her in English.

"Of course," she said.

He set down the wineglass and bottle and pulled out a chair. "This is the oldest wine in the house. A Faustino Rioja." He refilled her glass and then filled his own.

"You speak English," she said.

"I never said I didn't. I said I spoke enough languages already. I need to talk with you." He folded his hands on the table. "I see you've nearly finished the book."

"Yes."

"You've noticed that the number of pages in the two editions is roughly the same—until the last chapter. Would you like to know why?"

"I was trying to work through the original."

"I'll save you the time. And add a few things you ought to know. You've read what she says about the origin of the Basques."

"You believe it?"

"Of course. It was shortened by the translator, herself a Basque, for the same reason any of us would: it would reveal long-kept secrets."

"Then you're Basque, too."

"I didn't know it when I first came here. Looking back on my life, I should have. My father did not speak Euskera. He grew up in Malaga, far from Basque country, but he was a Basque. He didn't know it because he was an orphan, adopted by a Spanish couple when he was an infant. I discovered that his true parents died in a fire in Donostia, which is what we call San Sebastián."

"And what is it that the translator had to cut?"

"The fact that certain Basques die twice."

"What?"

"Those descended from the coastal Basques are amphibious, as Claudine says. After they give up this earthly life, they become marine creatures exclusively, for a year. Then they truly perish. When the time comes for this transition, they know it and prepare themselves. They enjoy another year of life, so long as it is aquatic at all times, not just eight hours a day."

Carmen stared at him.

"You don't believe it?" Fabius said.

"I don't know."

"Your great-grandmother describes the process in detail. She herself would undergo it." He paused. "Your mother did as well."

"What are you talking about?"

"Your mother didn't drown. She wasn't cremated."

"You lied to me?"

"It was her request."

"So she lied."

"Before you arrived for the funeral, she left here—by water."

Carmen pushed the books aside and leaned closer to him. "That's over a year ago."

"Yes. So now she's truly gone. I'm sorry to shock you like this. I planned to tell you at a more propitious time."

"When would that be?"

"One day out on the water, sailing," he said calmly. "But I have no choice now. It's time for me to prepare myself. I'm leaving today."

"Just like that?"

"In rare instances, we have more time. Usually it is like this. I've lived a hundred years. I'll live one more."

"You're sixty-eight."

He smiled. "Trust me, I have been in this life longer than that. Your family has been good to me. Now I'll go back to the place of our origins."

"Basque country?"

"No. Before that. Before Cádiz." He paused. "You understand?"

"I know what you're saying, but I don't understand."

"It's the truth."

Carmen drank some wine. "So this will happen to me as well. That's what you're telling me."

He nodded. "But only after you've lived a long life."

10

That was Fabius's goodbye. Carmen never saw him again.

A few hours later, she discovered that his ocean kayak was gone. He had left his keys on the kitchen counter. The house keys and a large brass key, embossed with a trident. The kitchen was tidy. His aprons were hanging on their hooks, but his sisters' photograph was gone.

His keys in hand, Carmen left the kitchen by the door Fabius always used, walked down the two short corridors she'd seen before, but instead of getting lost, she entered a much longer, well lit corridor. It was unremarkable. The walls white, with blue sconces, the ceiling blue. She passed rooms with more of those white doors from the shipwrecked *Sabina*. At the end of this corridor there was a blue door with a brass lock. It couldn't have been easier to reach.

She knocked twice, but she knew Fabius was gone. She unlocked the door and entered a large, circular blue room that smelled of the sea. Its circular windows were more like portholes, but larger. All of them looked onto the sea. The bed had been stripped and the room cleared of all possessions. The desk was bare, the closets and cabinets empty. The bathroom was also huge, tiled in blue and white, with brass fixtures. The sink, toilet, and shower stall were white. But it was the circular bathtub that drew Carmen into the room. It had recently been drained. Its deep blue tiles were still damp. Seven feet deep, with a diameter of fifteen feet, it was more like a pool than a tub. A man could submerge himself easily or float for many hours. Hours, she thought, when he could not remain in the sea if the weather was harsh or his work didn't allow it.

Carmen had already moved most of her things to her apartment in the city. That evening she gathered up what remained, her canvases and paints, her books. Passing by the room that opened onto the sea, she saw that the door was closed. She turned off the lights and locked up the house and walked down the stone path.

When she glanced over her shoulder, she saw, not the house she had just left, but the large house in the photograph and in her sketches, its windows lit up and the sea behind it a luminous blue. She gazed at it for a long moment before entering the forest. She didn't look back again, and she never returned to that place.

MICHAEL CONNELLY *is the author of 28 novels, many of which feature Detective Harry Bosch of the Los Angeles Police Department. He lives in Florida and California. He first saw Edward Hopper's "Nighthawks" at the Art Institute of Chicago while writing his first Bosch novel and was inspired to include the painting at the ending of the book.*

Nighthawks, 1942

NIGHTHAWKS

BY MICHAEL CONNELLY

Bosch didn't know how people in this place could stand it. It felt like the wind off the lake was freezing his eyeballs in their sockets. He had come totally unprepared for the surveillance. He had layers on but his top layer was an L.A. trench coat with a thin zip-in liner that wouldn't keep a Siberian husky warm in the Chicago winter. Bosch wasn't a man who gave much credit to clichés but he found himself thinking: I'm too old for this.

The subject of his surveillance had come down Wabash and turned east toward Michiganand the park. Bosch knew where she was going because she had headed this way on her lunch break at the bookstore the day before as well. When she got to the museum she showed her member pass and was quickly admitted entrance. Bosch had to wait in line to buy a day pass. But he wasn't worried about losing her. He knew where she would be. He didn't bother to check his coat because he was cold to the bone, and he didn't expect to be in the museum more than an hour—the girl would have to get back to the bookstore.

He moved through the galleries quickly on a direct route to the permanent Hopper exhibition. There he found her sitting on the one long bench. She had her notebook and pencil out and was already working. He had been surprised the day before to find she was not sketching in her notebook as she repeatedly glanced up and studied the painting. She was writing.

Bosch surmised that the Hopper painting was the biggest draw in the museum. Many people came for it and often carelessly stood in front her, blocking her view. She never cleared her throat to alert them. She never said anything. She sometimes leaned to her left or right to see around one of the blockers and Bosch thought he would see a slight smile on her lips, as though she were pleased with what the new angle of observation had brought her.

The lone bench was crowded with four Japanese tourists sitting in a row next to her. They looked like high school students come to study the master's most well known work. Bosch took a position on the other side of the gallery, behind the surveillance subject's back so she wouldn't notice him. He rubbed his hands together and tried to get some warmth into them. His joints were aching from the cold and the nine-block walk to the museum. He had found no interior space with an angle on the front doors of bookstore. He had waited outside, hovering around the entrance to a garage, for her to emerge at lunchtime.

Bosch saw a spot on the opposite end of the bench come open when one of the students got up. He moved toward it, sitting down and using the three students between him and the surveillance subject as a blind. Without leaning forward and exposing himself, he tried to look down the bench and possibly see what she was writing in her notebook. But she was writing with her left hand and that blocked his view.

He looked up at the painting when there was a moment the crowd cleared and it could be seen clearly. His eyes were drawn toward the man sitting alone at the counter, his face turned toward the shadows of the painting. There was a couple sitting across the counter from him. They looked bored. The man sitting alone was ignoring them.

"Iku jikan."

Bosch turned his eyes from the painting. An older Japanese woman was signaling the sitting students impatiently. It was time to go. The two girls and a boy stood up and scurried out of the gallery to join the rest of their classmates. Their five minutes with the masterpiece were up.

That left Bosch alone on the bench with the subject of his surveillance. Four feet of space on the bench separated them. Bosch realized that sitting down had been a strategic mistake. She could get a good look at him if she looked away from the painting and her notebook. She might remember him if this lasted another day.

He didn't move at first because that might draw her eye. He decided to wait two minutes and then get up. He would turn quickly away so she wouldn't see his face. In the meantime, she did not seem to notice his presence and he went back to looking at the painting. He wondered about the painter's choice to show the interior of the diner from the outside. To paint it from the shadows of night.

But then she spoke.

"Magnificent, isn't it?" she asked.

"Excuse me?" Bosch asked.

"The painting. It's pretty magnificent."

"That's what they say, yes."

"Who are you?"

Bosch froze.

"What do you mean?" he asked.

"Which one of them do you identify with?" she said. "You've got the man by himself, the couple who don't look all that happy to be there, and the man working behind the counter. Which one are you?"

Bosch turned from her to look at the painting.

"I'm not sure," he answered. "How about you?"

"Definitely the loner," she said. "The woman looks bored. She's checking her nails. I'm never bored. It's the one all alone."

Bosch stared at the painting.

"Yeah, me too, I guess," he said.

"What do you think the story is?" she asked.

"What, with them? What makes you think there's a story?"

"There's always a story. Painting is story telling. Do you know why it's called 'Nighthawks'?"

"No, not really."

"Well, the night part is obvious. But check out the beak on the guy with the woman."

Bosch did. He saw it for the first time. The man's nose was sharp and bent like a bird's. Nighthawks.

"I see it," he said.

He smiled and nodded. He had learned something.

"But just look at the light," she said. "All light in the painting comes from within the coffee shop. It is the beacon that draws them there. Light and dark, yin and yang, clearly on display."

"I would guess you are a painter but you are writing in your notebook, not drawing."

"Not a painter. But I am a story teller. A writer, I hope. One day."

He knew she was only 23 years old. It seemed too young to have accomplished anything yet as a writer.

"So you are a writer but you come to look at a painting," he said.

"I come for inspiration," she said. "I think I could write a million words about it. When I am having trouble I come here. It gets me through."

"What kind of trouble?"

"Writing is about what happens next. Sometimes that doesn't come so easily. So I come here and look at something like this."

She gestured toward the painting with her free hand, then nodded. Problem solved.

Bosch nodded too. He thought he understood inspiration and how it could travel from one discipline to another, how it could be harnessed for an endeavor seeming completely different. He had always thought that studying and understanding the sound of a saxophone had made him a better detective. He wasn't sure why or if he could ever explain it to himself or anybody else. But he knew that hearing Frank Morgan play "Lullaby" somehow made him better at what he did.

Bosch nodded at the notebook in her lap.

"Are you writing about the painting?" he asked.

"Actually, no," she said. "I am writing my novel. I just come here a lot in hope that something about the painting rubs off on me."

She laughed.

"I know, sounds crazy," she said.

"Not really," Bosch said. "I think I understand. Is your novel about someone alone?"

"Yes, very much so."

"Based on you?"

"Sometimes."

Bosch nodded. He liked talking to her even though it broke the rules.

"So that's my story," she said. "Why are you here?"

It took him by surprise.

"Why am I here?" he asked, buying time to think. "The painting. I wanted to see it in person."

"Enough to come back two days in a row?" she asked.

Bosch was caught. She smiled and pointed to her eye.

"They say a good writer is an observer," she said. "I saw you here yesterday."

Bosch nodded sheepishly.

"Couldn't help notice how cold you were," she said. "That jacket . . . you aren't from around here, are you?"

"No, not really," Bosch said. "I'm from L.A."

He watched her as he said it. His words were as freezing as the wind outside the museum.

"All right, who are you?" she asked. "What is this?"

Bosch waited in the foyer twenty minutes before Griffin's security man took him back to the office. Griffin was seated behind a large mahogany-topped desk. The same place he was sitting the day Bosch had met him.

Through the open curtain of the window to his right Bosch could see the still surface of a pool. Griffin was wearing a long-sleeved workout ensemble with a zip-up turtleneck. His face was flush from whatever activity accounted for a workout for him.

"Sorry to hold you up, Bosch," he said. "I was rowing."

Bosch just nodded. Griffin gestured to one of the chairs in front of his desk.

"Have a seat," he said. "Tell me what you've found."

Bosch stayed standing.

"This won't take long," he said. "The lead didn't pan out. I went to Chicago but it wasn't her."

Griffin leaned back in his seat, digesting Bosch's words. He was a man of wealth and power and was unused to being told that things didn't pan out. Things always panned out for Reginald Griffin, producer of three Academy Award–winning films.

"Did you speak to her?" he asked.

"Yes," Bosch said. "At length. I also checked out her apartment while she and her roommate were at work. I found nothing that indicated she was hiding her true identity. It's not her."

"You're wrong, Bosch. It was her. I know it."

"She ran away eight years ago. That's a long time and people change. Especially kids that age. The photo was not a good shot of her."

"You were supposed to be good, Bosch. Highly recommended. I should have hired someone else. Looks like I have to now."

"You won't have to bother. Just find a geneticist."

"What are you talking about?"

Bosch's hands had been in the pockets of his coat. He had zipped out the lining after returning from Chicago, but the El Niño rain pattern continued in the City of Angels and he needed the trench coat. It may not have kept him warm in Chicago but it would keep him dry in Los Angeles, even if it did make him look like a walking cliché. His daughter had reminded him of that. At least he wasn't wearing a fedora with it.

From the left pocket of the coat he produced a plastic bag. He leaned forward and placed it down on the desk.

"DNA sample," he said. "It's hair I took off her brush when I was in her apartment. Get a lab to extract DNA and then compare it to yours. You'll have scientific results then and you'll see, she's not your daughter."

Griffin grabbed the bag and looked at it.

"You said she has a roommate," he said. "How do I know this isn't her fucking hair?"

"Because her roommate is African-American and she's also a guy," Bosch said. "Any lab will be able to tell you the content of that bag comes from a Caucasian female."

Bosch put his hand back in his pocket. He wanted to get out of there. He knew he should have never taken the job in the first place. The stories Griffin's daughter had told him while sitting on the bench in front of the "Nighthawks" made it clear that he needed to vet his employers before agreeing to do anything for them. You live, you learn. Bosch was new at the private eye business. It had been less than a year since he pulled the pin at the LAPD.

Griffin pulled the plastic bag across the top of the desk and put it into a drawer.

"I'll have it checked," he said. "But I want you to stay with the case. You must have other ideas, all those years you spent on cold cases tracing people."

Bosch shook his head.

"You hired me to go to Chicago, follow the photo, you said," Bosch said. "I did that and it wasn't the right girl. I don't think I am interested in the rest. When your daughter wants you to know where she is, she'll reach out."

Griffin seemed incensed—either by Bosch's rejection or the idea that he should wait on his daughter to make contact.

"Bosch, we're not done here. I want you on the case."

"You can get anybody to do what I do. Just look in a phonebook. I'm not interested in continuing the relationship. We are, in fact, done."

Bosch turned toward the office door. Griffin's security man was there. He was looking over Bosch's shoulder at his employer, looking for a signal or some direction on what to do; let Bosch leave or stop him.

"Let him go," Griffin said. "He's useless—no wonder he demanded his money up front. She got to him. I know it was her in the photo but she got to him."

The security man opened the office door and stood to the side to let Bosch pass through.

"Bosch!" Griffin called.

Bosch was about to pass through the door. He stopped and then turned around to take Griffin's final verbal assault head-on.

"She told you about Maui, didn't she?" Griffin asked.

"I don't know what you're talking about," Bosch said. "I told you, it wasn't your daughter."

"I was drunk, goddamnit, and it never happened again."

Bosch waited for more but that was it. He turned and walked through the door.

"I'll show myself out," he said to the security man.

The door was closed behind him and the security man trailed him as Bosch made his way through the house to the front door. At one point he heard Griffin shouting again from his closed office.

"I was drunk!"

As if that were an excuse, Bosch thought.

Outside the house Bosch got into his car and drove off the property. He hoped the old Cherokee dropped oil on the cobblestone driveway.

When he was several blocks clear of the Griffin estate he pulled to the curb and grabbed the burner out of the cup holder between the seats. He called the one number that was programmed into the throw-away phone on a speed dial.

The call was answered after three rings.

"Yes?" a young woman's voice said.

"It's me," Bosch said. "I just left your father's house."

"Did he believe you?"

"I don't think so. But I don't know. He took the hair, said he'd have it tested. If he does that he might be convinced."

"And it won't come back to your daughter?"

"No, she's never been DNA typed anywhere. It will come back as no match. Hopefully he'll leave it at that."

"I'm going to move again. I can't risk it."

"It might be the smart thing."

"Did he mentioned Maui?"

"Yes, as I was leaving."

"The same story I told you?"

"He didn't tell the story but his bringing it up, that confirmed it for me. I knew I was doing the right thing."

There was a silence before she spoke again.

"Thank you."

"No, I should thank you. Did you figure out the photo yet?"

"Oh, yes, I did. It was from a book signing we had at the store with D. H. Reilly, the mystery novelist. The book he was signing—*No Trap So Deadly*—was optioned by my father's company. I didn't know that. At his office they have a clip service that pulls all media hits regarding their productions and properties. It helps them target promotions. It was just dumb luck. I was in the photo in background and he must've seen it when he was looking through all the newspaper clips on Reilly and the book he optioned."

Bosch thought about that for a moment. It seemed to work. A photo at a book signing tips off a search for a runaway daughter. Griffin had not told Bosch the origin of the photo he had given him when he hired him and put him on the case.

"Angela," Bosch said. "Considering all of this, I think you might want to change jobs too. You might even want to do more than just move house. You might want to change cities too."

"Okay," she said in a quite voice. "You are probably right. It's just that I love it here."

"Pick someplace warm," Bosch said. "Maybe Miami."

His attempt at humor fell flat. He heard only silence as Angela considered having to move again to avoid her father finding her.

During the silence Bosch flashed for a moment on the painting. The man sitting alone at the counter. He wondered how long Angela could last as a nighthawk, moving from city to city, always being at the counter by herself.

"Listen," he said. "I'm not going to get rid of this phone, okay? I know that was the plan but I'm going to hold on to it. You call me anytime, okay? If you need help or even if you just want to talk. You call me anytime, okay?"

"Okay," she said. "Then I guess I keep this phone as well. You can call me too."

Bosch nodded even though she couldn't see this.

"I'll do that," he said. "You take care."

He ended the call and slipped the burner into the pocket of his trench coat. He checked the sideview mirror for traffic coming up behind him. He waited for it to clear and then he pulled away from the curb. He was hungry and wanted to get something to eat. He thought one more time about the man sitting alone at the counter.

I am that man, he thought as he drove.

A former journalist, folksinger and attorney, **JEFFERY DEAVER** *is an international number-one bestselling author. His novels have appeared on bestseller lists around the world; they're sold in 150 countries and translated into twenty-five languages.*

The author of thirty-seven novels, three collections of short stories, and a nonfiction law book, and a lyricist of a country-western album, he's received or been shortlisted for dozens of awards. His The Bodies Left Behind *was named Novel of the Year by the International Thriller Writers association, and his Lincoln Rhyme thriller* The Broken Window *and a stand-alone,* Edge, *were also nominated for that prize.He's a seven-time Edgar nominee.*

Deaver has been honored with the Lifetime Achievement Award by the Bouchercon World Mystery Convention and by the Raymond Chandler Lifetime Achievement Award in Italy.

His book A Maiden's Grave *was made into an HBO movie starring James Garner and Marlee Matlin, and his novel* The Bone Collector *was a feature release from Universal Pictures, starring Denzel Washington and Angelina Jolie. Lifetime aired an adaptation of his* The Devil's Teardrop.

While his father was an accomplished painter and his sister is a talented artist, Deaver's last foray into art involved fingerpainting; sadly, his opus no longer exists, as his mother insisted that it be scrubbed off his bedroom wall.

Hotel by a Railroad, 1952

THE INCIDENT OF 10 NOVEMBER

BY JEFFERY DEAVER

December 2, 1954

General Mikhail Tasarich, First Deputy Chairman of the
Council of Ministers of the Union of Soviet Socialist Republics

Kremlin Senate, Moscow

Comrade General Tasarich:

I, Colonel Mikhail Sergeyevich Sidorov, of recent attached to the GRU,
Directorate for Military Intelligence, am writing this report regarding
the incident of 10 November, of this year, and the death associated
therewith.

First, allow me to offer some information about myself. I will say that
in my 48 years on this earth I have spent 32 of them as a soldier in the
service of Our Mother-Homeland. And those have been proud years, years

that I would not exchange for any sum. During the Great Patriotic War, I fought in the 62nd Army, 13th Guards Rifle Division (our motto, as you, Comrade, may recall, is: Not One Step Back! And, O, how we stayed true to that slogan!). I was privileged to serve under General Vasily Chuikov at Stalingrad, where you, of course, commanded the army that, during the glorious Operation Uranus, crushed the Romanian flank and encircled the German 6th Army (which merely months later surrendered, setting the stage for Our Mother-Homeland's victory over the Nazi Reich). I myself was wounded several times in the butchery that was the defense of Stalingrad but continued to fight, despite the wounds and hardships. For my efforts I received the Order of Bogdan Khmelnitsky, 3rd Class, and the Order of Glory, 2nd Class. And, of course, my unit, as yours, Comrade General, was honored with the Order of Lenin.

After the War, I remained in the military and joined the GRU, since I had, I was told, a knack for the subject of intelligence, having identified and denounced a number of soldiers whose loyalty to the army and to Revolutionary ideals was questionable. Everyone I denounced admitted their crime or was found guilty by tribunals and either executed or sent East. Few GRU officers had such a record as I.

I ran several networks of spies, which were successful in halting Western attempts to infiltrate Our Mother-Homeland, and I was promoted through the GRU to my recent rank of colonel.

In March of 1951 I was given the assignment of protecting a certain individual who was deemed instrumental in Our Mother-Homeland's plans for self-defense against the imperialism of the West.

The man I am referring to was a former German scientist, Heinrich Dieter, then aged 47.

Comrade Dieter was born in Obernessa, Weissenfels, the son of a professor of mathematics. His mother was a teacher of science at a boarding school near her husband's university. Comrade Dieter had one brother, his junior by three years. Comrade Dieter studied physics at the Martin Luther University of Halle-Wittenberg, which awarded him a bachelor's of science degree, and he received a master's of science in physics from Leopold Franzens University of Innsbruck. He completed his doctorate work in physics shortly thereafter at the University of Berlin. He specialized in column ionization of alpha particles. No, Comrade General, I too was not familiar with this esoteric subject but, as you will see in a moment, his discipline of study was to have quite some significant consequences.

While in school he joined the student branch of the Social Democratic Party of Germany (SPD) and the Reichsbanner Schwarz-Rot-Gold, which served as the party's paramilitary wing. But he quit these organizations after a time, as he showed little interest in politics, preferring to spend the hours in the classroom or laboratory. He was, it is asserted, part Jew, and accordingly could not join the Nazi Party. However, since he appeared apolitical and did not openly practice his religion, he was permitted to maintain his teaching and research posts. That leniency on the part of the Nazis could also be attributed to his brilliance; Albert Einstein himself said of Comrade Dieter that he had a formidable mind and was, rare among scientists, a man who could appreciate both the theoretical and the applicable aspects of physics.

When the Dieter family observed that people like themselves—intellectuals of Jewish heritage—would be at risk in Germany they made plans to emigrate. Dieter's parents and brother (and his family) successfully traveled from Berlin to England and from there to America, but Comrade Dieter, delayed in finishing a research project, was stopped on the eve of his departure by the Gestapo, based on a professor's recommendation that he be pressed into service to assist in the war effort. Owing to his research (concerning the aforementioned "alpha particles"), Comrade Dieter was assigned to assist with the development of the most significant weapon of our century: the atomic bomb.

He was part of the second Uranverein, the Nazi uranium project, jointly run by the HWA, the Army Ordnance Office, and RFR, the Reich Research Council of the Ministry of Education. His contributions were significant, though he did not advance far in rank or salary owing to his Jewish background.

Following Our Mother-Homeland's victory over the Nazis in the Great Patriotic War, Comrade Dieter was identified as one of the Uranverein scientists by our NKVD's Alsos Project officers in Germany. After fruitful discussions with the security officers, Comrade Dieter volunteered to come to the Soviet Union and continue his research into atomic weapons—now for the benefit of Our Mother-Homeland. He stated that he considered it an honor to assist in protecting against the West's aggression and their attempts to spread the poisonous hegemony of capitalism and decadence throughout Europe, Asia, and the world.

Comrade Dieter was transported immediately to Russia and underwent a period of reeducation and indoctrination. He became a member of the Communist Party, learned to speak Russian, and was helped to understand the lessons of the Revolution and the value of the Proletariat. He fervently embraced Our Mother-Homeland's culture and people. Once this period of transition was completed he was assigned work at the All-Union Scientific Research Institute of Experimental Physics at the premier Atomograd in the nation: the closed-city of Arzamas-16. It was to here that I was sent and assigned the job of protecting him.

I spent much time with Comrade Dieter and can report that he took to his work immediately, and his contributions were many, including assisting in the preparation of Our Mother-Homeland's first hydrogen bomb, detonated last August, you may recall, Comrade General. That test, the RDS-6, was a device of 400 kilotons. Comrade Dieter's team had recently been working to create a fissile device in the megaton range, as the Americans have done (though it is well known that their weapons are in all ways inferior to ours).

Like most such extra-national scientists vital to our national defense, Comrade Dieter was closely watched. One of my duties was to take measure of his personal loyalty to Our Mother-Homeland and report on same to all relevant ministries. My scrupulous observations convinced me of his devotion to our cause and that his loyalty was beyond reproach.

For instance, he was, as I mention, part Jew. Now, he knew that I had denounced certain men and women in Arzamas-16 for subversive and counterrevolutionary speech and activity; every one of those happened to be, by purest coincidence, a Jew. I inquired of Comrade Dieter if he was troubled by my actions and he assured me that, no, he would have done the same had anyone, friends or family, Jew or gentile, displayed even a whisper of anti-Revolutionary leaning. To prove that I harbored no ill will against the Children of David, I explained that one of my former assignments was identifying Jews as part of the ongoing Central Committee's program to resettle his people in the newly formed State of Israel as expeditiously as possible. He expressed to me his pleasure at learning this fact.

Comrade Dieter had no wife and I would arrange "chance meetings" between him and beautiful women, with the goal that he take a Russian-born wife. (This did not occur but he did have relations with some of them for varying lengths of time.) Each of these women reported to me in detail about their conversations, and not a single word of disloyalty ever passed Comrade Dieter's lips when speaking with them, even in moments that he believed were wholly unguarded.

Further, I can hardly count the many times when he and I would sit with a bottle of vodka, and I would regale him at length and in great detail about the philosophy of Marxist dialectic materialism, reading long passages. As his Russian was good but not perfect I would also read to him the lengthy reports of speeches by noble chairman Khrushchev, as they appeared in *Pravda*. He took great interest in what I read to him.

His loyalty was evident to me in one other aspect of his life: his passion for art.

A love of painting and sculpture was a tradition in his family, he explained; his brother was a professor of art history at a university in upstate New York and that brother's daughter, Comrade Dieter's niece, is a painter (and dancer) in the city of Manhattan. When he finally received permission from the Party to correspond with his family, all his letters were carefully vetted by me to make certain that nothing impugned the state or hinted at disloyalty (much less discussed his work). The subject was exclusively his, and his family's, love of art.

He described the rousing art scene here in Our Mother-Homeland, extolling the Soviet artists who labor to further the goals of the Revolution. He wrote glowingly to his family about the "Socialist Realist" movement that has typified our culture since the days of Comrade Lenin: paintings that are not only brilliantly executed but embrace the four pillars of Our Mother-Homeland values: Party-mindedness, ideology-mindedness, class-content and truthfulness. Among the art that he sent to his family were a postcard of a landscape by Dmitry Maevsky, another card of a thoughtful portrait by Vladimir Alexandrovich Gorb (of the famed Repin Institute of Art), and a poster announcing a forthcoming Party Congress, which

Comrade Dieter himself would be attending, illustrated with the rousing "Trumpeter and Standard-bearer" by Mitrovan Grekov, a work, of course, much revered by all patriotic countrymen.

His brother in return would send postcards or small posters of paintings that he believed Comrade Dieter might enjoy and that he might use to decorate his quarters. These cards, like the letters themselves, were vetted by the GRU technical division and found to contain no secret messages, microfilm, etc., though I did not think that likely. My concern with these gifts, for concern there was, Comrade General, lay elsewhere.

You are perhaps aware of the American Central Intelligence Agency's International Organizations Division. This insidious directorate (which the GRU was the first to uncover, I must add) has in recent years attempted to use art as a weapon—by promoting the incoherent and decadent American "abstract expressionism" to the world. This absurd defacing of canvasses, by the likes of Jackson Pollock, Robert Motherwell, Willem de Kooning and Mark Rothko, is considered by true connoisseurs of art to be sacrilege. Had these men (and the occasional woman) committed such self-indulgence here they would find themselves under arrest. The International Organizations Directive is the CIA's pathetic attempt to proclaim that the West values freedom of expression and creativity while Our Mother-Homeland does not. This is, on its face, absurd. Why, even the American President Harry Truman said of the abstract expressionist movement, "If that's art, then I'm a Hottentot."

But I was vastly relieved to note that Comrade Dieter's family—and obviously he—also rejected such nonsensical travesty. The paintings and sketches they sent him were realistic works that displayed traditional composition and themes not incompatible with those of the Revolution—by such Americans as Frederick Remington, George Innes, and Edward Hopper, as well as classic painters like the Italian Jacopo Vignali.

Indeed, some of the reproductions sent to Comrade Dieter were tantamount to agitprop supporting the values of Our Mother-Homeland! The Jerome Myers paintings, for instance, of immigrants struggling on the streets of New York, and those of Otto Dix, the German, whose paintings mocked the decadence of the Weimar Republic.

If ever anyone seemed enamored of his adopted home, it was Comrade Dieter. No, my instincts as an intelligence officer told me that if there were any risk regarding this singular man, it would not be his loyalty but that foreign agents or counterrevolutionaries would attempt to murder him, in an effort to derail Our Mother-Homeland's efforts in the field of atomic weapons. Protecting him from such harm became my whole life and I made certain he was protected at all times.

Now, having "set the stage," Comrade General Tasarich, I must turn to the unfortunate incident of 10 November of this year.

Comrade Dieter was active in the Party and attended Party Congresses and rallies whenever he could. These, however, were rare in the closed city of Arzamas-16 and so he would occasionally travel to larger metropolises in Russia or other nations within the Soviet Union to attend these events. One such gathering was that which I had mentioned earlier—described in the poster illustrated by the artist Grekov: the Joint Party Congress in Berlin, scheduled for November of this year, at which First Secretary Khrushchev and East German Prime Minister Otto Grotewohl would speak. The Congress would celebrate East Germany's recent autonomy and it was anticipated that plans would be announced for allegiances between the two nations. Everyone in Our Mother-Homeland was curious what direction the relationship between these former enemies would take.

I set about to make secure arrangements for the travel, contacting the MVD, Ministry of Internal Affairs, and the newly formed KGB, Committee for State Security. I wished to know if they had any intelligence of potential threats to Soviet citizens at the Congress and any word regarding risks to Comrade Dieter specifically. They said no, there was no such intelligence. Still, I proceeded as if there could well be a threat. I would not accompany him alone but would be aided by a KGB security officer, Lieutenant Nikolai Alesov. Both of us would be armed. Further, we would work closely with the Stasi (I am no fan of the East German Secret Police but one can hardly argue with their—dare I say ruthless?—efficiency).

Our instructions—from both GRU command and Our Mother-Homeland state security ministers—were to insure that Comrade Dieter was at no point in danger from counterrevolutionaries or foreign agents—and from criminals too, Berlin, of course, being well known as a hotbed of illegal activity perpetrated by the Roma, Catholics and Jews that have not been relocated.

We had additional orders too. If it turned out that Western agents or counterrevolutionaries made a move to kidnap Comrade Dieter, we were to make sure that "he was not able to supply our enemies with any classified information about the weapons program."

Our superiors did not elaborate, but it was clear what they meant.

I will be honest, Comrade General, that though I would have had some regrets, if the matter came down to it, I knew I could kill Comrade Dieter to prevent him from falling into the hands of Our Mother-Homeland's foes.

Arrangements thus made, on 9 November, the day before the Congress, we flew in a military aircraft to Warsaw and then took a train to Berlin. There, quarters had been arranged for us in Pankow, not far from Schönhausen Palace. It was a most elegant area, finer than any I had ever seen. As the conference was not until the next day, the three of us—myself, Comrade Dieter and Comrade security officer Alesov—attended the ballet in the evening (an acceptable version of *Swan Lake*, not up to the standards of the Bolshoi). After the performance we dined in a French restaurant (and joked that we need not use atomic bombs on the West; it will gorge itself to death!). We had cigarettes and brandy at the hotel and then retired. Comrade Alesov and I took turns remaining awake and guarding Comrade Dieter's door. The Stasi had searched the hotel for threats and assured us that the identities of every guest checked out satisfactorily.

Indeed, no danger presented itself that night. I must say, however, that despite the absence of hostile actors I got little sleep. This was not due to my duties in safeguarding Comrade Dieter, but rather because I kept thinking this: I am in the country of men who, just a few years earlier, had so viciously slaughtered so many of my fellow soldiers and who had wounded me. And yet here we were, each embracing nearly identical ideals. Such is the universal lesson of the Revolution and the invincibility of the Proletariat. Surely Our Mother-Homeland would conquer the world and live for a thousand years!

The next morning we attended the Party Congress, which proved to be a truly rousing event! Oh, what an honor to see First Secretary Khrushchev in person, as "The Internationale" played and men and women cheered and waved crimson flags. Half of East Berlin seemed to be present! Speech after speech followed—six hours, without stop. At the conclusion, we left in rousing spirits and, accompanied by a somber, weasel-faced Stasi agent, dined at a bierhaus. We then returned to the station to await the overnight train to Warsaw, where the Secret Police officer bade us farewell.

This station was the scene of the incident about which I'm writing.

We were seated in the departure lounge, which was quite crowded. As we read and smoked, Comrade Dieter set down his newspaper and stood, explaining that he was going to use the toilet before the train. The KGB agent and I of course accompanied him.

As we walked toward the facilities I noted nearby a middle-aged couple. The woman was sitting with a book in her lap. She wore a rose-colored dress. A man in trousers, shirt, and waistcoat stood beside her, smoking a cigarette. He was looking out the window. Curiously, on this chill evening, neither wore a coat or hat. I reflected that there was something familiar about them, though I could hardly place what it might be.

Suddenly Comrade Dieter changed direction and walked directly toward the couple. He whispered some words to them, nodding toward myself and Comrade Alesov.

I was immediately alarmed but before I could react, the woman lifted her book, beneath which she was hiding a pistol! She gripped the Walther and pointed it at me and Alesov, as the jacketless man pulled Comrade Dieter away. In American-accented Russian, she told us to throw our weapons to the floor. Comrade Alesov and I, however, drew ours. The woman fired twice—killing Comrade Alesov and wounding me, causing my pistol to fly from my grip, and I dropped to my knees in pain.

But immediately I rose, retrieved the gun and, preparing to shoot with my left hand, ran outside, ignoring my pain and without regard to my own personal safety. But I was too late; the agents, along with Comrade Dieter, were gone.

At the train station the Criminal Investigations Directorate of the National People's Army and the Stasi investigated but it was only a half-hearted affair—this was a matter between the West and Russia; no East Germans were involved. Indeed, they seemed to suspect that I myself had killed Comrade Alesov, as no witnesses were willing to come forth and describe what actually happened. The Stasi offered no justification for this theory other than the incredulity that a middle-aged woman would perpetrate such a crime. . . although, of course, the true answer is that it is easier to arrest a bird in the hand than go tramping through the bush in search of the real perpetrator—especially when that bird is in the employ of a rival security agency. That is, myself.

After two days they concluded that I was innocent, though they treated me like the worst Nonperson imaginable! I was escorted to the Polish border and ignominiously deposited there, where I had to beg the local— and extremely uncooperative—police for transportation to Warsaw for a flight to Moscow, despite my shoving my credentials as a senior member of the Russian intelligence corps into the face of everyone in uniform!

Upon my return home, I was attended to in hospital for my gunshot wound. Once released I was asked to prepare a statement for your Committee, Comrade General, describing my recollection of the events of 10 November.

Accordingly, I am submitting this report to you now.

It is clear to me now that the spiriting away of Comrade Dieter was an operation by the Central Intelligence Agency in Washington DC and carried out with the help of Comrade Dieter's brother and niece. It seems that the family's love of art was a fabrication. The reference to such an interest in the first letter sent by Comrade Dieter to America put his family on notice that he had come upon a way to communicate clandestinely with the intelligence agencies in the United States, in hopes of effecting his escape to the West. His brother and niece were not, as it now seems, involved in the arts at all but are, in their own rights, well-established scientists.

The CIA agents contacted by Comrade Dieter's brother were, without doubt, the ones who sent him the postcards depicting the paintings I referred to above. But they were not random choices; each painting had a meaning, which Dieter was able to work out. My thinking is that the messages were along these lines:

- The painting by Jacopo Vignali, a 17th century artist, of the Archangel Michael saving souls near death told him that the Americans did indeed wish to rescue him from life here in Our Mother-Homeland.

- The Frederick Remington painting called "The Trooper" depicted a man armed with a gun—meaning force would be involved in the rescue.
- The George Innes painting depicted the idyllic land of the New York valley, which is where his brother lived— the image beckoning him to join them.
- The message of "immigrating," that is, fleeing from East to West, could be found in the Jerome Myers work of the tenements of New York City.

You will recall that among the paintings that Comrade Dieter himself sent to America was the poster, incorporating Grekov's painting. The point of that missive was not the illustration itself, but the details of the Party Congress in East Berlin. The CIA rightly took this to mean that Comrade Dieter would be present at the event. Western Agents in Berlin could easily have surveyed hotels and train ticket records and confirmed when he, and his guards, would depart from East Berlin and from which station.

The Otto Dix postcard—of scenes in Germany—was the penultimate sent to Comrade Dieter from America and it confirmed that Berlin was in fact acceptable as the site of the contact with Western agents. The last postcard sent to Comrade Dieter was the most significant of all—the Edward Hopper painting.

This canvas was entitled "Hotel by a Railroad" and it showed two people: a middle-aged woman in a rose-colored dress, reading a book, and man without a jacket or hat, looking out the window. (This is why the couple in the station struck me as familiar; I had seen the postcard of the Hopper painting not long before.) This image informed Comrade Dieter how he might recognize the agents in East Berlin who would effect his escape, as they would be dressed in the garb of the people in Hopper's painting and affecting the same pose.

I have described how the abduction occurred. I have learned since then that, following the shooting in the station, a waiting car outside drove the two operatives and Comrade Dieter to a secret location in East Berlin, where they crossed to the West undetected. From there an American Air Force plane flew Comrade Dieter to London and then onward to the United States.

This is my recollection and assessment of the incident of 10 November 1954, Comrade General, and the events leading up to it.

I am aware of the letter from the Minister of State Security which states the KGB's position that I am solely at fault for the escape of Comrade Dieter from Our Mother-Homeland and his flight to America, as well as the death of Comrade Alesov. It is claimed that I did not appreciate Comrade Dieter's true nature: that he was not, in fact, a loyal member of the Party nor did he feel any allegiance to Our Mother-Homeland. Rather, he was simply feigning, while spending his hours learning what he might about our atomic bomb projects and awaiting the day when an escape to the West might be feasible.

Further, the letter asserts, I did not anticipate the plot that was concocted to effect such escape.

I can say in my defense only that the Comrade Dieter's subterfuge and his plan—communicating with the West through the use of artworks— were marks of genius, a strategy that I submit even the most seasoned intelligence officer, such as myself, could never discover.

Comrade Dieter was, as I say, a most singular man.

Accordingly, Comrade General Tasarich, I humbly beseech you to petition First Secretary Khrushchev, a former soldier like myself, to intervene on my behalf at my forthcoming trial and reject the KGB's recommendation that I be sentenced to an indefinite term of imprisonment in the East for my part in this tragic incident.

Whatever my fate, however, please know that my devotion to the First Secretary, to the Party, and to Our Mother-Homeland is undiminished and as immortal as the ideals of the Glorious Revolution.

I remain, yours in loyalty,
Mikhail Sergeyevich Sidorov
Lubyanka Prison, Moscow

CRAIG FERGUSON *has written films and television shows. He has written a couple of books and hours of stand-up comedy but squirms at the idea of calling himself an author; "vulgar lounge entertainer with artistic pretensions" might be more accurate. He wears pancake makeup and tells jokes which a proper author should never do and he is, these days, a reasonably cheerful soul, which means he lacks any credibility among the pseudointelligentsia.*

He is married to a spectacular woman he loves, father to beautiful clever children he loves, and caretaker to various cats and dogs (and a fish that "regenerates" every so often for the benefit of his youngest son) that he honestly doesn't really like. (One of the dogs is OK.)

He contributed to this collection because he is an enthusiastic fan of both Mr. Hopper and Mr. Block and is afraid of Mr. Block. He is also a fan of Elvis and St. Augustine but if you've read the story you already know that.

He worries about dying sometimes.

South Truro Church, 1930

TAKING CARE OF BUSINESS

BY **CRAIG FERGUSON**

The Reverend Jefferson T. Adams, beloved and respected minister of this parish for over fifty years, pulled deeply on the long fragile Jamaican-style reefer and held the smoke deep in his lungs. There was no sensation of getting high anymore, or indeed panic or paranoia or any of the other unpleasantness. No sensation at all really but he enjoyed the ritual.

He listened to the music from outside the church. It was too nice a day to go inside. Cold and still with a high milky cataract of cloud diffusing the sunlight enough to flatter the landscape, softening the edges and blanching out the imperfections like an old actor's headshot.

The sea was guilty and quiet, like it had just eaten.

He'd been to too many funerals anyway. You can't pastor for all that time and not get a little tired of it. Very tired.

Cold and still.

Not just the day.

Poor decrepit old bugger in the church. He'd been getting colder and slower for years until he just stopped altogether and froze.

The sound was beautiful. Local children from the Sunday school with a mournful and ethereal version of Elvis's "Rock a Hula Baby" from the awful 1961 movie "Blue Hawaii." Funny and silly and bizarre and sad.

Just like his life.

Billy had got him started on the Ganja after he told him about The Cancer. Showed him articles from the internet written by many "leading health professionals," Billy had said, in that odd way he had of sounding like an infomercial whenever he was telling you something he believed to be important.

Billy said, "Of course it won't cure you but it alleviates stress and combats the nausea from the chemo," a tidbit he quoted from the pompous hipster clerk who had sold him the marijuana at the dispensary in Portland. The clerk had implied while saying the opposite that in fact the marijuana might indeed cure cancer.

Jefferson had told Billy that he was not taking chemotherapy treatments, that he felt, now he was in his eighties, it was just a way of making things worse on the road to the inevitable and that Doctor Naismith didn't think it would have much effect anyway. Billy hadn't paid any attention to that. He had an endearing and infuriating way of being deaf to anything that got in the way of his theories. So the two old men took to sitting on the beach smoking fine legal herb and waiting for death or a cure. Also, Jefferson really enjoyed the marijuana. It made him feel calm and goofy and unafraid, which were things he was not when free of its influence.

At least not at first.

It had bonded him with Billy, really the last person he thought he'd have shared his final days with. Billy the distracted passionate believer in a myriad of mysteries who had hounded him for years with questions about Jesus and the disciples and the Ark of the Covenant and aliens and Atlantis and, for an alarming couple of weeks, the spiritual benefits of tantric sexual practice, which Billy lacked a partner for but was enthusi-astically practicing on his own.

Jefferson had explained patiently over and over again that, as an octo-genarian and Presbyterian, not to mention a minister of the church, many of these subjects were outside his area of expertise. Particularly, and please let's never bring up this subject again, the tantric sex.

He admired Billy's spiritual hunger, though; his desperate appetite for "The Unexplained" remained ravenous even as the man himself hurtled into his dotage. And Billy was compassionate, driving four hours to Port-land to buy good legal pot for the reverend every week even after Jefferson had told him it was unnecessary.

Billy liked the marijuana too, of course. He had learned to make a joint from an instructional video on YouTube. They had tried various methods of imbibing—the pinched single paper type joint favoured by incarcer-ated white supremacists and 1920s flapper girls—the idiot frat boy bong method—they even tried making brownies but years of being catered to by mothers and wives had left them both hopeless in area of food preparation. They eventually settled on the Rastafarian three-cigarette-paper-style joint with the cardboard roach. It seemed to be the most religious way of going about the business of getting high.

The ceremony of preparation was almost as important as the inhala-tion of the sacred smoke.

They had known each other for over seventy years, not friends all that time, of course, but in the same grades through elementary and high school. Jefferson had left town to go to divinity school, a credit to his deeply devout parents, and returned to become the third generation of Adamses to attend to the spiritual needs of the town. Everybody was very happy about this; the community then was almost all fishermen and their families and these are people who love continuity. It's reassuring when you deal with something as capricious as the sea.

Billy had taken over his father's auto repair shop and married Barbara French. They had two daughters who he lost touch with after Barbara had left him, with the girls, to shack up in Prescott,

Arizona, with a photocopier salesman she had met at a sales conference in Vancouver.

So Jefferson and Billy had been aware of each other but never connected in any real way until Jean had died. Jefferson had never entertained the thought that his wife, ten years his junior, would go before him but just a month after her sixtieth birthday and two months after his seventieth she had fallen over in the kitchen, having had a massive heart attack. The doctor told him later that she had probably been dead before she hit the floor, which was meant to be a comforting thought but Jefferson found little solace in it. It seemed such an unfairly *masculine* way to die, although she had always been a very robust woman.

Their only daughter, Molly, didn't even return for the funeral. She had fled to California after high school and, after becoming a Scientologist, considered her parents to be "suppressive persons" with whom she must avoid all contact when they had unwisely questioned the validity of her religion over their own.

His parishioners had been wonderful in the way that most people are after a sudden death, considerate and helpful and practical, but in the way of the world they were all ready to move on after Jean's death much sooner than Jefferson was. Not Billy, though. He kept showing up every night. Month after month. No doubt the fact that he had no one else to talk to helped fuel his altruism, but Jefferson found that he started to look forward to Billy's visits, putting the kettle on at seven o'clock every night getting ready for the inevitable.

As time drained away the two old men who had lived their entire lives a few miles from each other started to learn each other's stories and in the way of those who no longer care about ridicule or shame they told each other of their failings. As husbands, as fathers, as lovers, as men. Of course, this sharing of failings led to an affection between the two. A trust that only the condemned are capable of.

It was easy to learn about Billy, of course: he barely stopped talking and he'd tell you everything, but every so often he'd ask a question and shock you with the profundity of his attention to the answer.

He eventually got Jefferson's two biggest secrets out of him. One of which even Jean had been unaware of.

Jefferson was adopted and he was an atheist.

Billy was scandalized and intrigued by the adoption news. He had considered Jefferson a purebred Yankee—his name was Adams, for God's sake! Billy became obsessed with locating Jefferson's birth parents, which was impossible as the tracks had been covered up years ago by his adoptive parents, who never wanted the shame of their infertility to be discovered by the town. Jefferson had only learned of it himself from a deathbed confession from his mother by way of an explanation of why he was an only child and why his ears were so big.

He had dismissed the story as the last ramblings of a OxyContin-addled alcoholic geriatric at first but had asked his father about it, who was still alive at the time, although withering away at Primrose Pathways—a facility for senile clergymen who required twenty-four-hour care.

His father had confirmed the verisimilitude of his mother's story and added the shocking information that they had bought him as a baby from dirt-poor sharecroppers while on an evangelical trip to Mississippi just after Christmas in 1934 or '35.

Jefferson had told Jean, and for a while they had tried to unearth any further information, but both his parents had died that winter and there was no one else to ask or talk to.

"You'll never find who I was now, and anyway, everyone will be dead. What's the point?" Jefferson told Billy.

But Billy thought that it was important to know the truth about yourself, plus you could find out everything now because of the internet.

There was nothing to find out, of course. No record or website has that kind of ancient illegal information on it. The internet search eventually led to Billy's outlandish assertion that Jefferson was in fact the twin brother of the late Elvis Presley.

Elvis had been one of twins born to a poor sharecropper in Tupelo, Mississippi, at exactly that time. His brother Jesse was stillborn, but it was Billy's assertion that that was in fact untrue and that the devout but profoundly impoverished Gladys and Aaron Presley, fearing that they could not care for two babies, had sold one infant child to poor, barren, God-fearing church folk from the North.

Jefferson had actually started laughing when Billy told him this. A big, deep, throaty laugh, and Billy was grateful; he hadn't even seen the old man smile since his wife had died.

They left the secret of Jefferson's bloodline in the dust.

The other secret was more troublesome. That one only surfaced because of the dead whale.

It was a bright cold day in April and they had just finished a large spliff of extremely potent Mexican gold. The effect of the plant was so strong that any speech between them was impossible for a while, so they just sat at the top of the dunes looking with watering bloodshot eyes at the massive decomposing corpse of the mature North Atlantic right whale that had been dumped on the shore by a murderous spring tide the previous day.

Billy, of course, had been the first to speak, telling Jefferson he'd Googled the whale, and then both of them dissolving into hysterical laughter for ten minutes.

When they recovered and sat in the calming, almost post-coital bliss of shared drug-induced hilarity, Billy explained that he'd learned on Google that the North Atlantic right was one of the most endangered species on earth.

"They reckon there's only about five hundred or so left," he told Jefferson.

"I'm not surprised if they keep throwing themselves on beaches like this" Jefferson replied, after a long pause.

"It was old, I reckon it was dead before it hit land," said Billy.

"Like Jean," said Jefferson. "I miss her. It's been over ten years and I keep expecting her to turn up. Strange that, isn't it?"

"You'll see her again, when you go to your reward," said Billy in his softest, most conciliatory tones.

Jefferson gave a little laugh that Billy didn't like.

"You don't think so?" he asked.

Jefferson said that actually, no, he didn't. He said that he had seen a lot of people dispatched to their "reward" over the years. Young and old, good and not so good, healthy and sick, and they all kind of looked the same when they died. Sort of empty. Like it was over. Done.

Billy asked if he even believed in God, and Jefferson, much to his friend's distress, said that no, he didn't. He said that he used to, but that as he got older and life delivered more and more rare and smelly dead whales to his beach or other beaches up and down the coast, he thought it was a fairy story. Something to stop people losing their minds with despair. That's why he continued to be a clergyman long after he ceased to believe in the lie, because he saw it was a way for him to provide succor to people who would have been distraught without the Big Story.

"I read a book about that. *When Bad Things Happen To Good People.* It really helped."

"Billy, bad things happen to everybody. Good and bad. It has no pattern, it's all nonsense."

"You can't really believe that!"

"I can't believe anything else," said Jefferson sadly.

Billy was shocked that he'd been preaching what he believed to be a lie all these years. Jefferson said that he was just like an actor, playing a role for the entertainment and comfort of the customers.

"What's the point of preaching about God if you don't believe it?" squeaked Billy incredulously.

"I suppose it just sort of became a habit. I was just taking care of the family business. It's a job. Where's the harm?"

"The harm is that it's not the truth. You are not saying what you believe to be the truth!"

"In my opinion, the truth is vastly overrated," said Jefferson firmly.

Billy was profoundly uneasy about his friend's revelation but, using his almost superhuman powers of optimism and denial, he put it down to the effects of the cancer and the strong Mexican bud.

Billy had never once in his entire life entertained the notion of the absence of an all-powerful God who worked in mysterious ways, his wonders to perform. He wasn't an idiot; he was just blessed with Augustinian faith. He actually had a quote by St. Augustine in framed needlepoint on his kitchen wall.

"Trying to understand the mind of God is like trying to pour the ocean into a cup."

A gift from the wife who had deserted him for a better option.

They met by the whale every day and watched it decay, making sure they stayed upwind of it as after a while the stink became nauseating.

By the time the giant rib cage became visible looking like the ruins of an old church draped in rotting flesh, Jefferson stopped smoking the reefer.

He told Billy he no longer needed it, citing the example of Dr. Jekyll and Mr. Hyde.

Billy nodded knowingly.

"Because marijuana turned you into Mr. Hyde, a monster who didn't believe in God?" he asked, by way of confirming his theory.

"Absolutely not," replied Jefferson. "At a certain point in the story Dr. Jekyll realizes that he needs the potion to stop himself from turning into Mr. Hyde, the opposite of its original effect. The potion had changed him. That's happened to me. When I smoke now I get nervous and scared like I used to, but if I don't take it I feel better and relaxed and groovy."

"Do people still say groovy?" asked Billy.

"I do," answered Jefferson.

"So you still don't believe in God?"

"Yup. Still don't."

Billy decided he didn't want to talk about this anymore so he stopped, and Jefferson, being his friend, let him.

It was long into the summer and the whale carcass had almost disappeared by the time they put to sea. Billy had borrowed the little wooden boat with outboard motor from Dennis Mitchell, who had been a bit late on his payment for the new transmission on his truck and was looking for a way to extend his credit. Jefferson's physical decline was almost as dramatic as the dead whale's and he too was wasting away rapidly. The idea was that the two men would go fishing, but they both knew that it was just a last day out for the old minister before the end.

They puttered out of the old stone harbor into a gentle swell on an opaque grey sea. There was no wind and the distant horizon was obscured by a haze only marginally lighter in color than the water. The view was limited, but they were both old men who knew their way around. They knew where they were going.

Jefferson sat quietly looking out over the bow, and when they were out of sight of land Billy cut the engine. The two men sat in silence for a while. Unusually, it was Jefferson who spoke first.

"You know," he said, "I suppose, one way or another, when an atheist dies he's no longer an atheist."

They smiled at each other, but their moment was interrupted when the boat suddenly lurched violently to one side, almost pitching them both into the water.

"What the hell was that?" whispered Jefferson.

"I have no idea," said Billy.

They were still panicked when off to their side about fifteen feet from the tiny boat the enormous tailfin of an adult North Atlantic right whale breached the surface then slammed down again, baptizing them in freezing salty water and pitching the boat sideways once more.

"Quick, start the engine!" yelled Jefferson.

Billy pulled the ignition cord, but in the time-honored tradition of outboard motors it refused to start at the crucial moment. He was still trying when they felt the boat lift gently out of the water.

The whale was underneath the hull.

The boat rose slowly about two feet from the surface on the great creature's back, then gently and quietly the whale set it down again.

They looked over the side in awe of the monster that held the power of life over them. The head was next to the boat and it rolled on its side so that its black shining eye looked directly at them.

They watched silently as the giant beast moved slightly away and slowly circled their craft three times clockwise before returning to the murky depths without so much as a ripple on the surface.

The two old men stared at each other for a moment and then, as if they'd rehearsed it, they both yelled at the same time, screaming like victorious sports fans. They yelled and laughed and punched the air in triumph.

After a few moments they got quiet, catching their breath.

Billy held Jefferson's gaze. Made a decision, darted forward and pushed his friend over the side. No one spoke. No noise. Jefferson didn't cry out, but Billy watched him follow the whale out of sight.

The Reverend Jefferson T. Adams, beloved and respected minister of this parish for over fifty years, pulled deeply on the Jamaican-style joint and inhaled the smoke. He listened to the music inside the church and assumed Billy had chosen it. "Rock a Hula" indeed!

He couldn't help but smile.

Elvis Aaron Presley, dressed in one of the more outlandish sequined outfits of his later Vegas years, sidled up to him.

"Hey, brother, really good to see you."

Jefferson turned to him, noting that actually they really did look alike.

"This is just the hallucination of a dying brain, isn't it?" said Jefferson.

The old god of rock shrugged.

"I don't know, man. You can overthink these things," said the dead king.

It was no surprise to learn that **STEPHEN KING** *had no time for anthology commitments, but his feeling for the subject kept him from dismissing the proposal out of hand. "I love Hopper," he wrote, "so I'll table this for the time being." Later he chose the painting he'd write about—on the slim chance that he should find the time. "There's a painting, 'Room in New York.' I have a repro of it in my house, because it speaks to me." It evidently spoke persuasively, and "The Music Room" is the happy result.*

Room in New York, 1932

THE MUSIC ROOM

BY STEPHEN KING

T he Enderbys were in their music room—so they called it, although it was really just the spare bedroom. Once they had thought it would be little James or Jill Enderby's nursery, but after ten years of trying, it seemed increasingly unlikely that a Baby Dear would arrive out of the Nowhere and into the Here. They had made their peace with childlessness. At least they had work, which was a blessing in a year when men were still standing in bread lines. There were fallow periods, it was true, but when the job was on, they could afford to think of nothing else, and they both liked it that way.

Mr. Enderby was reading *The New York Journal-American*, a new daily not even halfway through its first year of publication. It was sort of a tabloid and sort of not. He usually began with the comics, but when they were on the job he turned to the city news first, scanning through the stories quickly, especially the police blotter.

Mrs. Enderby sat at the piano, which had been a wedding gift from her parents. Occasionally she stroked a key, but did not press any. Tonight the only music in the music room was the symphony of nighttime traffic on Third Avenue, which came in through the open window. Third Avenue, third floor. A good apartment in a sturdy brownstone. They rarely heard their neighbors above and below, and their neighbors rarely heard them. Which was all to the good.

From the closet behind them came a single thump. Then another. Mrs. Enderby spread her hands as if to play, but when the thumps ceased, she put her hands in her lap.

"Still not a peep about our pal George Timmons," Mr. Enderby said, rattling the paper.

"Perhaps you should check the Albany *Herald*," she said. "I believe the newsstand on Lexington and 60th carries it."

"No need," he said, turning to the funnies at last. "The *Journal-American* is good enough for me. If Mr. Timmons has been reported missing in Albany, let those interested search for him there."

"That's fine, dear," said Mrs. Enderby. "I trust you." There was really no reason not to; to date, the work had gone swimmingly. Mr. Timmons was their sixth guest in the specially reinforced closet.

Mr. Enderby chuckled. "The Katzenjammer Kids are at it again. This time they've caught Der Captain fishing illegally—shooting a net from a cannon, in fact. It's quite amusing. Shall I read it to you?"

Before Mrs. Enderby could answer, another thump came from the closet, and faint sounds that might have been shouts. It was difficult to tell, unless one put one's ear right up against the wood, and she had no intention of doing that. The piano bench was as close to Mr. Timmons as she intended to get, until it was time to dispose of him. "I wish he'd stop."

"He will, dear. Soon enough."

Another thump, as if to refute this.

"That's what you said yesterday."

"It seems I was premature," said Mr. Enderby, and then, "Oh, gosh—Dick Tracy is once more on the hunt for Pruneface."

"Pruneface gives me the willies," she said, without turning. "I wish Detective Tracy would put him away for good."

"That will never happen, dear. People *claim* to root for the hero, but it's the villains they remember."

Mrs. Enderby made no reply. She was waiting for the next thump. When it came—*if* it came—she would wait for the one after that. The waiting was the worst part. The poor man was hungry and thirsty, of course; they had ceased feeding and watering him three days ago, after he had signed the last check, the one that emptied his account. They had emptied his wallet at once, of almost two hundred dollars. In a depression as deep as this one, two hundred was a jackpot, and his watch might add as much as twenty more to their earnings (although, she admitted to herself, that might be a trifle optimistic).

Mr. Timmons's checking account at Albany National had been the real mother lode: eight hundred. Once he was hungry enough, he had been happy to sign several checks made out to cash and with the notation "Business Expenses" written in the proper spot on each one. Somewhere a wife and kiddies might be depending on that money when Father didn't come home from his trip to New York, but Mrs. Enderby did not allow herself to dwell on that. She preferred to imagine Mrs. Timmons having a rich mama and papa in Albany's Mansion District, a generous couple right out of a Dickens novel. They would take her in and care for her and her children, little boys who might be endearing scamps like Hans and Fritz, the Katzenjammer Kids.

"Sluggo broke a neighbor's window and is blaming it on Nancy," Mr. Enderby said with a chuckle. "I swear he makes the Katzenjammers look like angels!"

"That awful hat he wears!" Mrs. Enderby said.

Another thump from the closet, and a very hard one from a man who had to be on the verge of starvation. But Mr. Timmons had been a big one. Even after a generous dose of chloral hydrate in his glass of dinner wine, he had nearly overpowered Mr. Enderby. Mrs. Enderby had had to help. She sat on Mr. Timmons's chest until he quieted. Unladylike, but necessary. That night, the window on Third Avenue had been shut, as it always was when Mr. Enderby brought home a guest for dinner. He met them in bars. Very gregarious, was Mr. Enderby, and very good at singling out businessmen who were alone in the city—fellows who were also gregarious and enjoyed making new friends. Especially new friends who might become new clients of one business or another. Mr. Enderby judged them by their suits, and he always had an eye for a gold watch chain.

"Bad news," Mr. Enderby said, a frown creasing his brow.

She stiffened on the piano bench and turned to face him. "What is it?"

"Ming the Merciless has imprisoned Flash Gordon and Dale Arden in the radium mines of Mongo. There are these creatures that look sort of like alligators—"

Now from the closet came a faint, wailing cry. Within its sound-proofed confines, it must have been a shriek almost loud enough to rupture the poor man's vocal cords. How could Mr. Timmons still be strong enough to voice such a howl? He had already lasted a day longer than any of the previous five, and his somehow gruesome vitality had begun to prey on her nerves. She had been hoping that tonight would see the end of him.

The rug in which he was to be wrapped was waiting in their bedroom, and the panel truck with ENDERBY ENTERPRISES painted on the side was parked just around the corner, fully gassed and ready for another trip to the Pine Barrens of New Jersey. When they were first married, there had actually been an Enderby Enterprises. The depression—what the *Journal-American* had taken to calling the *Great* Depression—had put an end to that two years ago. Now they had this new work.

"Dale is afraid," continued Mr. Enderby, "and Flash is trying to buck her up. He says Dr. Zarkov will—"

Now came a fusillade of thumps: ten, maybe a dozen, and accompanied by more of those shrieks, muffled but still rather chilling. She could imagine blood beading Mr. Timmons's lips and dripping from his split knuckles. She could imagine how his neck would have grown scrawny, and how his formerly plump face would have stretched long as his body gobbled the fat and musculature there in order to stay alive.

But no. A body couldn't cannibalize itself to stay alive, could it? The idea was as unscientific as phrenology. And how thirsty he must be by now!

"It's so annoying!" she burst out. "I hate it that he just goes *on* and *on* and *on*! Why did you have to bring home such a strong man, dear?"

"Because he was also a well-to-do man," Mr. Enderby said mildly. "I could see that when he opened his wallet to pay for our second round of drinks. What he's contributed will keep us for three months. Five, if we stretch it."

Thump, and thump, and thump. Mrs. Enderby put her fingers to the delicate hollows of her temples and began to rub.

Mr. Enderby looked at her sympathetically. "I can put a stop to it, if you like. He won't be able to struggle much in his current state; certainly not after having expended so much energy. A quick slash with your sharpest butcher knife. Of course, if *I* do the deed, *you* will have to do the clean-up. It's only fair."

Mrs. Enderby looked at him, shocked. "We may be thieves, but we are *not* murderers."

"That is not what people would say, if we were caught." He spoke apologetically but firmly enough, just the same.

She clasped her hands in the lap of her red dress tightly enough to whiten the knuckles, and looked straight into his eyes. "If we were called into the dock, I would hold my head up and tell the judge and the jury that we were victims of circumstance."

"And I'm sure you would be very convincing, dear."

Another thump from behind the closet door, and another cry. Gruesome. That was the word for his vitality, the exact one. *Gruesome.*

"But we are *not* murderers. Our guests simply lack sustenance, as do so many in these terrible times. We don't kill them; they simply fade away."

Another shriek came from the man Mr. Enderby had brought home from McSorley's over a week ago. It might have been words. It might have been *for the love of God.*

"It won't be long now," Mr. Enderby said. "If not tonight, then tomorrow. And we won't have to go back to work for quite awhile. And yet . . ."

She looked at him in that same steady way, hands clasped. "And yet?"

"Part of you enjoys it, I think. Not this part, but the actual moment when we take them, as a hunter takes an animal in the woods."

She considered this. "Perhaps I do. And I *certainly* enjoy seeing what they have in their wallets. It's reminds me of the treasure hunts

Papa used to put on for me and my brother when we were children. But afterward . . ." She sighed. "I was never good at waiting."

More thumps. Mr. Enderby turned to the business section. "He came from Albany, and people who come from there get what they deserve. Play something, dear. That will cheer you up."

So she got her sheet music out of the piano bench and played "I'll Never Be the Same." Then she played "I'm in a Dancing Mood" and "The Way You Look Tonight." Mr. Enderby applauded and called for an encore on that one, and when the last notes died away, the thumps and cries from the soundproofed and specially reinforced closet had ceased.

"Music!" Mr. Enderby proclaimed. "It hath powers to soothe the savage beast!"

That made them laugh together, comfortably, the way people do when they have been married for many years and have come to know each other's minds.

JOE R. LANSDALE *is the author of over 45 novels and four hundred short pieces, including stories, novellas, nonfiction, and introductions. He has edited or co-edited a dozen anthologies. Some of his work has been filmed*—Bubba Hotep, Cold in July, Christmas with the Dead—*and is the inspiration for the TV series* Hap and Leonard. *His novels have won a number of awards, including the Edgar, the Spur, and nine Bram Stokers, as well as an award for Lifetime Achievement. He and his wife, Karen, live in Nacogdoches, Texas, with their pit bull and their cat.*

New York Movie, 1939

THE PROJECTIONIST

BY JOE R. LANSDALE

There's some that think I got it easy on the job, but they don't know there's more to it than plugging in the projector. You got to be there at the right time to change reels, and you got to have it set so it's seamless, so none of the movie gets stuttered, you know. You don't do that right, well, you can cause a reel to flap and there goes the movie right at the good part, or it can get hung up and the bulb will burn it. Then everyone down there starts yelling, and that's not good for business, and it's not good for you, the boss hears about it, and with the racket they make when the picture flubs, he hears all right.

I ain't had that kind of thing happen to me much, two or three times on the flapping, once I got a burn on a film, but it was messed up when we got it. Was packed in wrong and got a twist in it I couldn't see when I pulled it out. That wasn't my fault. Even the boss could see that.

Still, you got to watch it.

It ain't the same kind of hard work as digging a ditch, which I've done, on account of I didn't finish high school. Lacked a little over a year, but I had to drop out on account of some things. Not a lot of opportunities out there if you don't have that diploma.

Anyways, thought I'd go back someday, take a test, get the diploma, but I didn't. Early on, though, I'd take my little bit of earnings and go to the picture show. There was old man, Bert, working up there, and I knew him because he knew my dad, though not in a real close way. I'd go up there and visit with him. He'd let me in free and I could see the movies from the projection booth. Bert was a really fine guy. He had done some good things for me. I think of him as my guardian angel. He gave me my career.

While I was there, when I'd seen the double feature and it was time for it to start over, he'd show me how the projection was done. So when Bert decided he was going to hang it up, live on his Social Security, I got the job. I was twenty-five. I been at it for five years since then.

One nice thing is I get to watch movies for free, though some of them, once was enough. If I ever have to see *Seven Brides for Seven Brothers* again, I may cry myself into a stupor. I don't like those singing movies much.

Even if you wasn't looking at the picture, you had to hear the words from them over and over, and if the picture was kept over a week, you could pretty much say all the stuff said in the movie like you was a walking record. I tried some of the good lines the guys said to the girls in movies, the pickup lines, but none of them worked for me.

I ain't handsome, but I'm not scary looking either, but the thing is, I'm not easy with women. I just ain't. I never learned that. My father was quite the ladies' man. Had black, curly hair and sharp features and bright blue eyes. Built up good from a lot physical work. He made the women swoon. Once he got the one he wanted, he'd grow tired of her, same as he did with my mother, and he was ready to move on. Yeah, he had the knack for getting them in bed and taking a few dollars from them. He was everything they wanted. Until he wasn't.

He always said, "Thing about women, there's one comes of age every day and there's some that ain't of age, but they'll do. All you got to do is flatter them. They eat that shit up. Next thing you know, you got what you really want, and there's new mountains to conquer."

Dad was that kind of fellow.

Bert always said, "Guy like that who can talk a woman out of her panties pretty easy gets to thinking that's what it's all about. That there's nothing else to it. It ought not be like that. Me and Missy, we been married fifty years, and when it got so neither one of us was particularly in a hurry to see the other without drawers, we still wanted to see each other at the breakfast table."

That was Bert's advice on women in a nutshell.

Well, there was another thing. He always said, "Don't sit around trying to figure what she's thinking, cause you can't. And when it comes right down to it, she don't know what you're thinking. Just be there for one another."

Thing was, though, I never had anyone to be there for. I think it's how I carry myself. Bert always said, "Stand up, Cartwright. Quit stooping. You ain't no hunchback. Make eye contact, for Christ's sake."

I don't know why I do that, stoop, I mean, but I do. Maybe it's because I'm tall, six-six, and thin as a blade of grass. It's a thing I been trying to watch, but sometimes I feel like I got the weight of memories on my shoulders.

The other night Mr. Lowenstein hired a new usherette. She is something. He has her wear red. Always red. The inside of the theater has a lot of red. Backs of the seats are made out of some kind of red cloth. Some of the seats have gotten kind of greasy over time, young boys with their hair oil pressed into them. The curtains that pull in front of the stage, they're red. I love it when they're pulled, and then they open them so I can play the picture. I like watching them open. It gets to me, excites me in a funny way. I told Bert that once, thinking maybe he'd laugh at me, but he said, "Me too, kid."

They have clowns and jugglers and dog acts and shitty magicians and such on Saturday mornings before the cartoons. They do stuff up there on the stage and the kids go wild, yelling and throwing popcorn and candy.

Now and again, a dog decides to take a dump on the stage, or one of the clowns falls off his bike and does a gainer into the front row, or maybe a juggler misses a toss and hits himself in the head. Kids like that even better. I think people are kind of strange when you get right down to it, 'cause everything that's funny mostly has to do with being embarrassed or hurt, don't you think?

But this usherette, her name's Sally, and she makes the girls in the movies look like leftover ham and cheese. She is a real beauty. She's younger than me, maybe by six or seven years, got long blonde hair and a face as smooth as a porcelain doll. Except for red dresses the theater gives her to wear, she mostly has some pretty washed out clothes. She changes at the theater, does her makeup. When she comes out in one of those red dresses with heels on, she lights up the place like Rudolph's nose. Those dresses are provided by Mr. and Mrs. Lowenstein. Mrs. Lowenstein sews them to fit right, and believe me, they do. I don't mean to sound bad by saying it, but Sally is fitted into them so good that if she had a tan, it would break through the cloth, that's how tight they fit.

Mr. Lowenstein, he's sixty-five if he's a day, was standing with me back at the candy counter one time, and I'm getting a hot dog and a drink to take up to the projection booth. That's my lunch and dinner every day 'cause it's free. So this time, right when the theater is opening, just before noon, we see Sally come out of the dressing room across from us, same room the clowns and jugglers and dogs use. She comes out in one of those red dresses and some heels, her blonde hair bouncing on her shoulders, and she smiles at us.

I could feel my legs wilt. When she walked into the auditorium part of the theater to start work, Mr. Lowenstein said, "I think Maude maybe ought to loosen that dress a little."

I didn't say anything to that, but I was thinking, "I hope not."

Every day I'm up in the booth I'm peeking out from up there at Sally. She stands over by the curtains where there are some red bulbs. Not strong light, enough so someone wants to go out to the bathroom, or up to the concession stand, they can find their way without breaking a leg.

Sally, her job is to show people to their seats, which is silly, 'cause they get to sit where they want. She's an added expense at the theater, but way Mr. and Mrs. Lowenstein saw it, she's a draw for a lot of the teenagers. I figure some of the married men don't mind looking at her either. She is something. It got so I watched her all the time. Just sat up there and looked. Usually, I got bored, I looked down into the back row where there was a lot of boys and girls doing hand work and smacky mouth, but that always seemed like a wrong thing to do, watch them make out, and it seemed wrong what they did it in the theater. Maybe I was just jealous.

It got so I'd peek out at Sally all the time up there, since she had her that spot where she stood every night, that red bulb shining on her, making her blonde hair appear slightly red, her dress brighter yet. I'd got so caught up looking at her, that once, damn if for the first time in a long time, I forgot to change a reel and the picture got all messed up. I had to really hustle to get it going again, all them people down there moaning and complaining and stuff.

Mr. Lowenstein wasn't happy, and he gave me the talk afterward that night. I knew he was right, and I knew it didn't mean nothing. He knew flubs happen. He knew I was good at my work. But he was right. I needed to pay more attention. Still, it was hard to regret looking at Sally.

Right after this talk, things got shifted. Mrs. Lowenstein had long left the ticket stand out front, and had gone home ahead of Mr. Lowenstein. She had her own car, so it was me and him behind the concession counter, and I'm getting my free drink I got coming as part of my job, and Sally came out of the dressing room. She had on a worn, loose, flower-dotted dress, and she saw us and smiled. I like to think it was me she was smiling at. I knew I tried to stand up straight when she looked in my direction.

It was then that two men came in through one of the row of glass doors, and walked over to the stand. Now, I usually lock those doors every night, thirty minutes before the time they came in, but this time I'm messing with the drink, you see, and I hadn't locked the door yet.

After it was locked up, me and Mr. Lowenstein, and sometimes Sally, though she usually left a little ahead of us, would go out the back and Mr. Lowenstein would lock the back door. Every night he'd say, "Need a ride?" And I'd say, "No, I prefer to walk."

If Sally was there when we were, he'd ask her the same thing.

Sally, she walked too. In the other direction.

We did this every night.

I did prefer to walk. I took a ride once, but Mr. Lowenstein's car stunk so heavily of cigar smoke it made me sick. Dad used to smoke cigars and they smelled just that way, cheap and lingering. That smoke got into your clothes it took more than one run through the laundry to get the stink out.

But these guys came in because the door was unlocked when it should have been locked. Doesn't matter. They were they kind of guys that were going to come in eventually.

One of them was like a fireplug in a blue suit. He had a dark hat with the brim pushed back a bit, kind of style you saw now and then, but it made him look stupid. I figure it wasn't all looks. He had that way about him that tells you he isn't exactly lying in bed at night trying to figure out how electricity works, or for that matter what makes a door swing open. The other guy, he was thinner and smoother. Had on a tan suit and a tan hat and one of his pants legs was bunched up against his ankle like he had a little gun and holster strapped there.

They came over smiling, and the tall one, he looks at Mr. Lowenstein, says, "We work for The Community Protection Board."

"The what?" Mr. Lowenstein said.

"It don't matter," said the short stout one. "All you got to do is be quiet and listen to the service we provide. We make sure you're protected, case someone wants to come in and set fire to the place, rob it, beat someone up. We make sure that don't happen."

"I got insurance," said Mr. Lowenstein. "I been here for years, and I been fine."

"No," said the tall one. "You don't have this kind of insurance. It covers a lot that yours don't. It makes sure certain things don't happen that are otherwise bound to happen."

It was then that me and Lowenstein both got it, knew what they meant.

"Way we see it, you ain't paying your share," said the tall one. "There's people on this block, all these businesses, and we got them paying as of last week, and you're all that's left. You don't pay, you'll be the only hold-out."

"Leave me out of it," Mr. Lowenstein said.

The tall one gently shook his head. "That might not be such a good idea, you know. Stuff can go wrong overnight, in a heartbeat. Nice theater like this, you don't want that. Tell you what, Mr. Jew. We're going to go away, but we'll be back next Tuesday, which gives you nearly a week to think about it. But after Tuesday, we don't get, say, one hundred dollars a week, we got to tell you that you haven't got our protection. Without it, things here are surely going to ride a little too far south."

"We'll see you then," said the stout one. "Might want to start putting a few nickels in a jar."

Sally had stopped when they came in. She was standing there listening, maybe ten feet away. The stout one turned and looked at her.

"Sure wouldn't want this little trick to get her worn-out old dress rumpled. And I'm going to tell you, girlie, what you got poured into it is one fine bon-bon."

"Don't talk about her like that," Mr. Lowenstein said.

"I talk like I like," said the stout one.

"This is your only warning about circumstances that can happen," said the tall one. "Let's not have any unpleasantness. All you got to do is pay your weekly hundred, things go swimmingly."

"That's right," said the stout one. "Swimmingly."

"Hundred dollars, that's a lot of money," said Mr. Lowenstein.

"Naw," said the stout one. "That's cheap, 'cause what could happen to this place, you, your employees, that fat wife or yours, this nice little girl, the retard there, it could cost a lot more to fix that, and there's some things could happen money can't fix."

They went out then, taking their sweet time about it. Sally came over, said, "What do they mean, Mr. Lowenstein?"

"It's a shake-down, honey," Mr. Lowenstein said. "Don't you worry about it. But tonight, I'm taking you both home."

And he did. I didn't mind. I sat in the backseat behind Sally and looked and smelled her hair through the cigar smoke.

In my little apartment that night I sat and thought about those guys, and they reminded me of my dad quite a bit. Lots of bluster, more than bullies. People who were happily mean. I worried about Mr. and Mrs. Lowenstein, and Sally, of course, and I won't lie to you. I worried about me.

Next day I went to work same as usual, and when I was getting my lunch, my hot dog to take up into the booth, Sally came over and said, "Those men last night. Are they dangerous?"

"I don't know," I said. "I think they could be."

"I need this job," she said. "I don't want to quit, but I'm a little scared."

"I hear you," I said. "I need this job too."

"You're staying?"

"Sure," I said.

"Will you kind of keep a watch on me?" she said.

That was kind of like asking a sparrow to fight a chicken hawk, but I nodded, said, "You bet."

I should have told her to take a hike on out of there and start looking for other employment, because these kinds of things can turn bad. I've seen a bit of it, that badness.

But thing was, I was too selfish. I wanted Sally around. Wanted her to be where I could see her, but another part of me thought about that and knew I might not be able to do a thing to protect her. Good intentions weren't always enough. Bert used to say the road to hell was paved with good intentions.

That night after work, as Sally was starting to walk home, I said, "How about I walk you?"

"I'm the other direction," she said.

"That's all right. I'll walk back after I get you where you need to go."

"All right," she said.

We walked and she said, "You like being a projectionist?"

"Yeah."

"Why?"

"Decent pay, free hot dogs."

She laughed.

"I like it up there in the booth. I get to see all those movies. I like movies."

"Me too."

"It's kind of weird, but I like the private part of it too. I mean, you know, I get a little lonely up there, but not too much. Now and again I've seen a picture enough I'm sick of it, or don't like it, I read some. I'm not a good reader. A book can last me a few months."

"I read magazines and books," she said. "I read *The Good Earth*."

"That's good."

"You've read it?"

"No. But it's good you have. I hear it's good."

"It was all right."

"I guess I prefer picture shows," I said. "Doesn't take as long to get a story. Hour or two and you're done. Another thing I like is being up high like that, in the booth, looking down on folks, and seeing those actors in the movies, me running the reels. It's like I own those people. Like I'm some kind of god up there, and the movies, those actors, and what they do, they don't get to do it unless I make it happen. That sounds odd, don't it?"

"A little," she said.

"I run their lives over and over every week, and then they move on, and for me they don't exist no more, but now I got new people I'm in charge of, you see. They come in canisters. I can't keep them from doing what they do, but without me, they wouldn't be doing nothing. I got to turn them on for them to actually be there."

"That's an interesting perspective," she said.

"Perspective?" I said. "I like that. Like the way you talk."

She seemed embarrassed. "It's just a word."

"Yeah, but you got some words I don't have, or don't use anyway. Don't know how. I'm always scared I'm going to say them wrong, and someone will laugh. I was afraid to say canister just then, and I know that one."

"That's okay," she said. "I can't say aficionado right. I know I say it wrong, and I don't know how it's actually said. I need to hear someone that knows."

"I don't even know what that word means," I said. "Or how you would come about working it into a sentence."

"I try a little too hard to do that," she said. "I'm taking a few courses on the weekends. They got classes like that over at the college. I've only seen the word in a textbook."

"College, huh?"

"You should sign up. It's fun."

"Costs money, though."

"It's worth it, I can get a better job if I get an associate degree. I thought I might get married, but then I thought I'm too young for that. I need to do something, see something before I start wiping baby butts. Besides, the guys I've dated, none of them seem like husband material to me."

"Having a family may not be all that good anyway," I said. "It ain't always."

"I think I'd like it. I think I'd make a good wife. Not now, though. I want to live a little."

Right then I got to thinking maybe a family would be all right. Maybe I could do that with her. But it was just thinking. We passed by the drug-store on Margin Street, and I seen our reflection in the window glass. She looked like some kind of goddess, and me, well, I looked like a few sticks tied together with a hank of hair. Like I said, I don't think I got an ugly face, but I sure knew in that moment, I wasn't in her league. I saw too that the shop was closing down, and there were a couple guys and their girls coming out, arm-in-arm, and they were laughing and smiling.

I seen one of them guys look over at us, see Sally with me, and I could tell he was thinking, "How'd he manage that?" And then they turned and were gone.

We finally came to where she lived, which was a two-story brick building. It wasn't well lit up, but it was brighter than my place. At least there was a street light and a light you could see through the door glass into the hallway that led to the stairs.

"I live on the top floor," she said.

"That's good. High up."

"Oh yeah. You said you like being high up, at the theater."

"That's right."

"I look out the window at the people sometimes."

"I watch people too," I said. "It's not as good as the movies, but second or third time one plays, I start to watch people down in the seats, unless the movie is really good. Sometimes I can watch a movie every night and not get tired of it. Nothing is going to happen in it that I don't know about by then, and I like that too. I know who is who and who messes up and how it all ends. Real people. They can't do anything I can figure, not really. I like the movies 'cause I like knowing how it's going to come out."

"That's interesting," Sally said.

I wasn't sure she thought it was really all that interesting, and I wished then I'd talked about the weather, or some such, instead of how I was a god up in the projection booth. I can be such an idiot. That's what Dad always said, "You, son, are a loser and a goddamn idiot."

"All right," I said. "Well, you're here."

"Yes, I am. And thank you."

"Welcome."

We shuffled around there for a moment. She said, "Guess I'll see you tomorrow."

"Sure. I can walk you home again, you want."

"We'll see. Maybe. I mean, it depends. I'm thinking maybe I've blown it all out of proportion."

"Sure. You'll be okay."

I opened the glass door for her and she went inside. She turned at the stairs and looked back at me and smiled. I couldn't tell how real that smile was. Whatever she meant by it, it made me feel kind of small.

I smiled back.

She turned and came back. "It means someone who is a fan, who appreciates."

"How's that?"

"Aficionado," she said. "Or however it's supposed to sound."

She smiled and went back inside. I liked that smile better. I watched her through the glass door as she climbed up the stairs.

I showered and looked at my chest in the little medicine cabinet mirror while I dried off. The mirror was cracked, but so was my chest. It was all cracked and wrinkled from where I'd been burned.

I turned off the lights and went to bed.

Next morning I got up and went over to Bert's house. Missy was gone to do shopping, and though I would have been glad to see her normally, right then I was happy she was out.

Bert let me in and poured me some coffee and offered me some toast, and I took it. Sat at his table in their small kitchen and buttered the toast and put some of Missy's fig jam on it. They had about an acre of land out back of the house, and it had a fig tree on it, and they had a little garden out there every spring and part of the summer.

I ate the toast and drank the coffee, and we talked about nothing while I did.

When I finished eating, Bert poured me another cup of coffee, told me to come out and sit on the back porch with him. They had some comfortable chairs out there, and we sat side by side under the porch overhang.

"You want to tell my why you've really come over?" Bert said.

"There's some people come by the theater," I said. "Mooks."

"All right."

"They threatened Mr. Lowenstein, me, and Sally."

"Who's Sally?"

I told him all about her, and everything they'd said, what they looked like.

"I know who they are," he said. "But I don't know them, you understand?"

"Yeah."

"Look, kid. This isn't like in the old days. I'm seventy-four years old. Do I look like a tough guy to you?"

"You're tough enough."

"That time . . . That time there was no way out for you. Now, you got a way out. You quit that job and get another."

"I like it," I said.

"Yeah . . . All right. Yeah. I liked it to. I miss it sometimes, but I like better being home. I like being alive and being home to watch *Gunsmoke*. Me and Missy, we got it all right here. She put up with some stuff, and I don't want her to put up with any of that again."

"I hear you," I said.

"Not that I don't care, kid. Not that I don't bleed for you. But again, I'm seventy-four. I was younger then. And well, it was more immediate, and you being really young . . . You needed the help. You can walk away now. Or tell Lowenstein to pay the money. What I'd do. I'd pay the money."

"No," I said. "I can't."

"Your skin, kid, but I'm telling you, these guys are bad business. There's those two, and there's the three that run that place. Five, I think."

"How do you know?"

"I ain't as connected as I once was, back before I started running the projector, but I still know some people and I get word from them now and then. Look, how about this? Let me ask around."

"All right," I said.

I showed a picture that night that I didn't watch, or even remember. I was on time with changing the reels, but I spent all my time watching Sally down there under the red light. She looked nervous, kept looking this way and that.

They said they'd be back next week, and it had only been three days, so I figured for the moment we were fine. I was figuring what to do when next week came.

After the show closed that third night, Lowenstein said, "I'm going to pay them."

"Yeah," I said.

"Yeah. I got a good business here. That's a bite every week, but those guys, I can't do nothing about them. I called the cops next day, and you know what they told me?"

"What?"

"Pay them."

"They said that?"

"Yeah, way I figure it, kid, they have the cops in their pocket. Or at least the right cops. They get money from the businesses, and the cops get a little taste."

I thought that was probably true, things I knew about people.

I walked Sally home again that night, and when I got back to my place, Bert was sitting on the steps. There was a small wooden box on the steps beside him.

"Damn, boy. I was about to give up."

"Sorry. I walked Sally home."

"Good. You got a girl. That's a good thing."

"It's not like that," I said.

"She's the one you told me about, right?"

"Yeah. But it's not like that."

"How is it?"

"Well, it's not like that. I think she wasn't scared, she wouldn't bother with me. I mean she's always nice, but, hell, you know, Bert. There's me, and then there's this doll. Smart. She goes to night classes."

"Does she now?"

"Knows big words."

"How's she look?"

"Very nice."

"Big words and nice, that's fine, kid. You ought to try and touch base with that. You deserve it."

I looked at the box.

"Whatcha got there?"

He patted the box. "You know."

"Yeah. Guess I do."

"Asked around, these guys, they're muscling in on the territory. Giving the cops a bit of their juice. It's not like a big bunch of them. It's five guys, like I heard, way I told you. They think maybe they're going to become big bad business, and you know, they just might."

"All right," I said. "Just five."

"That's still a lot of guys."

"Certainly is. Mr. Lowenstein said he was going to pay them."

"That's good, kid. That's the best way all around. But, I got to tell you, month or two from now, it won't be one hundred dollars, it'll be two. They'll suck the place dry, then end up owning it. That's how they work. They already own the candy store on the corner. They just do a few places at a time till they got everyone in line, but they're growing. Pretty soon, all four blocks there, they'll own them. And then on from there, more blocks. Those kind of guys don't quit."

We were quiet for a while. Bert stood up.

"I got to go back," he said. "Told Missy I'd only be gone a little while, and I've been gone a long while."

"Did she see the box?"

"No. I was careful about it. What she knows is I had some bad ways before I quit and took to the projector. She don't know about you and me and what happened. She just thinks you're a swell kid. She don't know I got the box. Remember, you don't keep it, or what's in it. You get rid of it. I don't never want to see it again. These guys, they're up the end of the street. The Career Building. Top floor."

"Why's it called that?" I asked.

"No idea. But they ain't so big time they got bodyguards or nothing. They just got themselves and some plans."

I nodded.

"Lowenstein talked to the police," I said.

"Yeah, well, I can tell you without you telling me how that worked out. Keep your head up, kid. And remember, there are other theaters and other girls in other places. Ditch the box and take a hound out of here."

He clapped me on the shoulder as he passed. I turned and watched him hobble along the street, hands in his pockets.

That night I lay down on the bed with my clothes on, still wearing my shoes too. I lay there with the box beside me on the bed.

I remembered how my dad liked to come in with his women when we lived together, how he'd do what he did with them with me laying there nearby, just a kid.

I remembered that it wasn't enough for him, and when they were gone, he'd touch me. He liked to touch me. He said it was all right. It didn't feel all right to me.

One time I said that. That it was not right, that it was odd, and he pushed my chest down on the stove grate and held me there. I screamed and I screamed, but in that place where we lived, no one came. No one cared.

Except Bert. Bert and Missy lived there then. He had just started at the theater, doing the projection, and I'd go up there and talk with him, and one time, he sees me bleeding through my shirt. This was the time I was burned. It scabbed and the scabs busted and bled.

That's how he knew about me. I kind of spilled it all out when he asked how I was hurt. I opened my shirt. You could see the grate marks from the stove as clear as a tattoo.

Bert knew my dad. My dad, Bert said, did some work for certain men in the neighborhood that he knew. Work that involved his fists and some-times more than that.

I never knew what Dad did until then. I never asked and had never cared. I was happiest when he was gone and I was alone. I liked going to school just to be away from him, but like I said, I had to quit that before I finished.

I told Bert how Dad came in the night he burned me and tried to touch me, and I fought him. I was bigger by then, but I was no match. He held me down and did what he wanted, way he always did. It really hurt that time. He said it would hurt even worse if I fought him next time. Said I'd end up like Doris. That was my mother. I had suspected something bad happened to her, that she didn't just run away like he said, but right then I knew it, and I knew he was the one that did it.

He pushed me into the stove after that. He made me watch him heat it up and when it was hot, he pushed me into it. Said it was a lesson.

I didn't want to whine about what happened, but that time I was in the projection booth with Bert, I told him because I was angry. I felt like there was something wrong with me that my dad wanted to do that to me.

"It ain't you, kid. It's him. He's the one messed up, not you."

"I'm going to kill him," I said.

"He'll turn that around on you," Bert said. "I know who he is and what he is. He's worse than I thought, but he's not someone you can handle, kid. You'll just disappear."

I cried.

Bert put his arm around me, said, "All right, kid. It's going to be okay."

I ended up staying with Bert, which wasn't all that far from where I lived with Dad. Bert had just moved from the apartments where we were to a place around the corner. Word got around where Bert lived and that I was with him. Dad came by with another guy, a short fellow with a shiny bald head. He wasn't the kind of guy that wore a hat. You didn't see that much then, a guy without a hat.

"I've come to pick up my son," Dad said.

Dad was standing outside the door with that bald guy. Bert was holding the door open. He had a .45 automatic in his hand, out of sight behind the door frame. There was a screen between them. I was standing back in the little dump of a living room, out of sight. From the angle I was standing I could see them in the mirror across the way against the wall.

"He don't want to go," Bert said. "He's taking him a kind of vacation."

"I'm his father. He has to go."

"Naw. He don't have to do nothing."

"I could get the police."

"Yeah, you could," Bert said. "You could do that. But, the boy, he's got a story to tell."

"That's what it is, a story?"

"You think I think that?"

"I don't care what you think. Tell my son to come out."

"Not today."

"What I'm thinking, is we can come in and get him," the bald man said.

"I was thinking you might be thinking that," Bert said. "And I was thinking, you do that, it won't be such a good idea."

"They say you used to be something," the bald man said. "But now you run a projector."

"There's all sorts of people got opinions about me," Bert said. "You try and take that boy, you're able to talk later, you can form your own opinion, tell people, spread it around."

"All right," Dad said. "You keep him. For now. But he's coming home."

"You get lonely nights?" Bert said.

"It's best you watch your mouth," Dad said. "Best you watch yourself altogether."

"Unless you're going to get tough and eat your way through the screen, you ought to go on now," Bert said.

"You are setting yourself up for a world of hurt," Dad said.

"Am I?" Bert said.

"Guy like you with a nice wife, and a shitty, safe job at the picture show, that could all get stood on its head."

Bert went a little stiff.

"It's never good to threaten me," Bert said.

"What we're doing here," said the bald man, "is giving you chance to make it easy on yourself, or that threat as you call it, it'll turn into a promise."

"Why wait," Bert said, and brought the .45 around where they could see it. "Come on in."

Bert flipped the latch on the screen with the barrel of the .45.

"I'm giving you an invitation," Bert said.

"We got time," said Dad. "We got time and we got ways, and you have just stepped in the stink, mister."

"We'll see who stinks when it's all over," Bert said.

Dad and the bald man turned and walked away. I went over and stood near the door. I watched them get in a car, the bald man at the wheel.

Dad looked out the side window at the house. He saw me. He smiled the way a lion smiles.

So later I was sleeping on the couch, and Missy and Bert were in their room, or so I thought, but I rolled over and there's Bert across the way with a wooden box, and he's taking something out of it and putting it in his coat pockets, and going out the door.

I got up and put on my clothes and went over and looked at the box. The bottom of it was packed with cloth. Otherwise, it was empty.

Slipping out the door I went down the drive and looked around the hedges and saw Bert walking brisk-like. I waited until he was pretty far down, and then I followed. It was a long walk and the wind was high and there was a misty kind of rain.

Bert came to a corner and turned, and when I turned, I didn't see him anymore. I was out of the housing part of town, and there were buildings. I stood there confused, for a moment, and then I eased along, and when I got to the far side of the big building, I peeked around it. I saw Bert on one of the little porches off the building, in front of a door. He was under a light. He reached up with something and knocked the bulb out, then he took that something and stuck it in the door. I heard a snick, and a moment later, he was inside and out of sight.

I eased up to the porch, but I couldn't make myself go in. I waited there and listened, and after awhile I heard sounds like someone coughing loudly, and then there was a yell, and then that coughing sound again.

After a moment, the door pushed open and nearly knocked me off the porch. It was Bert.

"Damn, kid. What you doing here?"

"I followed you."

"I see that."

He took the automatic and held it up and unscrewed the silencer on the end of it. He put the silencer in one coat pocket, the gun in the other.

"Come on, fast. Not running, but don't lollygag neither."

"Did you?"

"Yeah. But not your old man. He's back at the apartments. That's what the bald bastard said when I asked."

"You asked?"

"Yeah. Nicely. And when he told me, I shot him. Couple times. There was another guy there I didn't know about, came out of the toilet. I shot him too. Might as well be straight with you, kid. They're deader than snow in July. Come on, hustle a little."

Stunned is how I felt, but happy too. I mean, those guys back there, they hadn't done nothing to me, not like Dad, but they were on his side. Probably thought I was telling lies. Probably thought a stove burn was something I deserved. Lot of guys thought like that around there. Your father's word was the law. And all those guys, they believed in a strict law. You were either for them or against them.

We came to the apartment where my dad lived, where I had lived with him. There was a hedge row that was never trimmed that led along both sides of the walk that went up to the apartment house. Inside, you had to go down the hall and make a turn to the left to get to our place.

Standing in the shadow of the hedge, Bert said, "You sure about this kid? Dead is dead. And he is your father."

"He's nothing to me, Bert. Nothing. He gets me back, he'll just kill me, and you know it. I'm nothing to him, just something to own and use and throw away. Like he did my mother. My mother was all right. I can still remember how she smelled. Then one day she wasn't there, and that's because of him. She's gone. He's here."

"Still, kid, he's your father."

"I'm all right with it."

Bert nodded. He took the gun and silencer out of his coat pockets and screwed the silencer into place. "You sit this one out. Go on home."

"You used to do stuff like this, didn't you, Bert?"

"All the time," he said. "I ain't proud of it. Except for tonight. These guys, your father. I'm all right with that. Maybe it'll make up for some of the other things I done."

"I'm staying with you, Bert."

"You don't want that, kid."

"Yeah, I do."

We went along the walk then and when we got to the door, Bert handed me the gun. I held it while he worked the lock and got it open with a little wedge. He pried the wood loose at the door. I gave him back the gun. We were inside so quickly and silently, we might as well have been ghosts.

When we got to Dad's door, Bert started with the wedge, but I grabbed his hand. We had an extra key stuck into the side of the door frame where it was cracked. You had to be looking for it to know it was there. We kept some putty over it the color of the wood. I reached around the frame and took out the putty and pulled out the key. I unlocked the door.

I could feel him in the room. I don't know how else to say that, but I could feel him. He was sitting in a chair by the bed, smoking a cigar, and about the time we saw him, he realized we were in the room.

"It's best you don't call out," Bert said.

Dad clicked the lamp by his chair. He was soaked in light and there was enough of it he could look out and see us. We stepped closer.

"I guess I should have known you'd come, Bert. I know who you are. I know what you've done."

"Shouldn't have threatened me," Bert said.

"Guy with me, Amos, he said you did some things some years back, for some boys he knew. He wasn't in the racket then, just on the outskirts. He said you were a kind of legend. We saw you the other day, standing in that doorway, you didn't look so legendary. Yet, here you are."

"Yep," Bert said. "Here I am."

"I'm not going to be all right, I yell or don't yell, am I?"

"Naw, you ain't."

That's when Dad grabbed at the lamp and tried to sling it at Bert, but the wire was too short and the plug didn't come out of the wall. The lamp popped out and back when the plug didn't give, rolled along the floor tumbling light, and then Dad was on his feet, in front of the chair, and he had a gun in his hand he'd pulled from the cushions.

Bert fired his automatic.

There was a streak of light and stench of gunpowder and a sound like someone coughing out a wad of phlegm, and then Dad sat back down in the chair. The gun he had dangled from his finger. He was breathing heavily. He tried to lift his hand with the gun in it, but he couldn't do it. He might as well have been trying to lift a steel girder.

Bert reached over and took Dad's gun from his hand and gave it to me to hold. He set the lamp up, then. The light from it lay on Dad's face like it had weight. Dad was white. I looked at him and tried to feel something, but I didn't. I didn't feel bad for him, and I didn't feel good about it. I didn't feel nothing. Not right then.

Dad was wheezing and there was a rattling in his chest. I guess the shot got him through one of his lungs.

"We can watch him die if it'll give you pleasure, or I can finish him, kid. Your call."

I lifted the pistol in my hand and pointed it at Dad.

Bert said, "Whoa."

I paused.

"No silencer," Bert said. He traded guns with me. "He can't do nothing, like you couldn't when you was a kid. Get up close and give it to him."

I moved close and put the barrel of the pistol to his head and pulled the trigger.

The gun coughed.

Now I had the box with the gun and silencer in it. Those many years ago, Bert had wiped my dad's gun clean with a dish rag, and dropped it and the gun on the floor. He had kept his own gun, though, and now I was to use it and get rid of it. I think it wasn't only about safety, about not getting caught. I think it was Bert's way to say he was done from then on.

Back then, when Dad was dead, we walked out of there silently and down the street quickly. I knew and Bert knew what we had done, and that was enough. We never talked about it again. Didn't even hint such a thing had happened.

I slept well for the first time in years. I finally got my own place, and eventually I took the projectionist job. Things had been all right until those guys came around.

Now things had come full circle. It wasn't just me I was protecting now, it was Sally and the Lowensteins. Under the gun and silencer there was the wedge Bert had used to jimmy the doors way back then. I saw there was a piece of paper under that.

There were three addresses listed on it. Two apartments were listed at the same general address.

The other had a place listed outside of town, almost out in the country. It was near the railroad tracks. For all the high roller talk those guys blew out, they were just like my father had been. Living on the margins, the rest of it going for booze and women. Big time in the lies, small time in their lives, as Bert once said.

I put the gun in my front pants pocket. The grip stuck out. I covered it with my shirt and stuck the silencer in the other pocket. I put the wedge in my back pocket, where I usually carried my wallet. I wouldn't need the wallet that night.

When I walked the gun, silencer and wedge were heavy in my pockets.

The first address was not far from where I was, not far from the theater.

Outside, I started to turn down the walk, and then I stopped. A car was parked at the curb. I knew that car. A man got out.

It was Bert.

"I decided maybe I ought to come," Bert said.

The apartments were easy and quick. Bert took the wedge from me and opened the doors. I went in and they were in bed together, naked, two guys. I had heard of such. I shot both of them in their sleep, Bert holding a flashlight on them so I could see it was them. They weren't the two who had come to see me, but they were part of the five, Bert said. The scammers, the thugs. It was over so quick they never knew they were dead.

At the other apartment we got in easy as before, but no one was there.

That bothered me, but there was nothing for it.

We drove out to the place on the edge of town and parked in a grove of pecan trees that grew beside the road, got out and walked up to the house. There was a light on inside. There were no houses nearby, though there were a couple within earshot, dark and silent.

We went to the windows and took a peek. There was a guy sitting on the couch watching TV. We could hear him laughing at something. The voices on the TV had canned laughter with them. He wasn't one of the two that had come to the theater, but Bert said he was one of the five.

Through an open doorway we saw the two who had threatened Mr. Lowenstein step into sight. They came out of the kitchen, each carrying a beer.

We stepped back from the window.

"Alright," Bert said. "That's all five, counting these three. They're together. That's all right. You don't have to worry about rounding up the one that wasn't at the apartment. He's the one on the couch."

"You're sure?"

"I know who they are," he said. "They been around awhile. It's the ones I was told about, ones bothering the block. Until recent they just been guys walking around after other guys, now they're trying to carve some territory. This is all of them."

"What do we do?"

"Well, it's easier to kill them in their sleep when they can't fight back. But I got an old saying. You get what you get."

"Meaning?"

"Meaning there's one more than I expected, and I got to go back to the car, kid."

We went back to the car. Bert got a sawed-off double-barrel shotgun out of the trunk. The stock was sawed down too. He opened it and slipped in two shells from a box in the trunk, and then he grabbed a handful of shells and stuck them in his pocket.

"Hoping I wouldn't need this. It goes boom real loud."

We walked back.

We waited out there in the bushes by the house for an hour or so, not talking, just waiting. I thought back on how it had been with Dad, me pushing that gun against his head, his eyes looking along that barrel at me. It was pretty nice. And those guys earlier that night. Didn't know them. Never talked to them, but considering they were all and of a same, I was alright with it. Maybe I was more like Dad than I wanted to be.

After awhile, Bert said, "Look, kid. We can come back another time when they're sleeping, maybe the other guy is back in his apartment then, splitting their numbers, or we can be bold and get it over with."

"Let's be bold."

"There's a door on either side of the living room, and if we go through the back, one of us coming out on either side, we can get them before they got time to think. Another thing, anyone else shows up, more of them there than we think, we got to finish things. Hear what I'm saying?"

I nodded.

"Don't get us in our own crossfire," Bert said. "That would be bad form, one of us shooting the other."

Slipping around back, Bert took the wedge and stuck it in the door and pulled and the door made a little popping sound. Nothing too loud. Nothing you could hear over the blare of that TV set.

Inside he went right and I went left.

Only the guy on my side saw us before we cut loose. He was the tall guy that came to the theater. He had tried to pull the gun out from under his pants leg, strapped to his ankle. He should have found a better place to keep it. I fired the silenced .45. It made that big tuberculosis cough and part of his face flew off.

That's when Bert cut down with the shotgun. One barrel, then the other. Both of those guys were dead. A lot of them was on the wall. The sound of that shotgun in the house was like two atomic bombs going off.

Bert glanced at the TV. "I hate that show, that canned laughter."

I thought for a moment he was going to shoot the TV.

We got out of there quick. Going out the back way. The canned laughed roared on the TV.

The only thing that had touched the door was the wedge, so no fingerprints to worry about.

I expected to see lights on in the houses down the way, but nothing had changed. Two shotgun blasts in the night must not have been as loud as they seemed to me. Maybe no one cared.

Bert put the shotgun on the seat between us and we drove away. He wheeled farther out of town, on down to the river. He drove down there and we pulled under the bridge, got out, wiped down the guns just for good measure, then threw them in the river, along with the wedge and the silencer.

When Bert pulled up at the curb in front of my place, I started to get out. "Hold it, kid."

I took my hand off the door lever.

"Listen here. You and me, we got a bond. You know that."

"The closest," I said.

"That's right. But I'm going to tell you something tough, kid. Don't come around no more. It's not a good idea. I done for you what I could. More than I meant to. I got my past in that river now, and I want to leave it there. I love you, kid. I ain't mad at you or nothing, but I can't have you around. I can't think on those kind of things anymore."

"Sure, Bert."

"Don't take it hard, okay?"

"No," I said.

"It ain't personal, but it's got be like that. And throw away that gun box. Good luck, kid."

I nodded. I got out. Bert drove away.

Next night I walked Sally to her apartment, and every night after that because she was scared. Walked her home until the day before the thugs were supposed to come around.

Sally and the Lowensteins were worried, but Mr. Lowenstein had put aside the money for them. He couldn't see a percentage on his side. Sally said she hated it, but was glad he was paying.

Mr. Lowenstein had read the papers, read about the murders in the apartment house and in the house outside of town, but he didn't put it together with those guys we had talked to. No way he could have. He talked about it, though, said the world was getting scary. I agreed it was.

On the last night I walked Sally, she said, "I'm not going to come back to work tomorrow. After Mr. Lowenstein pays them, I'll come back, so I won't need you to walk me for awhile. I think after he pays them, I'm going to be all right on my own."

"Okay," I said.

"I don't want to be there when they come around, even if he is paying. You understand?"

"Understood."

I stood there for a long moment with my hands in my pockets. I was glad she was safe.

"Sally, putting that ugly business aside, what do you think about you and me getting some coffee next week? You know, before work. We can even go to the movie on our day off, and for nothing."

I tried to say that last part with a smile since we see the movies all the time. Me up in the booth, her over by the seats.

She smiled back at me, but it wasn't much of smile. It was like she had borrowed it.

"That's sweet," she said. "But I got a boyfriend, and he might not like that."

"Never seen you with anyone," I said.

"We don't get out much. He comes around, though."

"Does he?"

"Yeah. And you know, I got the college stuff in the mornings and work midday and nights, then I got to study. My time is tight. We get the one day off, and there's so much to do, and I got to spend some time with my boyfriend, you know?"

"Yeah. Okay. What's this boyfriend's name?"

She thought on that a little too long. "Randy."

"Randy, huh? That's his name?"

"Yes. Randy."

"Like Randolph Scott. Like that movie we showed last week. *The Tall T.* You said you liked it."

"Yeah. Like that. His name is Randolph, but everyone calls him Randy."

"All right," I said. "Well, good luck to you and Randy."

"Thanks," she said, like I had meant it. Like I thought there really was a Randy.

Sally never did come back to work after that. And of course the thugs didn't show up. Mr. Lowenstein got to keep his hundred dollars. All along the block, those businesses, they got to keep their money too. Guess someone else like those fellows could come along, but what happened to those five, it's pretty discouraging to that kind of business. They don't know what kind of gang there is that owns this block. There was just me and Bert, but they don't know that.

I like it pretty good up there in the projection booth. Sometimes I look out where Sally used to stand, but she isn't there, of course. Mr. Lowenstein never hired another girl to take her place. He decided people would come anyway.

I saw Sally around town a couple of times, both times she was with a guy, and it wasn't the same guy. I'm pretty sure neither of them were named Randy. If she saw me she didn't let on. I wonder what she'd think to know what I did for her, for all of us.

What I do now is I show the movies and I go home. I used to walk by Bert's place every now and then. I'm not sure why. I read in the papers that his wife Missy died. I wanted to send flowers, or something, but I didn't.

Just the other day, I read Bert died.

I like my job. I like being the projectionist. I'm okay with it, being up there in the booth by myself, feeling mostly good about things like they are, but I won't kid you, sometimes I get a little lonely.

GAIL LEVIN *is Distinguished Professor of Art History, American Studies, Women's Studies, and Liberal Studies at The Graduate Center and Baruch College of the City University of New York. The acknowledged authority on the American realist painter Edward Hopper, she is author of many books and articles on this artist, including the catalogue raisonné and* Edward Hopper: An Intimate Biography *(both 1995). She has edited two anthologies on Hopper,* Silent Places: A Tribute to Edward Hopper, *for which she collected existing fiction that referenced Hopper (2000), and* The Poetry of Solitude: A Tribute to Edward Hopper, *for which she collected and introduced poetry about Hopper (1995). Gail Levin also worked as a curator, including at the Whitney Museum of American Art, where, from 1976 to 1984, she created landmark exhibitions on Edward Hopper and other topics. The present anthology is the first to publish fiction by Levin, who seconds Doris Lessing's observation in* The Golden Notebook: *"I have to conclude that fiction is better at 'the truth' than a factual record."*

Levin has also published and exhibited her photography, collages, and other artworks. A show of her collage memoir, "On NOT Becoming An Artist," was shown in May 2014 at the National Association of Women Artists in New York City and in 2015 in Santa Barbara, California; Santa Fe, New Mexico; and in the Berkshire Mountains of Massachusetts. She is currently working on several books resulting from her Fulbright grants in Asia, exploring links between Asian and American culture.

City Roofs, 1932

THE PREACHER COLLECTS

BY GAIL LEVIN

They call me "Reverend Sanborn." I was born Arthayer R. Sanborn,
Jr., in 1916, in Manchester, New Hampshire, son of Arthayer
and Annie Quimby Sanborn. I graduated from Gordon College,
a good Christian school in Wenham, Massachusetts, and then from
Andover Newton Theological Seminary. I served American Baptist
Churches in Woodville, Massachusetts, and in Woonsocket, Rhode
Island, before I went to Nyack, New York, where I led the First Baptist
Church, located on North Broadway. My job came with the security
of a home, just next to the church, where I lived with my wife, Ruth,
and our four children.

Before long I met at church our neighbor and long-time parishioner,
Marion Louise Hopper. An aging spinster, she lived alone in her family's
old house next door to the church. She liked to boast that her younger
brother, and only sibling, was a famous artist, named Edward. Edward

Hopper, however, appeared to want as little as possible to do with Nyack and his sister.

In early April 1956, Marion became ill and called Edward for help. He and his wife, Jo, had to rush up to Nyack from Manhattan. The doctor diagnosed Marion as having gallstones and a dangerous blood condition. She was then seventy-five and living in an old house with a decrepit furnace and water pipes that could scarcely do their job. The house was depressingly dark since Marion scrimped by using only twenty-five-watt lightbulbs. Her cat was emaciated and sick.

Her brother, just two years younger than his sister, found the role of rescuer disturbing. He complained that his ears had begun to ring; he ran to New York to see his own doctor, leaving Jo to deal with Marion. Jo found her sister-in-law disagreeable, complaining to me, "She and I make each other ill, we disturb each other so much." Nothing serious was wrong with Edward, so he had to come back to Nyack to help Jo, check on Marion, and make sure that her furnace was working as a late spring snowstorm struck. Jo, however, informed me that henceforth she expected Marion's "noble" friends at church to prove their idea of worthiness. That is where I came into the picture.

Marion's dependence on the church grew as she aged and became more feeble and reclusive. I saw to it myself that the church ladies' auxiliary looked in on her as needed. But I also made a point of getting to know her myself. I had Marion give me the key to her house—just in case of an emergency. I got the idea to buy the poor shut-in a television set and soon she was hooked on watching soap operas. That got her off my back. While she was glued to the television set, I took it upon myself to explore the old house from top to bottom. I thought that I should check up on the condition of the roof and so one day went up into the attic.

Looking around, I was surprised to find not leaks, but stacks and stacks of early artwork by Edward Hopper: piles of drawings, oil paintings, and illustrations. After I returned several times and rummaged around, I found valuable historical documents including the letters young Edward had written to his family during the three trips he made to Europe just after completing art school. The more I learned the more I became concerned about what would happen to all these treasures after Marion's death. Indeed, I could not get their fate off my mind. Marion's only heirs were her brother and sister-in-law, and they were just a few years younger than Marion. None of them had produced any children, who could look after their estate.

I began to reflect that to save these artworks from oblivion could not only be justified, but that the savior would be a hero. So I stepped up to prevent harm from coming to Hopper's artworks. I knew that vagrants might occupy an abandoned house. An empty house could be set on fire. The antique furniture and precious artworks could be stolen, damaged, or destroyed. Marion certainly would not give me permission to remove these artworks. They belonged to Edward. But he had all but abandoned them years ago, moving to New York. I alone cared for these artworks more than anyone else in the world. I saw their value. I went to the library and read about Edward Hopper. I studied and made myself an expert. I researched the Hopper family's genealogy, dating back to its arrival in 17th-century New Amsterdam.

As time went on, I found ways to make myself useful to Edward and Jo Hopper. For them, coming to Nyack from Manhattan was an unwelcome chore. It was nearly impossible during the half of the year that they spent living in South Truro on the far end of Cape Cod. When the old couple returned to New York City, late each October, they drove via Nyack, where Edward left their car at the family home. Only at this time and when they came to retrieve the car in the spring did they plan to see Marion. They were not close to her. She remained out of sight and forgotten.

Marion had little understanding of her brother's life in New York. When he had a retrospective show at the Whitney Museum in 1964, she asked to attend the opening party and to bring her friend Beatrice and me. I was eager to go. But Edward, then eighty-two, could not be bothered by his sister's request. He wrote to her: "This is the one time in the year when I can meet museum directors, critics and collectors of importance and I shall have to devote all my time to them (and will have no time for you, Dr. Sanborn and Beatrice.)" He was most ungrateful.

Still less did Edward have time to worry about the abandoned artworks in the attic of his boyhood home. At first, I just rescued a few of the smaller drawings and paintings, taking them home to study. I especially loved a drawing he had done of that same attic and some early self-portraits that he had painted in oil. Marion never even noticed. In the beginning, I had no idea of the monetary value of Hopper's art. In fact, the works of Hopper's early years, made long before he became famous, had never been on the market. At the time he made these things, he could not sell anything, since no one wanted his art.

The Bible says in Ephesians 4:28, "He who steals must steal no longer; but rather he must labor, performing with his own hands what is good, so that he will have something to share with one who has need." I know that my labors as a researcher and my efforts to save the works by Hopper that passed through my hands justify my deeds. I have shared my profits with my wife and our three sons and a daughter and nine grandchildren—all needing educations, weddings, and security in life. Such valuables should not go to waste!

Marion remained in the family home until May 1965, when a burglar wearing a pink mask broke in, held a hand over her mouth, and forced her upstairs. Nearly eighty-five, her health went downhill. When the housekeeper hired by Edward and Jo insisted upon taking her vacation over the Fourth of July, they had to come and act as Marion's nurses for a week. I volunteered to drive them up to Nyack from the city and then back home. On July 16, Marion was taken to the hospital and she died the next day. Once again, I drove to the city to fetch the elderly couple and conducted Marion's funeral in Nyack.

Edward was not interested, so that Jo was left alone to sort through the house's store of family heirlooms and old photographs. She spent about six weeks in Nyack. She told me that Marion had been "a pack rat like me . . . She not so fond of me, but from across the grave, I felt her gladness I wasn't throwing our her treasures or selling the hundred-year-old birthplace." She complained that Edward had abandoned her to the task, and had left her "breathing in the dust of a century."

I bided my time until Jo and Edward left Nyack. I still had the key to the house filled with Hopper's art, family papers, and antiques. As Edward's health began to fail, I continued to remove works from the attic trove. My concern for a valuable antique Dutch cupboard inspired me to move it out of the empty house and to store it with a neighbor. Had the frail Edward or Jo come calling, I could claim that I had put it there just to keep it safe. But once the Hoppers' three estates were settled, I planned to possess the object that I so desired. I alone cared for it. I deserved it.

Edward's health continued to deteriorate. In December 1966, he was in so much pain that Jo had to call an ambulance to rush him to the hospital. She phoned and told me that he had had a double hernia operation. She said that she had to postpone the cataract surgery that she needed to correct her dimming vision. Edward was back in the hospital the following July. Also affected by glaucoma, Jo slipped in the studio as she was preparing to go to visit Edward in the hospital. She broke her hip and leg, joining him in the same hospital, where they remained for three months. Due to glaucoma, her eyes proved inoperable.

Released from the hospital in December 1966, the Hoppers found daily life hard to manage. They lived on the top floor of an old row house, up seventy-four steps. They were in no condition to check up on their possessions in the house in Nyack. Nine months after his hernia operation, Edward was back in the hospital with heart problems. He returned home, barely able to eat. On May 15, 1967, he died in his studio, two months short of his eighty-fifth birthday.

Abandoned by friends who had cared only for the more famous Edward, Jo had no one to turn to but me. I had conducted Edward's funeral in Nyack. To do so, I had to fly back from Pittsburgh, which I was visiting at the time. Jo referred to me as a "13th disciple"—"a husky, good looking football coach content to shepherd a flock of Nyack ladies . . . doing needed and often arduous practical good offices for them that would include going out in the kitchen and making lunch for Marion." For my services, she paid me $500 from the estate, a mere pittance for my sustained efforts in their behalf.

Jo was left vulnerable and alone. She was ill and her vision was impaired. She and Edward had no surviving family members. She knew that she should attend to probating the will and disposing of the property in Nyack, but she concluded that she was "all so alone and nearly blind" so that she "better let it alone." She struggled to cope with daily life. Her leg was slow to heal and she felt like a prisoner on the top floor of that nearly empty building in the city. New York University had purchased the row house and, unable to evict the Hoppers, waited for their deaths to finish renovating.

In Jo's vulnerability, I saw opportunity. Few visited Jo after Edward's death, but I took the trouble to. At the end of one visit, when her vision was compromised and she was barely able to move about the studio, I adopted one of Edward's unsold canvases, a picture of *City Roofs* from 1932. It was abandoned and forlorn until I gave it a good home. I got Jo to change her will and write me into it. Unfortunately, she did not leave me any art and I did not know that she kept meticulous track of the whereabouts of Edward's artworks. She continued to write in the ledger books that she had started soon after their marriage in which she recorded whenever works left the studio for exhibition, sale, or gifts. Later I claimed that she gave me *City Roofs* because I knew that she would have if she could have appreciated my efforts to save Edward's work in Nyack. Instead, in her shaky hand, she had noted that this painting that I took had not been sold and was "here in studio."

Jo Hopper died on March 6, 1968, twelve days before her eighty-fifth birthday and less than ten months after she had lost Edward. Upon hearing, I rushed to the neighbor to retrieve the Dutch cupboard that I had hidden there, successfully removing it from the estate for myself. No one remembers Jo's funeral. There wasn't one. Who would have attended?

When Jo's will was probated, it was announced that Edward's entire "artistic estate" had been left to the Whitney Museum. I kept on looking after the empty house and adding bit by bit to my little collection of early Hopper until the executor for the estate, a local lawyer in Nyack, put the house on the market in 1970, two years after Jo's death. It was sold to a Mrs. Linet, who thought that she bought the house and its contents. I had asked her for a few meager things from the house, but she turned me down. She lost a fortune because she was greedy. Because of her stinginess, she forced me to act. I informed the estate lawyer and told him about the art in the attic. Neither the lawyer nor the Whitney Museum had bothered to check on what was in the Nyack house and so they knew nothing about those works.

Before the closing, my son and I removed the rest of the art from the attic. I kept some more art and all of the memorabilia and documents for my collection, but delivered the rest, on the advice of the executor, to Hopper's art dealer, John Clancy. From there, the art eventually reached the museum. The buyer was surprised to find that there was no more art in that attic and sued the estate, canceling the sale. The odd bits of furniture left in the house were later put on auction to benefit the church.

After these last additions to my collection, I slowly began to put Hopper's works up for auction. I wrote letters to warn the auction houses that the objects I consigned were to be sold anonymously. I did not yet want to call attention to myself. Eventually I learned that to get higher prices, I needed to give the remaining works a history of ownership by someone who knew the artist, because that would testify to their authenticity.

I was amazed when the Boston Museum of Fine Arts paid more than sixty thousand dollars for an early Hopper self-portrait that I had given to my friend, another underpaid preacher, to sell. I was surprised and pleased by the rising values for Hopper's art. I had hundreds of drawings from the years of Hopper's maturity as well as many early works, including some eighty paintings. What I lacked was any written evidence that either Edward or Jo Hopper ever gave me any work of art.

In 1972, I called Kennedy Galleries in New York. They dealt in American art. I had seen their ads for work by Hopper in art magazines at the library. They sent their employee to Nyack to assess my collection. I showed him only a small selection, not telling him that I had much more art. Without any qualms about how I got these works of art by this leading American artist, this prominent gallery offered me a consignment deal for everything that I showed them. That same day they wrote me a check for $65,000 as a deposit against future sales. I rushed to deposit the check in the local bank and as soon as it cleared, I submitted a letter to the First Baptist Church and resigned. As I began my retirement, I was fifty-six years old. I would devote my remaining years to researching and marketing the work of Edward Hopper.

It turned out that my sales were competing against those of the Whitney Museum, which was slowly selling Edward's work from Jo's bequest. In 1976, the museum was called out for selling off what they referred to as "duplicates" of Edward's art. The museum did not know what to do with so many Hoppers. The museum found itself attacked in *The New York*

Times by its art critic, Hilton Kramer, who claimed that the museum was squandering its legacy. The Whitney certainly proved by this that they did not need the works in my collection.

Looking to stop the bad publicity, the museum obtained a grant from a foundation and hired a young art historian to research Edward Hopper and write a complete catalogue of his work, studying the objects in Jo's bequest. The hiring of Gail Levin as curator of the Hopper Collection was praised in the *New York Times* by Hilton Kramer, who wrote, "She brings both a keen eye and a scholarly intelligence to the large task that awaits her."

The article spoke to me, since I realized that to assure the sale of the works in my collection, I needed Miss Levin to authenticate all of the Hoppers that I still had. As soon as I read this piece, I immediately went to see her. I lost no time, piling a small selection of the works that I had collected into a suitcase and taking it right into her office at the Whitney. I appeared as my retired self: calm, rested, suntanned, and since it was such a balmy late June day, I wore Bermuda shorts.

I explained to Miss Levin that I had been a close friend of Edward and Jo Hopper's. I opened my suitcase and revealed a selection of Hopper's boyhood works. A new curator still in her twenties, she was interested and curious in all that I brought in. Then she started in asking me for any inscriptions, personal notes, in short anything that would have documented how I obtained these works of art that I told her had been gifts. I told her I had nothing to show.

As she pursued her research, she would later discover that Jo carefully recorded the gifts that Edward Hopper gave to her and to others in the record books that she kept whenever works left the studio. The only exception turned out to be documented by Jo in her diary. I had not yet realized this unfortunate detail. But on that day, Miss Levin had barely started her research. She had no reason as yet to suspect me.

That summer Miss Levin made an appointment to visit my wife, Ruth, and me in our vacation home in Newport, New Hampshire. I purchased it with sales of some of Hopper's works, but she did not need to know that. She came up from New York to see the works in our Hopper collection stored there, but I kept many of them hidden from her on that first visit. I did not want to overwhelm this naïve but inquisitive young lady or provoke too many more questions.

Miss Levin was too curious. She questioned how we happened to have so many of the sketches for Hopper's mature paintings. She surmised correctly that these would not have been stored in the Nyack attic with Hopper's boyhood works. My wife, Ruth, told her by way of explanation, "As one of the legatees, Reverend Sanborn was allowed to buy from the contents of the New York studio after the art had been sent to the Whitney. The entire contents were valued at just over $100. We took advantage of that offer to purchase a low boy, a high boy, and several other pieces of antique Dutch furniture. Lo and behold, we found underneath the dresser-drawer linings stacks of Hopper's drawings." Miss Levin seemed satisfied with that explanation.

She followed up by visiting us in our winter home in Melbourne Beach, Florida, where I kept more of my Hopper collection. She arranged to have a professional photographer record at the museum's expense each of our Hoppers for the complete catalogue of his work that she was producing for the museum. This would authenticate them for posterity. She was doing just what I needed her to do.

That same winter, Lawrence Fleischman of Kennedy Galleries organized a show of Edward Hopper's works. All of the early works and some of the later drawings were from my collection. He added other works bought elsewhere and did not acknowledge my singular efforts in his catalogue. I felt annoyed by this and would not do further business with him. He enlisted both Miss Levin and Lloyd Goodrich, who had directed Hopper's shows at the Whitney, to write essays in the catalogue. Neither one wrote about me.

When Miss Levin organized her first show of Edward Hopper at the Whitney in 1979, I loaned many of his illustrations and some drawings from my collection. I had saved them from the Nyack attic, when no one else was interested in what was there. I was surprised to read that although she thanked me, she did not acknowledge me as the close friend of Edward and Jo Hopper that I had told her I had been. All along she appeared to doubt what I had told her. Why then should I share my Hopper documents with her as she requested?

I had kept all of the Hopper family photographs and documents from the attic for my own collection. I got the letters that Hopper wrote home to his family from Paris and the illustrated letter that he sent to his mother from his trip to Santa Fe in 1925, shortly after he married Jo. I also got two of Hopper's record books, one of which I sold to Kennedy Galleries. It turned out Lloyd Goodrich gave the Whitney those record books that Jo had left to him in her will. My two never made it into the estate.

In 1980, Miss Levin opened her second big Hopper show at the Whitney Museum, "Edward Hopper: The Art and the Artist." Once again she gave me what I considered inadequate credit for my extensive work on Hopper. In the end, I had loaned her some of Hopper's letters and other documents and she had quoted from them and even made copies of them without getting my permission to do so. I went to see her boss, the museum's director, Tom Armstrong. He wanted the main record book that I still had in my possession. I said, "Well, we can talk." It turns out that Miss Levin was claiming to her boss that I had stolen the works that I had taken from Hopper's studio and the Nyack attic. Armstrong and I agreed that this should never become public. He offered to fire Miss Levin if I gave up the record book and some other things. We made a deal. The rest, as they say, is history. My role as a collector of Edward Hopper is now secure. My children and grandchildren will take care of my legacy.

Gail Levin served as curator of the Edward Hopper Collection at the Whitney Museum of American Art from 1976 to 1984. Her project of a catalogue raisonné of Hopper's work was published by W. W. Norton and Co. for the Whitney in 1995.

Arthayer R. Sanborn, Jr. died on November 18, 2007 at the age of 91, in his home in Celebration, Florida. Of the others named in this story, only the author remains alive.

WARREN MOORE *is Professor of English at Newberry College, in Newberry, SC. His novel* Broken Glass Waltzes *was published in 2013, and he has had stories appear in a variety of small and online magazines, and in 2015's* Dark City Lights. *He lives in Newberry with his wife and daughter, and thanks his father (who introduced him to Hopper) and his mother (who introduced him to Marge.)*

Office at Night, 1940

OFFICE AT NIGHT

BY WARREN MOORE

Margaret heard the train rumble by as Walter looked at the papers on the desk. The cord on the window shade swung, whether from the train's vibrations or from the breeze through the window, she didn't know. She couldn't feel either, nor did she feel the blue dress—her favorite—clinging to her curves. All she saw was Walter, and all he saw were the files in the pool of light from the desk lamp.

She had put the papers in the file cabinet and rested her arm atop the folders what seemed like—could have been—a lifetime ago. The phrase brought a faint smile to Margaret's face. Any time could be a lifetime, depending on how long you lived. And she had thought from time to time that she and Walter might have a lifetime together. Before she had died.

Margaret Dupont had never liked her name. She would have liked a movie star name like Jean or Bette, but her name? It made people think of the woman from the Marx Brothers movies. She stuck with it, though, because she had to, after all, and she liked her middle name, Lucille, even less. She had been named after a maiden aunt who had died young, and from time to time, she wondered if there had been a jinx on the name. But her grandmother liked the name, and as a cousin told Margaret when she was a teenager, "I guess she just wore your mother down." Yep—she could imagine her mother in the hospital, exhausted, saying, "What the hell, *Margaret* it is." She wouldn't have said it out loud, though—Mother wasn't going to talk like that in public, any more than she'd take a step with a lit cigarette. It wasn't ladylike.

But Margaret hadn't been ladylike as a child, either, and that was probably one of the reasons she and Mother had gone for weeks at a time without speaking sometimes. Mother was small; Margaret was big, like her daddy, who had been big enough to hitch to a plow by the time he was nine, which is when he stopped going to school. Mother got a couple more years in before she had to leave school, and a few years later, she married Daddy and came to the city. Margaret had come along a few years later, the second and last child—so big it nearly killed her mother, a claim she heard too often.

Margaret was big for her age—"Large Marge," bigger than most of the boys, even, at least until she got sick. Scarlatina, the doctors told her parents, and it weakened her heart and slowed her growth, but she was lucky to have gotten off that easily—not everyone lived through that. But she stuck with life, because she had to, and it hadn't even occurred to her that there was a choice. And her growth slowed, but even then she was too tall, almost six feet, for heaven's sake, and what kind of boy would want a big old thing like that? But she had to miss a year of school and make it up after, so she was a year older than the other kids in high school, and so that much bigger, even. "Large Marge," and clumsy to fit it. She had thrown a knee out of joint at a school dance, but the embarrassment of crumpling to the gymnasium floor had hurt worse than the knee's displacement.

But she was smart, and she stayed in school and finished it, because Mother and Daddy wouldn't have had it any other way. And she could work, had worked summers and after school, and did what was needed around the house, when her parents were working—her sister was seven years older, and had married and started a family of her own. Margaret had won the typing medal in high school. And she could draw—her sketches had even been used in newspaper ads from the local department store, with her name and all.

It didn't matter, though, in Greensburg. She'd always be "Violet and Ernie's girl," or "the Tree," or "Moose," or "Large Marge." The town wasn't big enough for her to be anyone else. So she had to go someplace that was.

When she told Mother and Daddy that she wanted to go to the city—and all three of them could hear *New York* in those words—Mother asked if she had lost her mind, that she'd do no such thing, and when Margaret said she could, she had saved her money, she had looked up safe places where girls could stay—the Barbizon, the Rutledge!—Mother said any child that wanted to run off to the city was bound to become a whore, or marry an Italian. When Margaret said that she didn't think either of those would be necessary, Mother slapped her and stalked from the room. Margaret stood there, and didn't let her eyes water until Mother had left, and Daddy had started to cry. "Couldn't you just go to Atlanta?"

Margaret did cry, then, but only as she said she had to try someplace big—someplace with opportunities, and stores that might want to see her portfolio, and art. Daddy shook his head and left the room, his shoulders shaking as he walked away. Margaret left three days later, without speaking to Mother again. When she tried to talk to Daddy, he'd just start to cry, and if that happened one more time, she knew she might not be able to go at all. She packed her things and caught the train, as no one waved goodbye. Later that night, she found ten dollars had been tucked into an envelope in her suitcase. The only word on it was "Daddy."

The coach fare to New York was more than that, but she paid—with her own money, and even giving a quarter to the porter—and rode the shuddering coach for what may have been thirty hours ("Remember," she said to herself, "Buy a watch!"), but felt as though it could have been thirty years. She ate soup in the dining cars, tucking extra crackers into her purse for snacks along the way. On the second day of the trip, a young soldier in the coach smiled at her and tried to start a conversation, and while Margaret didn't have much to say to him, she wondered at the idea that a man might want to talk to her—tall, ungainly, Large Marge. He got off the train somewhere in Ohio, handing her a hastily written address and telling her to write him once she got to be a famous ar-TEEST. She said that might be a while, but thanked him. She knew she'd never see him again, though—Ohio was a place she didn't want to pass through more than once.

Surely in New York, there might be someone for her. She imagined him—tall like Daddy, taller than her. Blonde hair and a kind voice—and a love of art, of course. But she'd have to be careful—she had read the magazines, and knew there were men in the city who would use a girl and throw them away, and to have to return to Greensburg, to Mother—best not to think of that.

She had dozed off, with her head against the window, and awoke with a start when the conductor touched her lightly on the shoulder and said, "Pennsylvania Station, miss. End of the line." She blushed as she stood, gathered her purse and stepped from the passenger car to find her luggage—well, a suitcase and makeup kit, and her portfolio. She bought a map at the newsstand, and looked up the Barbizon. It looked to be about two and a half miles, but she hadn't come here to spend all her money on cab fare. She began to walk north, up Seventh Avenue toward Central Park and then east.

It took Margaret almost two hours to reach the hotel. She could have made it in half the time, but she kept stopping, almost stunned by the towers around her, and the people everywhere. The thought circled through her head: "This is what New York looks like." Then it changed: "This is what New York looks like *with me in it.*" Finally, she found the hotel—it was the biggest building she had ever seen—before today.

She walked into the lobby, approached the desk. "I'd like a room, please."

The clerk, a woman, reminded her of her elementary school librarian—pinch-faced and stern, with the ability somehow to look down at Margaret despite being at least a head shorter. "What's the reservation under?"

"I'm afraid I don't have a reservation."

"Any references?"

"You mean, like for a job?"

"No, miss. To stay at the Barbizon, we require three letters of recommendation. We're quite selective about the young ladies who reside here."

"Well, I don't have anything like that. I'm new to the city, and didn't know anything about that. Couldn't you just—"

"I'm sorry," the librarian said. "That simply isn't possible. Good day."

The blood began to drain from Margaret's face as the older woman turned away. She stepped back from the counter, feeling her knees wobble a bit. She ducked her head as she stepped back through the doors, onto the street. It was afternoon, and the streets were already falling into the shadows of the tall buildings. She walked, toward the park, then south. As the street numbers grew lower, the language on the signs changed from English to German, and then occasionally to English again. Some of the German signs said something about a Bund—Margaret wondered if those were the people she had seen in the newsreels.

Her luggage grew heavier and heavier as she walked through the upper Eighties, and she was wondering why she had been such a fool as to do this, and whether Mother and Daddy would claim her body when she died in an alleyway, when she saw a house with a hand-lettered sign reading "Rooms to Let." She knocked on the door.

The woman who answered had her hair pulled back into a bun, but she looked kinder than the woman at the Barbizon and she looked at Margaret, and at her luggage, and said, "Room, cold breakfast, and dinner for five dollars a week. Two weeks in advance." Her voice was pleasant, and sounded foreign—like Margaret would have imagined a leprechaun's to be. Before she thought, she asked, "Are you Irish?"

The woman scowled. "Would that be a problem, missy?"

Margaret blinked. "Oh, no, ma'am. I just thought you talked pretty, like one of those priests in the movies."

"You sound like a hillbilly yourself, you know."

"Maybe I am. But I'm a hillbilly who needs a place to sleep, and I've got ten dollars."

"Fifteen, girl. The ten are advance; the five is for this week."

Margaret ran some figures in her head. She'd need to get a job pretty quickly, but what she could see over the woman's shoulder, into the hallway and the dining room at the side, looked clean. "Fifteen, then."

She handed the woman her cash, glancing into her own purse as she did so. She corrected herself: she'd need to get a job really quickly. "What's your name, hillbilly?"

"Margaret Dupont. Miss Margaret Dupont. And you are?"

"Mrs. Dorothy Daly—not that the 'Mrs.' does me a whit of good, with Himself gone two years now." She crossed herself. Margaret wanted to smile—she had never seen that outside of a movie, either. But she kept a straight face. "So, Peggy, you're a big thing, aren't you? Bet you eat a lot."

"I try to watch my figure," Margaret said—what she had read about those rude New Yorkers had some truth to it, she guessed. "And why did you call me Peggy?"

"Short for Margaret, girl," Mrs. Daly said, shaking her head. Before Margaret could figure that out, Mrs. Daly said, "Don't just stand there like a gump—let's get you in before dinner."

The room was small—in Greensburg, it would have been cramped— with a single bed, a washbasin, a nightstand and a chest of drawers. The mirror atop the nightstand was missing a bit of its silvering, but it would do well enough. And she could put her things down at last. She focused again on Mrs. Daly's voice as she discussed house rules. "No guests upstairs, and no more than four showers a week. I've a clean house, but not a palace. There's a phone down the hall. Five minute limit, and no long distance without paying up front."

"That'll be fine." *I've no one to call, anyway.*

"And Peggy?"

"Yes?"

"Bring your suitcases down once you've emptied them."

"Oh! Do you store them for us?"

"You could say that, hillbilly, or you could say they're collateral. You're not likely to skip if you've nothing to carry your things in, are you?"

Margaret did as she was told, except for the portfolio, which she saw as more of a sample book than a piece of luggage. The dinner was chicken, potatoes, and green beans—a meal she had eaten many times before, had *cooked* many times before, but it didn't taste like the food from home. But it wasn't soup or crackers, and she cleaned her plate. She thought of getting a second helping, but she remembered Mrs. Daly's comment about her size, and decided to pass. The meal was enough, and she could get by on two meals a day for a while.

Mrs. Daly introduced her to the other tenants, ranging from an old man to a woman who may have been thirty to Margaret's nineteen. She promptly forgot their names, as the weight of the day and the weight of the meal pulled her toward sleep. After a decent interval, she went upstairs to her room and fell asleep as if she had been clubbed. Tomorrow was Thursday, time to look for a job.

And Friday became time to look for a job as well, as did the following weeks. Apparently Mr. Roosevelt's big ideas hadn't made it to the department stores yet, because none of them needed so much as a window dresser, much less a sketch artist. She thought she had a nibble in the fashion district, but nothing happened there either. And she almost regretted slapping the bartender who offered her a waitressing job—in exchange for what he called a "finder's fee," but one in which no money would change hands. Almost. But she didn't want to prove Mother right.

As she walked through the garment district once again (an hour from the rooming house), she saw a rather run-down office building, which she assumed held rather run-down offices. Well, she was feeling rather run-down herself—and running out of time and money, even on the two-meal-a-day plan. Before long, she might have to ask Mrs. Daly if she could wash dishes or cook in exchange for some of the rent. But for now, she could keep looking.

So she walked into the building, and looked for, and then at, the directory. There were offices listed on the tenth, seventh, sixth, and third floors, and Margaret figured she might as well start at the top and work her way down, so there would be fewer steps at the end of the day after she had struck out. She rode the elevator to the top floor, where it took her about ninety seconds to learn that Garlandson Architects Inc. didn't need anyone, thank you, miss. Three flights of stairs later, she found herself on the seventh floor, which didn't surprise her a bit, but which also failed to yield a position with Parker and Son, whatever it was that they did. As she got to speak neither to Mr. Parker nor his son (his Son?), she didn't even get to learn what their business was, other than not hiring anyone. Likewise, the booking agent down the hall—a Mr. Landsberg—told her she was out of luck unless she could dance. Margaret almost gave it a try, but she told Mr. Landsberg sorry, but she wasn't a showgirl.

"Maybe you should try it sometime," Landsberg said. "You've got the figure for it. How tall are you?"

Margaret was so surprised by the idea that she might have a figure for anything that she told the truth. "Five-eleven and a half."

Landsberg shook his head. "No, sweetheart, that's too tall for the Rockettes. But if you change your mind, give me a call."

"Probably better for everyone if I don't," she said to herself in the hallway. A showgirl's figure? Large Marge? She looked down at herself. Her legs *were* long, and pretty well toned from all the walking she had done recently, and the two-meal plan kept her slim, too—even Mrs. Daly would occasionally push a second helping at her in the evening. Well, she guessed there might be a bright side to that much, anyway.

Another flight took her to the sixth floor, which was primarily vacant. *Like my prospects,* she thought, but in the interest of completeness, she walked the hallways until she saw a door at the end of the hall. "Walter Schroer, Title Attorney" was gold leafed on the pebbled glass, and the letters were new enough not to start flaking. At least, not yet. She could see a silhouette through the glass, and she knocked at the door.

"Come in," said a voice—a man's voice, and a pleasant one at that. Margaret did, and he said, "Oh, you must be the girl from the agency. What took you so long?"

For an instant, she thought about lying, saying yes, she *was* that girl from the agency, but she didn't think it would be a good idea, especially if the real girl from the agency (what agency?) were to show up in the middle of things. So she said, "I'm not sure what you mean—I'm just here looking for work. But if you're expecting someone—"

"Well, I *was*," the man said, "but she doesn't seem to be here."

Margaret looked around. The office was small—not much larger than her room at Mrs. Daly's. The man—who she figured was Mr. Schroer, as the office hardly seemed big enough for too many other people—had a small desk, brown wood on the green carpet. A filing cabinet was behind his right shoulder against a wall of the strangely angled room. The room's shape reminded her of a cough drop, or a card from a Rook deck before the sides were tapped into a neat pile. A smaller desk sat catty-cornered to her right, and a typewriter sat there. On the man's desk, a desk lamp was positioned to illuminate a blotter, and a telephone rested by his left elbow.

Schroer looked at her as she looked around. "Can you type?" he asked her.

"Yes, sir, about 60 to 65 words per minute."

He whistled. "Can you file?"

"Well, knowing the alphabet helps with the typing."

He smiled. "And can you take dictation? Let's see. Sit over there." He gestured toward the typewriter. "There's a pad and pen in the desk drawer." Indeed, there were. "You ready, Miss . . . ?"

"Dupont," Margaret said. "Mar—Peggy Dupont." She liked the sound, and maybe the new name would bring a change of luck.

"OK, Mar-Peggy," Schroer said, and then she smiled. "October 19, 1935. Dear Mr. McGillicuddy—two *d*'s—I am happy to inform you that the title to the parcel of land designated Plat Z219X3 is free of liens. Furthermore, no easement will be necessary, as right-of-way is included in the rights to the property. The necessary papers are enclosed. At your service, I remain, Sincerely, Walter Schroer. Read it back." She did, and as she finished, he said, "Not bad. Type it up, please." So she did that as well. "May I see it?"

"It's your office," she said, a little surprised at her own, well, sassiness. Mother would have had a conniption. But she handed him the paper, and he said, "Nicely done." He went back to the desk, picked up the phone, and placed a call.

"Ajax Personnel? Yes, this is Walter Schroer. Misfiled? It happens, I suppose. Don't bother. I think the position is filled. Thank you. Goodbye." He looked back at Margaret. "Well, Mar-Peggy, judging from your voice, I'm guessing you aren't from Brooklyn. Where did you learn to type and take dictation?"

"Greensburg High School, sir. In Greensburg, Tennessee."

"I didn't know they typed there."

She narrowed her gaze. "Not all of us do."

"Probably why they kicked you out." She started to stand up, but he gestured to her, both arms out, palms down. "Settle down, Mar-Peggy."

"Do you have to keep doing that? Peggy is fine."

"Good to know. Have you ever been a secretary before? No? Well, if seventeen-fifty a week is fine, then you can be one now. The going rate is twenty, but good luck finding a job that pays the going rate. I'd start by keeping an eye on the death notices. Also, you can answer the phone, which shouldn't be hard, as it doesn't ring very often."

"Seventeen-fifty is very satisfactory, Mr. Schroer."

"This office isn't big enough for Misters and Misses. Unless there's a client in here, Walter will do."

Mother wouldn't have approved of that at all, but then, this wasn't Greensburg. "OK, Walter."

"Very good. Now what do you know about property law?"

Nothing, as it happened, so he spent the afternoon telling her what a title was, and what he did, and where the City Register Office was, where he would be sending her from time to time, and where the deli was, where she could bring him a sandwich tomorrow at lunch, and it was five o'clock when he finally said, "Any questions?"

No more than a million, she thought, but she said, "You gave me a lot of information. And thank you for giving me a chance."

He shrugged. "Thank Ajax. See you tomorrow at nine."

"Yes, sir." The three miles to the rooming house were the shortest she'd ever walked, until the next morning. At last, she was no longer walking through the city with her in it—she felt as though she walked through her city.

It had taken Margaret a while to get used to being dead, she thought. Well, really just a couple of weeks, and she didn't exactly know what the rules were, or how long she had to learn them—forever, perhaps? Or would she lose interest in being . . . well, a ghost, she guessed, or maybe what they called a haint back in Greensburg, eventually, and just become something else or become nothing? Whatever was coming, she couldn't say, but she would have liked to know how things worked.

Her body, for example. She knew where it was—back in Greensburg in the family plot, at least that's what she figured when she heard that Daddy had claimed it. She was a little surprised that she didn't have to go where it did. In fact, she couldn't—she tried, but then she realized she didn't know how to do that, or even if that were possible—but she hoped it had been a nice funeral. Her aunt Connie loved a good funeral, but especially loved it when the next of kin would "take on," weeping, wailing, throwing themselves at the grave, that sort of thing. Margaret didn't figure that would have happened at her funeral—Mother wouldn't have stood for it. Sorry, Aunt Connie. But it might have been nice to hear the music.

Still, she was in New York, and being a ghost had some advantages. She didn't have to pay rent anymore, and it didn't make much difference to her whether she was inside or out, awake or, well, not asleep, exactly, because she didn't get tired anymore. Sometimes, though, she would be looking around, or moving about the city, and then she wouldn't feel like it, and she'd blink and it would be hours, or even a couple of days later. Either way, regardless of where she had been when she blinked, she'd find herself either in the office, or in front of Mrs. Daly's rooming house, where she had—

Well, where she had died. It wasn't anything dramatic, she guessed, but it most definitely had been fatal. No crime in the street or being hit by a taxi, or anything, just falling the wrong way. She had been thinking about the new honeysuckle perfume she had bought at Macy's, when her heel had broken on the curb, or maybe her knee had gone out again—she couldn't really recall now, and the particulars didn't especially matter—and she fell and as her head rushed toward the sidewalk she thought *This is going to hurt* but it didn't, and the next thing she knew, she was behind Mrs. Daly, who was talking to a neighbor about that great tall girl who had fallen and just died, out like a candle (Mrs. Daly said, crossing herself), and how her poor father had come to take the girl's things back to wherever she was from and left nothing but a room to rent again.

And Margaret figured that was sad, but it didn't bother her all that much, because it wasn't like she hurt, and she could go to the shows and museums, the park, and really anywhere in the city, and she didn't have to pay admission or anything, and no one bothered her, of course. She thought some of the animals may have noticed her—cats in alleys and windowsills, birds, and it seemed the squirrels in Central Park cocked their heads a certain way when she was around—but no people. And she could walk all day without getting tired or hungry, and that was fine with her as well.

She saw other ghosts (the word still seemed strange, maybe even a little uncomfortable, like *unwed mother* or *Negro*, but it was the word she had) around the town, but if they had noticed her, they didn't mention it—perhaps one didn't do that sort of thing. They minded their business, and she minded hers, and that was fine, she guessed.

There wasn't much she could *do*, though, really. She could pass through things—that was one of the first things she had tried, once she had heard Mrs. Daly—but that also meant things passed through her, most of the time, anyway. As the days went by, she found that if she concentrated, she could ride in a streetcar, cab, or subway train and travel with it, instead of just standing there like a gump as it passed through her. But she couldn't pick things up or move them, at least nothing more than specks of dust, and that took concentration and time, and when she was finished, she wouldn't want to concentrate, and she'd blink and be back to the rooming house or the office, but later.

She wasn't entirely sure what she looked like, or what it was the animals, and perhaps the other, well, the others, saw when they encountered her. When she thought about it, looking down where her body had been, she thought she looked about the same—her favorite blue dress with the white collar (had she been buried in that? Died in it? She didn't know, but she liked the dress), stockings, dark shoes. No girdle, but she hadn't needed one before either, and alas, no one had ever been in a position to comment on it. She thought she had seen her reflection in a shop window once, a blue flower that matched her dress in her dark hair, but she couldn't be sure, and perhaps it was a trick of the light. Perhaps *she* was a trick of the light as well, but she didn't feel like such a thing.

How *did* she feel? Like the third carbon of herself: legible but faint, perhaps a bit smeary. Useful for a file copy, but not something to send to a client. But she was still in the city that had become her city, the city where she had been Peggy, even if she had been betrayed by clumsy old Large Marge when she fell.

She missed Walter, though. They had worked together for six months before she died, and she had liked being around him. It was work, yes, but he seemed like a nice boss, and he was terribly good looking, which didn't hurt, but he was also a perfect gentleman.

Darn it. She had been ladylike, of course—Mother wouldn't have had it any other way—but she knew that some men had noticed her, seeing a flicker in their eyes as she walked down the street, or hearing some banter from the counter man at the deli. There were times she thought Walter had as well—to tell the truth, that was why she had bought the perfume.

He had been in love once before, with a girl who had died of infantile paralysis when he was in law school, but he only talked about her once on a slow afternoon, and she had seen the pain in his eyes and changed the topic. Maybe one day something could have happened with Walter. She had seen it in dozens of picture shows, the boss falling for the secretary, and sometimes it worked out. Maybe it would have, eventually.

But Peggy hadn't gotten to eventually. Even so, she wondered if that was why she found herself at the office so often. Walter was there a lot, too, sometimes working late into the night. Had he done that when she had worked there, coming back after she had left in the afternoon? Probably not—a good secretary, she thought, made that unnecessary.

Walter was thinking out loud again. He had done that when she worked for him, and she enjoyed being a sounding board. He was looking over a client's files, but it was incomplete. One of the Ajax girls must have messed it up—Peggy saw the steno book sitting in the chair by the filing cabinet. Sloppy; she had always placed it next to the typewriter, so she didn't have to hunt for it later.

The whole office looked a little shabbier than she remembered it being. Had it really been this small, this worn? It took a moment to understand the difference. The room had once held all these things, but had also held room for her opportunities. Now those were gone. She was gone. For the first time, really, since she had died, she felt cheated.

But only for a moment. She had come to the city without knowing what was ahead, and it had taken her in, and even in a short time, she had felt a part of it. She had been someone she never could have been in Greensburg—she had been Peggy Dupont.

And what could she be now? She didn't know, but she hadn't known before, either. But she had found her way to the city, and had found her way in it, if briefly. She could find a way to whatever came next as well. She thought about the others she had seen, flickering through the city, not speaking to her, doing whatever errands they felt called to do. Why had she seen so few of them? Maybe they were there because they didn't realize they didn't have to be.

She had been trapped in Greensburg, until she chose not to be. She had been stranded, alone, until she chose not to be. And if she chose not to be here anymore? Well, she didn't know, but she had liked what she had found before. Why not see what else was there?

And with that, Peggy Dupont knew what she had wanted all along— to be free, and she was. Free of Greensburg, free of Mother, free of the large body that had betrayed her, and now, free to go wherever she could imagine. She remembered lines from a long poem in high school:

The world was all before them, where to choose
Their place of rest, and Providence their guide.

She had a feeling that there was more than the world before her, just as the city had been bigger than the small office, and she knew that her travels before then were the tiniest clumsy steps. She had other journeys. But there was Walter, who had been kind. Had she loved him? She no longer knew, but she knew he had been kind. Perhaps she could do him a small kindness in return.

She saw the missing sheet of paper, resting askew in the open file drawer. She concentrated harder than she ever had before, and maybe it was that or maybe it was the breeze and vibration of the passing train, but the paper fluttered to the floor near the desk. Walter didn't see it, studying the rest of the file, but he would soon enough.

And he did, a few minutes later, but Peggy was gone, and it wasn't until the next morning, as he gathered the file for the closing, that Walter Schroer caught the faintest scents of dust and honeysuckle.

JOYCE CAROL OATES *is the author of a number of novels and story collections including, most recently,* The Man Without a Shadow *and* The Doll-Master: Tales of Terror. *She is a member of the American Academy of Arts and Letters and a recipient of the Bram Stoker Award, the National Book Award, the O. Henry Award, and the National Medal in the Humanities, among others.*

Eleven A.M., 1926

THE WOMAN IN THE WINDOW

BY JOYCE CAROL OATES

Beneath the cushion of the plush blue chair she has hidden it.

Almost shyly her fingers grope for it, then recoil as if it were burning-hot.

No! None of this will happen, don't be ridiculous.

It is eleven A.M. He has promised to meet her in this room in which it is always eleven A.M.

She's doing what she does best: waiting.

In fact, she is waiting for him in the way that he prefers: naked. Yet wearing shoes.

Nude he calls it. Not *naked*.

(*Naked* is a coarse word! He's a gentleman and he feels revulsion for vulgarity. Any sort of crude word, mannerism—in a woman.)

She understands. She herself disapproves of women uttering profanities.

Only when she's alone would she utter even a mild profanity—*Damn! God damn. Oh hell . . .*

Only if she were very upset. Only if her heart were broken.

He can say anything he likes. It's a masculine prerogative to say the coarsest cruelest words uttered with a laugh—as a man will do.

Though he might also murmur—*Jesus!*

Not profanity but an expression of awe. Sometimes.

Jesus! You are beautiful.

Is she beautiful? She smiles to think so.

She is *the woman in the window.* In the wan light of an autumn morning in New York City.

In the plush blue chair waiting. Eleven A.M.

Sleepless through much of the night and in the early morning soaking in her bath preparing herself for *him.*

Rubbing lotion onto her body: breasts, belly, hips, buttocks.

Such soft skin. Amazing . . . His voice catches in his throat.

At first, he scarcely dares touch her. But only at first.

It is a solemn ritual, creamy-white lotion smelling of faint gardenias rubbed into her skin.

In a trance like a woman in a dream rubbing lotion into her skin for she is terrified of her skin drying out in the radiator heat, arid airlessness of The Maguire (as it is called)—the brownstone apartment building at Tenth Avenue and Twenty-third where she lives.

From the street The Maguire is a dignified-looking older building but inside it is really just *old.*

Like the wallpaper in this room, and the dull-green carpet, and the plush-blue chair—*old.*

Dry heat! Sometimes she wakes in the night scarcely able to breathe and her throat dry as ashes.

She has seen the dried-out skin of older women. Some of them not so very old, in their sixties, even younger. Papery-thin skin, desiccated as a snake's husk of a skin, a maze of fine white wrinkles, terrible to behold.

Her own mother. Her grandmother.

Telling herself don't be silly, it will never happen to *her*.

She wonders how old his wife is. He is a gentleman, he will not speak of his wife. She dares not ask. She dares not even hint. His face flushes with indignation, his wide dark nostrils like holes in his face pinch as if he has smelled a bad odor. Very quiet, very stiff he becomes, a sign of danger so she knows to retreat.

Yet thinking, gloating: *His wife is not young. She is not so beautiful as I am. When he sees her, he thinks of me.*

(But is this true? The past half-year, since the previous winter, since the long break over Christmas when they were apart [*she* was in the city; *he* was away with his family in some undisclosed place very likely Bermuda for his face and hands were tanned when he returned] she has not been so certain.)

She has never been to Bermuda, or any tropical place. If *he* does not take her, it is not likely that she will ever go.

Instead, she is trapped here in this room. Where it is always eleven A.M. Sometimes it feels to her as if she is trapped in this chair, in the window gazing out with great yearning at—what?

An apartment building like the building in which she lives. A narrow shaft of sky. Light that appears fading already at eleven A.M.

Damned tired of the plush-blue chair that is beginning to fray.

Damned tired of the bed (he'd chosen) that is a double bed, with a headboard.

Her previous bed, in her previous living quarters on East Eighth Street, in a fifth-floor walkup single room, had been a single bed, of course. A girl's bed too small, too narrow, too insubstantial for *him*.

The girth, the weight of *him*—he is two hundred pounds at least.

All muscle—he likes to say. (Joking.) And she murmurs in response *Yes*.

If she rolls her eyes, he does not see.

She has come to hate her entrapment here. Where it is always eleven A.M. and she is always waiting for *him*.

The more she thinks about it the more her hatred roils like smoldering heat about to burst into flame.

She hates him. For trapping her here.

For treating her like dirt.

Worse than dirt, something stuck on the sole of his shoe he tries to scrape off with that priggish look in his face that makes her want to murder him.

Next time you touch me! You will regret it.

Except: at work, at the office—she's envied.

The other secretaries know she lives in The Maguire for she'd brought one of them to see it, once.

Such a pleasure it was, to see the look in Molly's eyes!

And it is true—this is a very nice place really. Far nicer than anything she could afford on her secretary's salary.

Except she has no kitchen, only just a hot-plate in a corner alcove and so it is difficult for her to prepare food for herself. Dependent on eating at the automat on Twenty-first and Sixth or else (but this is never more than once a week, at the most) when *he* takes her out to dinner.

(Even then, she has to take care. Nothing so disgusting as seeing a female *who eats like a horse*, he has said.)

She does have a tiny bathroom. The first private bathroom she'd ever had in her life.

He pays most of the rent. She has not asked him, he volunteers to give her cash unbidden as if each time he has just thought of it.

My beautiful girl! Please don't say a word, you will break the spell and ruin everything.

What's the time? Eleven A.M.

He will be late coming to her. Always he is late coming to her.

At the corner of Lexington and Thirty-seventh. Headed south.

The one with the dark fedora, camel's-hair coat. Whistling thinly through his teeth. Not a tall man though he gives that impression. Not a large man but he won't give way if there's another pedestrian in his path.

Excuse me, mister! Look where the hell you're going.

Doesn't break his stride. Only partially conscious of his surroundings.

Face shut up tight. Jaws clenched.

Murder rushing to happen.

The woman in the window, he likes to imagine her.

He has stood on the sidewalk three floors below. He has counted the windows of the brownstone. Knows which one is *hers.*

After dark, the lighted interior reflected against the blind makes of the blind a translucent skin.

When he leaves her. Or, before he comes to her.

It is less frequent that he comes to her by day. His days are taken up with work, family. His days are what is *known.*

Nighttime there is another self. Unpeeling his tight clothes: coat, trousers, white cotton dress shirt, belt, necktie, socks and shoes.

But now the woman has Thursdays off, late mornings at The Maguire are convenient.

Late mornings shifting into afternoon. Late afternoon, and early evening.

He calls home, leaves a message with the maid—*Unavoidable delay at office. Don't wait dinner.*

In fact it is the contemplation of the woman in the window he likes best for in his imagination this girl never utters a vulgar remark or makes a vulgar mannerism. Never says a banal or stupid or predictable thing. His sensitive nerves are offended by (for instance) a female shrugging her shoulders, as a man might do; or trying to make a joke, or a sarcastic remark. He hates a female *grinning.*

Worst of all, crossing her (bare) legs so that the thighs thicken, bulge. Hard-muscled legs with soft downy hairs, repulsive to behold.

The shades must be drawn. Tight.

Shadows, not sunlight. Why darkness is best.

Lie still. Don't move. Don't speak. Just—don't.

It's a long way from when she'd moved to the city from Hackensack needing to breathe.

She'd never looked back. Sure they called her selfish, cruel. What the hell, the use they'd have made of her, she'd be sucked dry by now like bone marrow.

Saying it was sin. Her Polish grandmother angrily rattling her rosary, praying aloud.

Who the hell cares! Leave me alone.

First job was file clerk at Trinity Trust down on Wall Street. Wasted three years of her young life waiting for her boss Mr. Broderick to leave his (invalid) wife and (emotionally unstable) adolescent daughter and wouldn't you think a smart girl like her would know better?

Second job also file clerk but then she'd been promoted to Mr. Castle's secretarial staff at Lyman Typewriters on West Fourteenth. The least the old buzzard could do for her and she'd have done a lot better except for fat-face Stella Czechi intruding where she wasn't wanted.

One day she'd come close to pushing Stella Czechi into the elevator shaft when the elevator was broken. The doors clanked opened onto a terrifying drafty cavern where dusty-oily cords hung twisted like ugly thick black snakes. Stella gave a little scream and stepped back, and she'd actually grabbed Stella's hand, the two of them so frightened—*Oh my God, there's no elevator! We almost got killed.*

Later she would wish she'd pushed Stella. Guessing Stella was wishing she'd pushed *her.*

Third job, Tvek Realtors & Insurance in the Flatiron Building and she's Mr. Tvek's private secretary—*What would I do without you, my dear one?*

As long as Tvek pays her decent. And *he* doesn't let her down like last Christmas, she'd wanted to die.

It is eleven A.M. Will this be the morning? She is trembling with excitement, dread.

Wanting badly to hurt him. Punish!

That morning after her bath she'd watched with fascination as her fingers lifted the sewing shears out of the bureau drawer. Watched her fingers test the sharpness of the points: very sharp, icepick-sharp.

Watched her hand pushing the shears beneath the cushion of the blue plush chair by the window.

It is not the first time she has hidden the sewing shears beneath the cushion. It is not the first time she has wished him *dead.*

Once, she hid the shears beneath her pillow on the bed.

Another time, in the drawer of the bedside table.

How she has hated him, and yet—she has not (yet) summoned the courage, or the desperation, to kill him.

(For is not *kill* a terrifying word? If you *kill*, you become a *killer.*)

(Better to think of punishment, exacting justice. When there is no other recourse but the sewing shears.)

She has never hurt anyone in her life!—even as a child she didn't hit or wrestle with other children, or at least not often. Or at least that she remembers.

He is the oppressor. *He* has murdered her dreams.

He must be punished before he leaves her.

Each time she has hidden the shears she has come a little closer (she thinks) to the time when she will use them. Just *stab, stab, stab* in the way he pounds himself into her, her body, using her body, his face contorted and ugly, terrible to behold.

The act that is unthinkable as it is irrevocable.

The shears are much stronger than an ordinary pair of scissors, as they are slightly larger.

The shears once belonged to her mother who'd been a quite skilled seamstress. In the Polish community in Hackensack, her mother was most admired.

She tries to sew too. Though she is less skilled than her mother.

Needing to mend her clothes—hems of dresses, underwear, even stockings. And it is calming to the nerves like knitting, crocheting, even typing when there is no time-pressure.

Except—*You did a dandy job with these letters, my dear! But I'm afraid not "perfect"—you will have to do them over.*

Sometimes she hates Mr. Tvek as much as she hates *him.*

Under duress she can grip the shears firmly, she is sure. She has been a typist since the age of fifteen and she believes that it is because of this skill that her fingers have grown not only strong but unerring.

Of course, she understands: a man could slap the shears out of her hand in a single gesture. If he sees what she is doing, before the icepick-sharp points stabs into his flesh.

She must strike him swiftly and she must strike him in the throat.

The "carotid artery"—she knows what this is.

Not the heart, she doesn't know where the heart might be, exactly. Protected by ribs. The torso is large, bulky—too much fat. She could not hope to pierce the heart with the shears in a single swift blow.

Even the back, where the flesh is less thick, would be intimidating to her. She has a nightmare vision of the points of the shears stuck in the man's back, not deep enough to kill him, only just wound him, blood streaming everywhere as he flails his arms and bellows in rage and pain . . .

Therefore, the neck. The throat.

In the throat, the male is as vulnerable as the female.

Once the sharp points of the shears pierce his skin, puncture the artery, there will be no turning back for either of them.

Eleven A.M.

Light rap of his knuckles on the door. *Hel-lo.*

Turning of the key. And then—

Shutting the door behind him. Approaching her.

Staring at her with eyes like ants running over her (nude) body.

It is a scene in a movie: that look of desire in a man's face. A kind of hunger, greed.

(Should she speak to him? Often at such times he seems scarcely to hear her words, so engrossed in what he sees.)

(Maybe better to say nothing. So he can't wince at her nasal New Jersey accent, tell her *Shhh!*)

Last winter after that bad quarrel she'd tried to bar him from the apartment. Tried to barricade the door by dragging a chair in front of it but (of course) he pushed his way in by brute strength.

It is childish, futile to try to bar the man. He has his own key, of course.

Following which she was punished. Severely.

Thrown onto the bed and her face pressed into a pillow, scarcely could she breathe, her cries muffled, begging for him not to kill her as her back, hips, buttocks were soundly beaten with his fists.

And then, her legs roughly parted.

Just a taste of what I will do to you if you—ever—try—this—again. Dirty Polack!

—•—

Of course, they'd made up.

Each time, they'd made up.

He had punished her by not calling, staying away. But eventually he'd returned as she'd known he would.

Bringing her a dozen red roses. A bottle of his favorite Scotch whiskey.

She'd taken him back, it might be said.

She'd had no choice. It might be said.

No! None of this will happen, don't be ridiculous.

She is frightened but she is thrilled.

She is thrilled but she is frightened.

At eleven A.M. she will see him at the door to the bedroom, as he pockets his key. Staring at her so intently she feels the power of being, if only for these fleeting moments, female.

That look of desire in the man's face. The clutch of the mouth like a pike's mouth.

The look of possession as he thinks—*Mine.*

By this time she will have changed her shoes. Of course.

As in a movie scene it is imperative that the woman be wearing not the plain black flat-heeled shoes she wears for comfort when she is alone but a pair of glamorous sexy high-heeled shoes which the man has purchased for her.

(Though it is risky to appear together in public in such a way the man quite enjoys taking the girl to several Fifth Avenue stores for the purchase of shoes. In her closet are at least a dozen pairs of expensive shoes he has bought for her, high-heeled, painful to wear but undeniably glamorous. Gorgeous crocodile-skin shoes he'd bought her for her last birthday, last month. He insists she wear high-heeled shoes even if it's just when they're alone together in her apartment.)

(Especially high heels when she's *nude.*)

Seeing that look in the man's eyes thinking—*Of course he loves me. That is the face of love.*

Waiting for him to arrive. And what time is it?—eleven A.M.

If he truly loves her he will bring flowers.

To make it up to you, honey. For last night.

He has said to her that of all the females he has known she is the only one who seems to be happy in her body.

Happy in her body. This is good to hear!

He means, she guesses, adult females. Little girls are quite happy in their bodies when they are little/young enough.

So unhappy. Or—happy . . .

I mean, I am happy.

In my body I am happy.

I am happy when I am with you.

And so when he steps into the room she will smile happily at him. She will lift her arms to him as if she does not hate him and wish him dead.

She will feel the weight of her breasts, as she raises her arms. She will see his eyes fasten greedily on her breasts.

She will not scream at him *Why the hell didn't you come last night like you promised? God damn bastard, you can't treat me like shit on your shoe!*

Will not scream at him *D'you think I will just take it—this shit of yours? D'you think I am like your damn wife, just lay there and take it, d'you think a woman has no way of hitting back?—no way of revenge?*

A weapon of revenge. Not a male weapon but a female weapon: sewing shears.

It is appropriate that the sewing shears had once belonged to her mother. Though her mother never used the shears as she might have wished.

If she can grasp the shears firmly in her hand, her strong right hand, if she can direct the blow, if she can strike without flinching.

If she is that kind of woman.

Except: she isn't that kind of woman. She is a *romantic-minded girl* to whom a man might bring a dozen red roses, a box of expensive chocolates, articles of (silky, intimate) clothing. Expensive high-heeled shoes.

THE WOMAN IN THE WINDOW

A woman who sings and hums *tea for two, and two for tea, you for me and me for you, alone* . . .

Eleven A.M. He will be late!

God damn, he hates this. *He is always late.*

At the corner of Lexington and Thirty-first turning west on Thirty-first and so to Fifth Avenue. And then south.

Headed south into a less dazzling Manhattan.

He lives at Seventy-second and Madison: upper east side.

She lives in a pretty good neighborhood (he thinks)—for her.

Pretty damn good for a little Polack secretary from Hackensack, N.J.

Tempted to stop for a drink. That bar on Eighth Avenue.

Except it's not yet eleven A.M. Too early to drink!

Noon is the earliest. You have to have preserve standards.

Noon could mean lunch. Customary to have drinks at a business lunch. A cocktail to start. A cocktail to continue. A cocktail to conclude. But he draws the line at drinking during the midday when he will take a cab to his office, far downtown on Chambers Street.

His excuse is a dental appointment in midtown. Unavoidable!

Of course five P.M. is a respectful hour for a drink. Almost, a drink at five P.M. might be considered the "first drink of the day" since it has been a long time since lunch.

Five P.M. drinks are "drinks before dinner." Dinner at eight P.M. if not later.

Wondering if he should make a little detour before going to her place. Liquor store, bottle of Scotch whiskey. The bottle he'd brought to her place last week is probably almost empty.

(Sure, the woman drinks in secret. Sitting in the window, drink in hand. Doesn't want him to know. How in hell could he not know? Deceitful little bitch.)

There's a place on Ninth. Shamrock Inn. He can stop there.

Looks forward to drinking with her. One thing you can say about the little Polack, she's a good drinking companion, and drinking deflects most needs to talk.

Unless she drinks too much. Last thing he wants to hear from her is complaints, accusations.

Last thing he wants to see is her face pouty and sulky and not so good-looking. Sharp creases in her forehead like a forecast of how she'll look in another ten years, or less.

It isn't fair! You don't call when you promise! You don't show up when you promise! Tell me you love me but—

Many times he has heard these words that are beginning to bore him.

Many times he has appeared to be listening but is scarcely aware which of them is berating him: the girl in the window, or the wife.

To the woman in the window he has learned to say—*Sure I love you. That's enough, now.*

To the wife he has learned to say—*You know I have work to do. I work damn hard. Who the hell pays for all this?*

His life is complicated. That is actually true. He is not deceiving the woman. He is not deceiving the wife.

(Well—maybe he is deceiving the wife.)

(Maybe he is deceiving the woman.)

(But women expect to be deceived, don't they? Deception is the terms of the sex contract.)

In fact he'd told the little Polack secretary (warned her) at the outset, almost two years ago now—(Jesus! that long, no wonder he's getting to feel trapped, claustrophobic)—*I love my family. My obligations to my family come first.*

(Fact is, he's getting tired of this one. Bored. She talks too much even when she isn't talking, he can hear her *thinking*. Her breasts are heavy, beginning to droop. Flaccid skin at her belly. Thinking sometimes when they're in bed together he'd like to settle his hands around her throat and just start squeezing.)

(How much of a struggle would she put up? She's not a small woman but *he's* strong.)

(The French girl he'd had a "tussle" with—that was the word he'd given the transaction—had put up quite a struggle like a fox or a mink or a weasel but that was wartime, in Paris, people were desperate then, even a girl that young and starved-looking like a rat. *Aidez-moi! Aidez-moi!* But there'd been no one.)

(Hard to take any of them seriously when they're chattering away in some damn language like a parrot or a hyena. Worse when they screamed.)

Set out late from his apartment that morning. God damn, he resents his God-damn wife suspicious of him for no reason.

Hadn't he stayed home the night before? Hadn't he disappointed the girl?—all because of the wife.

Stiff and cold-silent the wife. God, how she bores him!

Her suspicions bore him. Her hurt feelings bore him. Her dull repressed anger bores him. Worst of all her boredom bores him.

He has imagined his wife dead many times, of course. How long have they been married, twenty years, twenty-three years, he'd believed he was lucky marrying the daughter of a well-to-do stock broker except the stock broker wasn't that well-to-do and within a few years he wasn't a stock broker any longer but a bankrupt. Asking to borrow money from *him*.

Also, the wife's looks are gone. Melted look of a female of a certain age. Face sags, body sags. He has fantasized his wife dying (in an accident: not his fault) and the insurance policy paying off: forty thousand dollars free and clear. So he'd be free to marry the other one.

Except: does he want to marry *her?*

God! Feeling the need for a drink.

It is eleven A.M. God damn bastard will be late again.

After the insult and injury of the previous night!

If he is late, it will happen. She will stab, stab, stab until he has bled out. She feels a wave of relief, finally it has been decided for her.

Checks the sewing shears, hidden beneath the cushion. Something surprising, unnerving—the blades of the shears seem to be a faint, faded red. From cutting red cloth? But she doesn't remember using the shears to cut red cloth.

Must be the light from the window passing through the gauze curtains.

Something consoling in the touch of the shears.

She wouldn't want a knife from the kitchen—no. Nothing like a butcher knife. Such a weapon would be premeditated while a pair of sewing shears is something a woman might pick up by chance, frightened for her life.

He threatened me. He began to beat me. Strangle me. He'd warned me many times, in one of his moods he would murder me.

It was in defense of my life. God help me! I had no choice.

Hears herself laugh aloud. Rehearsing her lines like an actress about to step out onto the bright-lit stage.

Might've been an actress, if her damn mother hadn't sent her right to secretarial school. She's as good-looking as most of the actresses on Broadway.

He'd told her so. Brought her a dozen blood-red roses first time he came to take her out.

Except they hadn't gone out. Spent the night in her fifth-floor walkup, East Eighth Street.

(She misses that, sometimes. Lower East Side where she'd had friends and people who knew her, on the street.)

Strange to be naked, that is *nude* yet wearing shoes.

Time for her to squeeze her (bare) feet into high heels.

Like a dancer. Girlie-dancer they are called. Stag parties exclusively for men. She'd heard of girls who danced at these parties. Danced *nude.* Made more in a single night's work than she made in two weeks as a secretary.

Nude is a fancy word. Hoity-toity like an artist-word.

What she has not wanted to see: her body isn't a girl's body any longer. At a distance (maybe) on the street she can fool the casual eye but not up close.

Dreads to see in the mirror a fleshy aging body like her mother's.

And her posture in the damned chair, when she's alone—leaning forward, arms on knees, staring out the window into a narrow shaft of sunshine between buildings—makes her belly bulge, soft-belly-fat.

A shock, first time she'd noticed. Just by accident glancing in a mirror.

Not a sign of getting older. Just putting on weight.

For your birthday, sweetheart. Is it—thirty-two?

She'd blushed, yes, it is thirty-two.

Not meeting his eye. Pretending she was eager to unwrap the present. (By the size of the box, weight of what's inside, she guesses it's another pair of God damn high-heeled shoes.) Heart beating rapidly in a delirium of dread.

If he knew. Thirty-nine.

That was last year. The next birthday is rushing at her.

Hates him, wishes he were dead.

Except she would never see him again. Except the wife would collect the insurance.

She does not want to kill him, however. She is not the type to hurt anyone.

In fact she wants to kill him. She has no choice, he will be leaving her soon. She will never see him again and she will have nothing.

When she is alone she understands this. Which is why she has hidden the sewing shears beneath the cushion for the final time.

She will claim that he began to abuse her, he threatened to kill her, closing his fingers around her throat so she had no choice but to grope for the shears and stab him in desperation, repeatedly, unable to breathe and unable to call for help until his heavy body slipped from her twitching and spurting blood, onto the green rectangle of light in the carpet.

His age is beyond forty-nine, she's sure.

Glanced at his I.D. once. Riffling through his wallet while he slept openmouthed, wetly snoring. Sound like a rhinoceros snorting. She'd been stunned to see his young photograph—taken when he'd been younger than she is right now—dark-haired, thick-dark-haired, and eyes boring into the camera, so intense. In his U.S. Army uniform, so handsome!

She'd thought—*Where is this man? I could have loved this man.*

Now when they make love she detaches herself from the situation to imagine him as he'd been, young. *Him*, she could have felt something for.

Having to pretend too much. That's tiring.

Like the pretense she is *happy in her body.*

Like the pretense she is *happy when he shows up.*

No other secretary in her office could afford an apartment in this building. True.

Damn apartment she'd thought was so special at first now she hates. *He* helps with expenses. Counting out bills like he's cautious not to be overpaying.

This should tide you over, sweetheart. Give yourself a treat.

She thanks him. She is the good girl thanking *him*.

Give yourself a *treat!* With the money he gives her, a few tens, a rare twenty! God, she hates him.

Her fingers tremble, gripping the shears. Just the feel of the shears.

Never dared tell him how she has come to hate this apartment. Meeting in the elevators old women, some of them with walkers, eyeing her. Older couples, eyeing her. Unfriendly. Suspicious. How's a secretary from New Jersey afford The Maguire?

Dim-lit on the third floor like a low-level region of the soul into which light doesn't penetrate. Soft-shabby furniture and mattress already beginning to sag like those bodies in dreams we feel but don't see. But she keeps the damn bed made every day whether anyone except her sees.

He doesn't like disorder. *He'd* told her how he'd learned to make a proper bed in the U.S. Army in 1917.

The trick is, he says, you make the bed as soon as you get up.

Pull the sheets tight. Tuck in corners—tight. No wrinkles! Smooth with the edge of your hand! Again.

First Lieutenant, he'd been. Rank when discharged. Holds himself like a soldier, stiff backbone like maybe he is feeling pain—arthritis? Shrapnel?

She has wondered—*Has he killed? Shot, bayoneted? With his bare hands?*

What she can't forgive: the way he detaches himself from her as soon as it's over.

Sticky skin, hairy legs, patches of scratchy hair on his shoulders, chest, belly. She'd like him to hold her and they could drift into sleep together but rarely this happens. Hates feeling the nerves twitching in his legs. Hates sensing how he is smelling her. How he'd like to leap from her as soon as he comes, the bastard.

A man is crazy wanting to make love, then abruptly it's over—*he's* inside his head, and *she's* inside hers.

The night before waiting for him to call to explain when he didn't show up. From eight P.M. until midnight she'd waited rationing whiskey-and-water to calm her nerves. Considering the sharp-tipped shears she might use against herself, one day.

In those hours sick with hating him and hating herself and yet—the leap of hope when the phone finally rang.

Unavoidable, crisis at home. Sorry.

Now it is eleven A.M. Waiting for him to rap on the door.

She knows he will be late. He is always late.

She is becoming very agitated. But: too early to drink.

Even to calm her nerves too early to drink.

Imagines she hears footsteps. Sound of the elevator door opening, closing. Light rap of his knuckles on the door just before he unlocks it.

Eagerly he will step inside, come to the door of the bedroom—see her in the chair awaiting him . . .

The (nude) woman in the window. Awaiting him.

That look in his face. Though she hates him she craves that look in his face.

A man's desire is sincere enough. Can't be faked. (She wants to think this). She does not want to think that the man's desire for her might be as fraudulent as her desire for him but if this is so, why'd he see her at all?

He does love her. He loves something he sees in her.

Thirty-one years old, he thinks she is. No—thirty-two.

And his wife is ten, twelve years older at least. Like Mr. Broderick's wife, this one is something of an *invalid.*

Pretty damned suspicious. Every wife you hear of is an *invalid.*

How they avoid sex, she supposes. Once they are married, once they have children that's enough. Sex is something the man has to do elsewhere.

What time is it?—eleven A.M.

He is late. Of course, he is late.

After the humiliation of last night, when she had not eaten all day anticipating a nice dinner at Delmonico's. And he never showed up, and his call was a feeble excuse.

Yet in the past he has behaved unpredictably. She'd thought that he was through with her, she'd seen disgust in his face, nothing so sincere as disgust in a man's face; and yet—he'd called her, after a week, ten days.

Or, he'd showed up at the apartment. Knocking on the door before inserting the key.

And almost, in his face a look of anger, resentment.

Couldn't keep away.

God, I'm crazy for you.

In the mirror she likes to examine herself if the light isn't too bright. Mirror to avoid is the bathroom mirror unprotected and raw lit by daylight but the bureau mirror is softer, more forgiving. Bureau mirror is the woman she *is*.

Actually she looks (she thinks) younger than thirty-two.

Much younger than thirty-nine!

A girl's pouty face, full lips, red-lipstick lips. Sulky brunette still damned good-looking and *he* knows it, *he* has seen men on the street and in restaurants following her with their eyes, undressing her with their eyes, this is exciting to him (she knows) though if she seems to react, if she glances around, he will become angry—at *her*.

What a man wants, she thinks, is a woman whom other men want but the woman *must not seem to seek out this attention or even be aware of it*.

She would never bleach her hair blond, she exults in her brunette beauty knowing it is more real, earthier. Nothing phony, synthetic, showy about *her*.

Next birthday, forty. Maybe she will kill herself.

Though it's eleven A.M. he has stopped for a drink at the Shamrock. Vodka on the rocks. Just one.

Excited thinking about the sulky-faced woman waiting for him: in the blue plush chair, at the window, nude except for high-heeled shoes.

Full lips, lipstick-red. Heavy-lidded eyes. A head of thick hair, just slightly coarse. And hairs elsewhere on her body that arouse him.

Slight disgust, yet arousal.

Yet he's late, why is that? Something seems to be pulling at him, holding him back. Another vodka?

Staring at his watch thinking—*If I am not with her by eleven-fifteen it will mean it's over.*

A flood of relief, never having to see her again!

Never the risk of losing his control with her, hurting her.

Never the risk she will provoke him into a *tussle*.

She's thinking she will give the bastard ten more minutes.

If he arrives after eleven-fifteen it is over between them.

Her fingers grope for the shears beneath the cushion. There!

She has no intention of stabbing him—of course. Not here in her room, not where he'd bleed onto the blue-plush chair and the green carpet and she would never be able to remove the stains even if she could argue (she could argue) that he'd tried to kill her, more than once in his strenuous lovemaking he'd closed his fingers around her throat, she'd begun to protest *Please don't, hey you are hurting me* but he'd seemed scarcely to hear, in a delirium of sexual rapacity, pounding his heavy body into her like a jack hammer.

You have no right to treat me like that. I am not a whore, I am not your pathetic wife. If you insult me I will kill you—I will kill you to save my own life.

Last spring for instance when he'd come to take her out to Delmonico's but seeing her he'd gotten excited, clumsy bastard knocking over the bedside lamp and in the dim-lit room they'd made love in her bed and never got out until too late for supper and she'd overheard him afterward on the phone *explaining*—in the bathroom stepping out of the shower she'd listened at the door fascinated, furious—the sound of a man's voice when he is *explaining to a wife* is so callow, so craven, she's sick with contempt recalling.

Yet *he* says he has left his family, he loves *her*.

Runs his hands over her body like a blind man trying to see. And the radiance in his face that's pitted and scarred, he needs her in the way a starving man needs food. *Die without you. Don't leave me.*

Well, she loves him! She guesses.

Eleven A.M. He is crossing the street at Ninth and Twenty-fourth. Gusts of wind blow grit into his eyes. The vodka is coursing along his veins.

Feels determined: if she stares at him with that reproachful pouty expression he will slap her face and if she begins to cry he will close his fingers around her throat and squeeze, squeeze.

She has not threatened to speak to his wife. As her predecessor had done, to her regret. Yet, he imagines that she is rehearsing such a confrontation.

Mrs. ___? You don't know me but I know you. I am the woman your husband loves.

He has told her it isn't what she thinks. Isn't his family that keeps him from loving her all he could love her but his life he'd never told anyone about in the war, in the infantry, in France. What crept like paralysis through him.

Things that had happened to him, and things that he'd witnessed, and (a few) things that he'd perpetrated himself with his own hands. And if they'd been drinking this look would come into his face of sorrow, horror. A sickness of regret she did not want to understand. And she'd taken his hands that had killed (she supposed) (but only in wartime) and kissed them, and brought them against her breasts that were aching like the breasts of a young mother ravenous to give suck, and sustenance.

And she said *No. That is your old life.*

I am your new life.

He has entered the foyer. At last!

It is eleven A.M.—he is not late after all. His heart is pounding in his chest.

Waves of adrenaline as he has not felt since the war.

On Ninth Avenue he purchased a bottle of whiskey, and from a street vendor he purchased a bouquet of one dozen blood-red roses.

For the woman in the window. *Kill or be killed.*

Soon as he unlocks the door, soon as he sees her, he will know what it is he will do to her.

Eleven A.M. In the plush-blue chair in the window the woman is waiting nude, except for her high-heeled shoes. Another time she checks the shears hidden beneath the cushion that feel strangely warm to her touch, even damp.

Stares out the window at a narrow patch of sky. Almost, she is at peace. She is prepared. She waits.

Multiple award winning author **KRIS NELSCOTT** *is best known for her Smokey Dalton mystery series. The first Smokey Dalton novel,* A Dangerous Road, *won the Herodotus Award for Best Historical Mystery and was short-listed for the Edgar Award for Best Novel; the third,* Thin Walls, *was one of the* Chicago Tribune's *best mysteries of the year. Both* Days of Rage *and the most recent Smokey Dalton novel,* Street Justice, *have been nominated for the Shamus Award for Best Private Eye Novel of the Year.* Entertainment Weekly *says her equals are Walter Mosley and Raymond Chandler.* Booklist *calls the Smokey Dalton books "a high-class crime series" and* Salon.com *says "Kris Nelscott can lay claim to the strongest series of detective novels now being written by an American author."*

Nelscott's next novel A Gym of Her Own *features a side character from the Smokey Dalton series, and will appear in spring of 2017. The character in this story comes from an as-yet-untitled project that she's developing. Stories about Lurleen have also appeared in the anthology series* Fiction River.

Nelscott also has her own secret identity: she's one of several pen names for bestselling writer Kristine Kathryn Rusch. To find out more about Nelscott or sign up for her newsletter, go to krisnelscott.com. To find out about everything she writes, go to kriswrites.com.

Hotel Room, 1931

STILL LIFE 1931

BY **KRIS NELSCOTT**

She first noticed outside Memphis: they didn't ride segregated in the box cars. At the time, she was standing outside yet another closed bank. The line of aggrieved customers wrapped around the block—men in their dusty pants, stained workshirts, caps on their heads; women wearing low heels, day dresses, and battered hats.

Lurleen looked just different enough to attract attention. Her green cloche hat was a bit too new, her coat a little too heavy. Her shoes were scuffed just like everyone else's, but hers were scuffed from too much travel, not age and wear.

She clutched the double handles of her brown duffel, and stared at the missed opportunity. The sign in the window had a desperate scrawl: *Out Of Cash. Come Back Tomorrow*. There was no date and no signature. She couldn't tell if "tomorrow" was yesterday, three days ago, or truly, the next day.

And she didn't want to ask the dusty, discouraged folks who stood in line like there was a chance there would be cash. She'd seen this in six other towns in the past two months, and each time, she was startled they weren't smashing the glass windows, opening the doors themselves and taking what was left.

Maybe everyone in the crowd knew there was nothing left. Nothing left at all.

She sighed, wrapping her gloved fingers tight around the duffel's thick handles, trying to act like the duffel was empty, waiting for cash instead of lined with it. She knew better than to travel with so much money, but she had no choice now.

She wasn't sure which banks to trust, considering how many she'd seen shuttered and forlorn on her trip here. She worried that if she trusted all of her savings to one of these institutions, she'd never see another dime.

She understood why people were buying safes and putting them in their homes.

But she no longer had a home. Not any more.

She hadn't sold the house. In the end, she'd seen no point. It had become little more than a shack. On bad days, wind blew through the cracks in the wall, filling the four rooms with more dirt than she could clean off in an afternoon.

By the time Frank had passed, she'd had enough of that place. After she'd buried him in the family plot, and packed up using the two bags from her travels before Frank, still clean and sturdy like they'd been used just the week before.

She'd taken undergarments, and one clean dress, choosing to buy new as she went along. She'd taken the money Frank had left her—all $200 of it, planning to retrieve her own money, along the way.

She'd made a mistake for love.

Women did that. They forgot themselves somewhere in the brown eyes and warm smiles, in the last chance for babies that never did arrive, and a future that promised some kind of comfort—which never did arrive either.

Before she'd met Frank, she'd been a solitary woman on a solitary road, doing good works as only she'd known how.

She'd been younger, more resilient, believing in human kindness, despite all she'd seen.

Until . . .

She squinted at the line, unmoving around that closed bank. She shook her head slightly. It would take only one sentence to turn that despairing crowd into a mob—venting its anger in the exact wrong direction, screaming blue murder.

One sentence, and its vile variations.

One sentence that she hoped she'd never hear again.

"He done it!"

They ran past her, screaming, fists raised, faces red. Lurleen pressed herself against the post near the general store, her dolly clutched in one hand. Her mama stood just inside the door, holding her sister Noreen's arm. Noreen twisted away, trying to free herself, but she couldn't.

Daddy wasn't here. He was in Atlanta buying supplies for the store. Mama spent money on a telegram, but she didn't hear back. And so Mama had to handle it, and Noreen lied.

Two nights ago, Noreen had been clutching and clawing with George Tarlin, telling Lurleen to stop watching because that was grown-up business. Lurleen tried to tell Mama it was George Tarlin, not that nice boy who sat near the tree on the bad side of town, reading books and asking after Lurleen's dolly.

But Noreen, she said it was the nice boy. It'd always been the nice boy. And he'd been the one what hurt her. Not George Tarlin who slapped her across the face yesterday morning when she told him he couldn't marry her without Daddy's permission. No, she'd said that bruise was the nice boy.

Rumors spread like crazy and now everyone knew that Noreen was "soiled" and the nice boy done it and he was gonna pay.

He done it, they said. And he did pay.

He was the first one Lurleen saw, hanging from a tree outside of town. Eyes gone by the time she saw him, face half ripped off, clothes torn and covered in blood. After Daddy'd come home, she'd gone with him over Mama's objections. Weak objections.

Mama wanted Lurleen to know what them nice boys could do.

So Daddy took her to the place where all the yelling and cheering had come from, and then he said he was sorry he done it. He made her sit in the wagon, eyes closed, while he went and done something to that body, something that sounded meaty, like an axe to a chicken neck.

And Noreen, she never was the same. She didn't talk to no one, and they all said it was because of that nice boy, because of what he done. George Tarlin didn't want her no more, because of what that boy had done.

But that boy didn't do nothing.

Both Lurleen and Noreen knew that.

And the night before she died by her own hand with Daddy's too-sharp razor, Noreen said to Lurleen, "Baby girl, you gotta know one thing. Lies, they can kill you. They can kill everything. Don't you lie about what you done. Don't you lie about nothing, you hear?"

And Lurleen, she promised.

She didn't lie about nothing for a long time. Then she lied about everything.

Because, she'd slowly realized, lying about everything was the only way she could ever find the truth.

Lurleen shook her head. Lines and crowds and upset folk—they always brought a fear up, a fear of what people could do.

Which was why she looked away from the line, away from the shabby Memphis bank that had taken a good fifty dollars of her hard-earned money and would never give it back, and watched as a train went by.

Maybe it was the bank or the crowd or the memory. Maybe it was the despair—not that she was short of money, but she was *shorter* of money than she had been.

When those box cars went past, side door open, and men sitting on the edge, legs dangling, clothes filthy, she had an uncharacteristic thought. She saw the faces, dirt-streaked as the clothes, and realized she was looking at pale skin beneath some streaks and dark skin beneath other streaks.

And she thought: *Oh, that's going to cause problems.*

Then she caught herself. She didn't oppose mixing. Not like everyone else did. In her pre-Frank life, she'd even known couples who were mixed (and sometimes trying to hide it). She'd long ago realized that skin color was no different than hair color. Maybe because of that nice boy she'd met when she was little, the one her sister's lies had killed. He'd had dark skin. He'd loved reading. George Tarlin never had. He hadn't been nice neither.

But the problems . . .

Lurleen no longer had illusions. She knew that here, in this place where the war was still being fought and Confederate veterans still being honored, where the romance of the past trumped the truth of it, mixing like that was as bad a recipe as that lie—*he done it*—combined with a pointed finger.

She turned away, and trudged back to the train station, where she'd left her other bag with one of the porters who guarded such things for people who actually had money.

She needed to focus on herself now. That was what she had said when she left West Texas; that was what she had meant.

She was on a voyage of discovery, seeking something better, just like—it seemed—half the country. Only she was doing it in actual train cars, sitting on seats, riding like the first-class lady she was, with other first-class white folk she didn't want to talk to, because she knew she'd hate them as a matter of principle.

She needed to collect the money she'd left behind when she'd left her second life behind. Her before-Frank life. She couldn't've done it before he died, and he'd waited one year too long to leave this good earth.

Now all the little banks were going. The individual banks, the ones that didn't have branches, but were funded by locals who made the decisions themselves.

The little banks, the ones whose owners looked a woman in the eye, and said, *It's a new era, sister. Women can vote, so yes, you can open an account here without your husband.* And they'd meant it too. She'd thought she was supporting those banks, thought she was doing good. Turned out, all she was doing—as Frank would've said if he'd known—was pissing her money away, one seemingly smart decision at a time.

Only a few stops left. Nashville, Roanoke, Richmond, then points north. Real North. Yankee North, where she hadn't been since before the Great War. Funny that Before-Frank she'd worked for folks in Yankee North—*colored* folks in Yankee North—and she hadn't been up there since she graduated from Barnard.

Not quite true, of course. None of that was quite true. There was graduation, the apartment, the temporary job as a typist, and Elliot. And then, her father, of course, saving her from a life with That Jew, dragging her home, where Elliot did not follow, *could not* follow, as Elliot had said in that expensive telephone call she had made from her father's general store. *You understand, sweetheart, right?*

No, she hadn't understood either man and by the time she had gone north again—just for a moment (a moment that she didn't count)—Elliot was already married to someone "more suitable," his mother had said, looking at Lurleen with grim disapproval.

Lurleen had fled then, vowed not to marry, and when she learned that Elliot had died in the Battle of Argonne Forest, she pretended she didn't care.

But she didn't stop the work she'd started, work she'd started to impress him.

She hadn't stopped until . . .

She leaned her head back and closed her eyes, ignoring the half dozen books in her black suitcase. She had read whatever newspaper she tucked between the handles of her duffel so that it looked like she was carrying papers instead of paper money. But she found herself thinking more than reading.

She'd thought she was being so practical fourteen years ago. She'd taken the money Elliot's mother had pressed upon her to forget the engagement ever happened, saying, *We shall never speak of this again.* Apparently, an upper-class Jewish family in New York City was as embarrassed by a middle-class Christian girl from West Texas as the girl's West Texas family was by the fact that their daughter had fallen for a Jew. Only no one had seen the liaison back in Texas. There had been a lot of witnesses in among their Barnard-Columbia friends.

A lot of them who felt that Lurleen and Elliot were a love match, just like Lurleen had. Before that trip. The one she didn't count.

The one where Elliot's mother offered her a shocking five thousand dollars to forget she'd ever known him. To destroy his love letters, tear up the portrait they'd had commissioned for their engagement, and give back the ring.

She had taken the money, destroyed the letters, torn up the portrait, and given his mother the ring. Out of spite. Out of anger. Out of a hope that taking such a vast sum would somehow harm Elliot and his inheritance.

But later, when she read his obituary, she'd learned just how much the family was worth, and realized that the fortune they had given her—the money that was more than her father earned in the last ten years of his life—was barely pocket-change to them.

That was why Elliot could focus on Good Works. Why he didn't need to earn a living. He knew the living would come to him.

The scheme Lurleen used was Elliot's. Initially, they were going to do it together—he and Lurleen. They would change the world, use her pale skin and red-blond hair as camouflage. He would map everything out, use his law degree for assistance, and make sure they got the right information.

Elliot had been the one who had established the contact with the National Association for the Advancement of Colored People. He'd been the one who had deduced that their investigative arm needed investigators who could talk to Southern whites, get them to open up, get them to admit the horrors they were committing on a daily basis. He'd been the one who called what they were going to do Good Works, when (she later realized) it was the excitement that appealed to him.

The risk, the danger.

The same risk and danger that had sent him Over There against his mother's wishes.

His plan for their Southern Good Works had sounded so good in theory, but in practice—well, in practice Lurleen had learned that he would have been a burden had he come along, with his curly black hair, the beard that appeared midafternoon whether he wanted it to or not, and his unmistakable New York accent. He'd've gotten them thrown out of urban center after urban center—or what passed for urban centers in the pre- and post-war South.

But his idea with the money, scattering it to banks in different communities, in case they were robbed or lost what they had—that idea had been smart. She always had an emergency fund one train ride away—and sometimes she'd needed every dime.

It hadn't been his fault that she had left the money sit for seven years.

The Frank years.

She got money out of the bank in Nashville, but not the bank in Roanoke. That bank wasn't just closed, it was gone entirely—had been since 1926. Apparently there'd been a banking crisis then, one she hadn't heard about.

The bank in Richmond was open when she arrived, but didn't have all of her funds. They offered her $25 of her initial $50 savings, and she took it, figuring the remaining $25 plus the interest it had (in theory) earned since 1917 would never arrive.

And then she'd gone on to New York.

The train arrived in Pennsylvania Station in a hiss of steam, accompanied by shouts from the conductors—*Last stop! Penn Station! This train will close for service! Last stop!*

She took her bags. She felt grimy and windblown, even though she hadn't left the train for hours.

She followed her fellow passengers out the door, down the stairs and onto the platform and then she did like every other rube did around her—she looked up.

The grandness took her breath away. Stairs leading off the platform, up to the main area, and from here, she could already see steel arches and so much light that it hurt her eyes.

The platform smelled of steam and German soft pretzels, perfume and sweat. She clung to her bags, alert for the pickpockets and thieves who haunted every large railway station she'd been to, and walked up the stairs with her head held high.

She'd looked like a rube once. She wasn't going to do it again. Now, she needed to look like a New York lady who knew where she was going.

It wasn't easy. Penn Station looked nothing like she remembered. Oh, the bones had been here before the war—the steel columns, the light— but the people hadn't. Not in such crowds, with such noise. And there were no vendors, at least that she remembered. Back then, everything had seemed new, like a museum waiting for patrons, and now it had a layer of grime mixed with the echo of a thousand voices.

New York. Yankee North's rapid heartbeat.

She had forgotten how alive this place was.

She'd already revealed herself as a rube, so she took one last rube step and stopped at the information desk, round and large as the station itself, and sitting in the middle of the flow of people. The tired man running it barely met her gaze, but he did tell her there were hotels all over the area, and they wouldn't be full in the middle of the afternoon.

"But," he said, "a lady like you needs to avoid most of them. If you were my girl, I'd tell you to go to the Hotel New Yorker, just across the way, Eighth and 34th. Take the exit over there. They'll treat you fine and you'll be safe."

Then he turned away, missing the fact that her eyes had filled with tears. No one had worried about her safety since Frank took ill, and even before then, the bloom had been off the rose. He'd seen her as a wife. A failure of a wife, really, since she hadn't had the housekeeping skills and the babies never came. Those passionate moments, those exciting moments of love back in the early days—gone as if they had never been.

She made herself stop thinking about Frank, because thinking about Frank led to that resounding loneliness she felt in the last six months of his life, that realization that when he died (not if, *when*) no one would care what she did.

She hovered close to the information booth and stared at the exit across the great hall with its steel arches and marvelous light. The words "To Eighth Avenue" were calligraphed on a sign that she could read from here.

What would she get when she went there? A hotel room and . . . what? A job? There were no jobs, not even for qualified people. And she really didn't need one, even with a quarter of her money stolen or lost or destroyed by banks she should never have trusted.

The other banks had made up for some of it. Years of interest, good years much of it, paid some of the losses.

And she had to figure out what to do with her cash. After the Bank of the United States made the national news for failing in December, she had decided to reclaim her money from *her* banks—just like the rest of the country had. That had provided her with a travel goal, although ending up here, where the Bank of the United States had been based, with a duffel filled with cash seemed foolhardy now.

Part of her still believed, apparently, that anything that came out of New York was just fine. Fine and good and desirable.

Like Elliot had been.

A man bumped her, and she swiveled, hitting him in the leg with her solid black case. He tripped, hands open and empty enough for her to realize he probably hadn't been pickpocketing—or he hadn't succeeded because she had caught him. She glared at him, and he stumbled forward without an apology.

Her hand tightened around her duffel. The newspaper was still threaded through the handles, and no one could get in it without moving the paper and touching the latch.

She had to pay attention, though, because, God knew, no one else cared.

She walked across the wide open hall, up the stairs, heading toward the street. She emerged on Eighth Avenue to noise and thin sunlight and honking horns. Paved roads and the smell of gasoline. No horses at all— that was a change—and so was the sight across from her.

A building so large she couldn't see the top of it without craning her neck. The wings were set back from each other, covered with windows. A man walked around her, said, "Gawk on your own time, sister," before he disappeared into the crowd.

Her cheeks flushed and she moved aside. True rube. She'd worked so hard when she traveled on her own all those years ago to look like a native, only to fail in the city where she had spent her most formative years.

Above the gold-plated doors, an overhang shielded pedestrians. The words *Hotel New Yorker* ran across in bold letters.

She crossed the road, careful not to gawk any more, although it was hard. A car honked as it went by her. She had to dodge behind a large black car, parked in front of the curb. A bellboy was pulling suitcases from the trunk as an older man in uniform extended a hand to a woman getting out of the passenger seat.

Lurleen wished she'd thought to clean up on the train. That grimy coat of travel dirt made her feel like the white trash girl Elliot's mother had seen—not understanding that even in the South (especially in the South) there were more layers to society than met the eye.

Lurleen managed to get through the doors before one of the bellboys saw her. She noted him across the large marble lobby, and scurried to the registration desk before he could reach her. She resolutely did not gawk at the chandeliers hanging from the gold-plated ceiling or the second floor balcony railings that looked like they were made of etched glass.

The man behind the desk did not question her presence at all. Maybe it was the cloche hat or the stylish clothes, no matter how travel rumpled they were.

The rooms, he told her, started at $3.50 per night, and what kind of accommodations did she want? Something small and comfortable, she said, keeping her voice down. And how long does madam want to stay? he asked. The "madam" gave her pause—no one had called her that before.

But she was no green girl, not any longer, nor, apparently, could she pass for one.

"I don't know how long I'll stay," she said in response to his question. "A few days at least."

And she gave him the last crisp ten dollar bill she had in her wallet, placing it "on account." In exchange, he gave her a room key for one of the mid-range floors (his words) with a view of Eighth Avenue. It would be, he said, quieter.

The entire place had an air of quiet, surprising in the city, which she had remembered as smelly and noisy and difficult. But she hadn't expected any place like this.

The bellboy reached her side, and offered to take her bags. If she didn't let him, she would be calling attention to herself.

"I'll carry the duffel," she said, and walked away from him, the way she'd seen other society matrons do in smart hotels back south. He trailed behind her, carrying the black suitcase.

She had an entire gauntlet of employees to go through—the bellboy, the elevator operator, a maid on her floor, all wishing her a good afternoon. Lurleen inclined her head, and let the bellboy open her room with her key, showing her all the special features—the radio with four stations, the private bath, and the windows that opened upward, making it (he said) nearly impossible to throw anything out of them.

She wanted to ask about "nearly impossible," and how they knew that, but refrained. Instead, she gave him two bits—too much, probably, but she wanted him out of the room—and when he left, she pulled off her hat and placed it on the dresser, smoothing her hair with one hand.

Then she removed her coat, hanging it over the chair shoved tight against the brown desk, kicked off her shoes and slipped out of her grimy dress. She sat on the edge of the bed, at sixes and sevens for the moment, knowing she should bathe, but not quite ready to.

She didn't want to sleep on the clean white sheets when she was this filthy. But she had to decide what to do.

She needed to organize her money, place some of it in her wallet, and stash some of it elsewhere. She couldn't leave it in the room. A hotel this fancy had to provide a safe for its guests, although it made her nervous. But she certainly didn't trust any bank, even with its private security boxes. There would be no guarantee the doors would be open in the morning.

She could probably refuse maid service, but that would make people suspicious—why was she doing that? What did she have to hide?

She hadn't thought it through, this goal. New York, as if it were the holy grail. The be-all and end-all. She didn't want to return to school, and she didn't know what else was available.

Perhaps she would find her way to the NAACP offices, and finally introduce herself to Mr. White. He had received her postcards over the years, unsigned most of them, all of them showing unsightly pictures of horrid things—lynchings, mostly, but some of men burning alive, and others of the crowd "enjoying" the moment.

Most had dates on the back, and she'd sent them to Mr. White so that he could investigate the case for the anti-lynching campaign ten years ago.

It seemed like an eternity. Would he even remember her? She remembered him, the warmth of his voice on the handful of very expensive telephone calls, even as she gave him the list of names, the people who would tell her about the horrors.

She no longer had her notebooks. Before she had fled to West Texas with Frank, she had boxed them up and shipped them to 69 Fifth Avenue, Suite 518, NY NY, a place she had never been. She had never even known if they had arrived.

Maybe she should find out. After all that time on the trains, the walk would do her good.

After she bathed. After she rested.

After she had a while to figure out her plans.

She knew she had been atoning.

Long ago, Lurleen had figured out that her travels through her native South had nothing to do with Good Works, and everything to do with Noreen. Maybe if Noreen had told the truth, she would still be alive. She and that nice boy, whose name Lurleen could never remember, would both be living apart somewhere, their lives and deaths not touching. They'd have separate but equal families, and separate but equal houses, and separate but equal lives.

Although Lurleen had seen enough to learn that separate did not mean equal. Usually it meant separate and *un*equal.

All the things she'd seen. All the lies she'd told. In her search for the truth.

Sometimes, she was Lureen Taylor, with "people" in Atlanta. Sometimes she was Noreen Drayton, visiting cousins a few miles away. Sometimes, she was Mrs. Vasey, come to see if the school teacher job was still open. And sometimes, she stopped only for an afternoon, and had told just enough lies to determine that the people in that small town—whatever it was—had a nose for the truth.

She'd leave before she got run out of town, before she ever got started.

But other places, she burrowed into the community for a week, a month, a summer. She was a widow woman, or a spinster with no hope of ever marrying, or a married woman whose daddy had given her funds for the new house, the house she was surprising her husband with.

Amazing how many people believed the lies. Especially since she had an ear for accents and knew the difference between an Atlanta accent north of Piedmont and New Orleans accent from the Garden District. She spoke like a native of Huntsville and could manage enough Alabama to fool someone from the Carolinas. Arkansas was a bit too dense for her tongue, and she never did manage the variations between Memphis and Nashville, but she could cover it all with her Atlanta accent, because people from Atlanta always roamed.

She rarely got caught. There was that near miss in Arkansas in 1919. Some of the local women got her out. And then there was the afternoon she met Frank in Dallas. She'd been followed into that diner by some men because she asked too many questions. She'd slipped into Frank's booth, where he sat alone with coffee and sweet apple pie, and asked him to indulge her for just a moment.

He thought the men were toughs, after a woman for what was under her skirts, and she never disabused him. They got to talking and that led to a correspondence, which led to a future months later, after she had given up by fleeing Waco.

Along the way, though, she'd found a lot of truth. Whispered stories over shared dinner in a boardinghouse. Pride, as someone showed her a postcard with a family member posing beside a corpse. Warnings that she best stay out of a particular side of town, lest she see something untoward, done by one of them boys with their shifty eyes.

Her mission always meant talking to the despicable ones, the murderers and their families, the townspeople who saw lynchings as entertainment. She'd always arrived too late, drawn by the postcard or a photograph or a rumor, and pulling out information for articles that would appear in the *Amsterdam News* or *The Crisis, The Defender* or *The Atlanta Independent.* Conversations with attorneys who needed just that one bit of evidence, that one piece of news that might help their client.

She'd even spoke to the great Darrow, nearly risking her identity for a case he would eventually abandon.

All excitement and fear and real true living, doing something she actually believed in. Elliot's Good Works. Noreen's atonement.

And for a while, Lurleen's life.

It took half the night of dithering to figure out her money. She put twenty ones in her wallet, one hundred in four different envelopes stuffed in her purse, another hundred in another envelope at the bottom of her suitcase, and still another hidden in one of the bathroom tiles.

The rest stayed in the duffle, wrapped in layers of undergarments and nightgowns. A box with her wedding ring and pearl necklace sat on top of it all, the reason, she told the hotel manager when she asked to put the duffel in the safe, that she was entrusting it to his care. Still and all, she tied two strings around the duffle, using her father's old double knots so she would know if anyone broke in.

She walked down the island from the hotel, heading—she knew— toward 69 Fifth Avenue, which, according to her map, crossed at West 14th. She had forgotten the particular pleasures and discomforts of walking through the city. Men in sharp suits, hurrying to work; women in nice dresses, window-shopping. Both stepping past the men in shabby suits or dirty work pants, the older men wearing signs around their necks—*Will Work For Food*—the women in threadbare dresses sitting behind them, listless children on their laps.

Lurleen averted her eyes just like everyone else did—too much misery, and none of it hers. She found three open banks along her route. She hadn't investigated any of them, but she didn't care. Everyone had believed that the Bank of the United States had been one of the most solid banks in the country. The best bank in New York, someone had proclaimed not six months before it shuttered, reminding everyone that banks had never been safe.

But they were safer than carrying her money in her purse or in that duffel all the time. She had enough money to lose a bit more.

She deposited $90 in each of the banks, keeping two fives from each envelope, and giving one each to the first two shabby women with families that she saw. Strange, she thought as she walked, she expected the men to drink the money away. But she thought the women would buy something for the children.

The gifts didn't make her feel better. Because each block, each half-block really, she saw at least five more people who needed money, needed enough money to survive longer than a week or a month. They needed jobs and help and a roof over their heads.

By the time Lurleen reached West 14th, she walked with her eyes averted once again, her hand on her purse. If she hadn't looked up after she crossed Sixth Avenue, she wouldn't have seen the flag, rippling defiantly in the cool spring wind. Half a block away, the message was clearer than it probably was up close:

A Man Was Lynched Yesterday.

It blinked out, became something else for a half a moment—the man in Waco, screaming as they dragged him down the Main Street, yelling for help, his dark panicked eyes meeting hers. She'd followed, drawn to the first—the only—lynching that had ever happened on her watch.

She had recorded all of it, took what names she knew, even made haphazard sketches, not that she needed to since the local newspaper photographer took shot after shot, and probably made some of them into postcards.

The young man had screamed and screamed, and she had stumbled away, finally. There was no one to go to for help, no one to stop it, no one to speak sense. The authorities had all been present—the police, two judges, several lawyers, the mayor—all of them, and they had been cheering, or in one case, passing judgment, telling the young man he was guilty.

He done it!

She hadn't saved him. Instead, she'd fled to Dallas on the afternoon train, writing her notes, locals asking what she was doing, and she'd—

She'd gone to Frank, and fallen in love, or so she told herself.

Because love was the only thing that could've made her give up the Good Works. Because good women like her, good *moral* women, they didn't run away. They stepped in, talked sense to the men, made everything better.

And she never had.

Lurleen shook off the memory, made herself look away from the flag, and continued forward. She was walking toward that brown building. She needed to keep its lower levels in sight, not its flag. Not its pronouncement.

But she couldn't help herself.

Another half block and she saw another sign spread across windows on the same floor:

The Crisis

Crisis. Indeed. There were several. And they all were intertwined into something she still didn't entirely understand.

But she knew what the sign actually referred to. *The Crisis* was the NAACP's magazine, and she'd read it faithfully for years. Not even Frank could get her to stop. He would shake it at her—*why are you reading this filth?* he'd ask, and she'd tell him, implore him, really, to look and see the literature inside, the poets, the stories, the *voices.*

But he hadn't. And really, she hadn't expected it of him. He was as open-minded as he could be, given how he was raised. He never harmed another soul, but he didn't see issues with the separation of the races either.

They'd only argued about it once, and then she'd stopped. Because she would have had to reveal what was behind her travels all those years if she spoke any further. And she knew if she told Frank that she had been an investigator for the NAACP—an unpaid investigator, who helped with evidence for the lawyers—he would have . . . well, she never wanted to find out. But she guessed it would have been anything from giving her the occasional *I don't understand you* look to tossing her out on her ear.

A shudder ran through her. Then she realized she was standing like a rube again, in the middle of the sidewalk, staring at the flag and the words in the window.

She pulled her purse closer and crossed Fifth Avenue, and forced herself to walk into the building itself. It was done with clean lines and lots of gold trim, just like the hotel. A bank of elevators waited on the other side of the marble floor, some of the doors open, revealing the operators standing inside.

She went into the nearest elevator and said primly, "Fifth floor please," without looking at the operator. This was the day not to look at anyone.

The elevator smelled of tobacco and the hint of another woman's perfume. The car shuddered slightly as it rose, but Lurleen didn't mind. It still felt like magic to her.

The door opened, and the hallway appeared, some kind of scuffed tile or some cheaper flooring that resembled the marble below. Dozens of glass frosted doors were closed, making it all look even more foreboding.

"Fifth floor, miss," the operator said, clearly waiting for her to get out.

She swallowed, nodded, and stepped into the hallway. She waited until the elevator doors closed before she walked down the hall, searching for the door marked 518.

It wasn't hard to find. It was slightly ajar, and from inside, she heard the click of typewriters, the hum of voices.

Her throat had gone completely dry. She peered through the crack in the door, saw men and women bent over desks, the women typing, the men on the phones. Papers and posters lined the wall, some warning blacks to be on guard, others proclaiming *For A Full Democracy, Join The NAACP.*

Everyone inside had dark skin. Everyone.

She didn't belong.

She turned away, only to hear a female voice say, "May I help you?"

Lurleen took a deep breath. She could say, *No, sorry, this is the wrong office,* and no one would be the wiser.

But she had more courage than that—or she had, once upon a time.

She turned. "I . . . um . . . came to see Mr. White."

The woman leaning against the door was young and pretty. Her hair was pulled away from her face, revealing compassionate eyes. "Come on in," she said. "I know he's here."

Lurleen's stomach tightened. She stepped through the frosted door, into a world of desks and ringing telephones, index cards in a wooden case pushed against the wall, and even more conversation than she had heard from the hallway.

Everyone in the room looked up at her, then looked away, most without meeting her gaze, and she realized she had done it again. She had given herself a destination with no real purpose. What would she say to Mr. White? That she'd been honored to investigate for him? Had she been honored? Had she really thought of him as anything at all, except a voice on the telephone, a name on an envelope?

"Mr. White is in a conference." A young man had come up to her. He was taller than Frank and wore a suit with a stiff collar. His brown eyes reminded her of the eyes of the young man she had seen lynched in Waco. "May I help you?"

She shook her head. She needed to leave. She had no real reason for being here, and she was bothering these good people.

"They're discussing that matter in Alabama," the young man said as if she should know what that matter was. "They should be done soon if you'd just like to wait."

She stood awkwardly, uncertain what to do. So many eager faces, so many busy hands, everyone around her working hard, believing in what they were doing, striving to change the world.

For all her "good works," she hadn't tried to change the world at all, not even when she worked for the NAACP. Instead, she had been studying the world's sickness from a distance—her world's sickness—and using her own privilege to "help," when really, maybe, she had been nothing more than a voyeur, peering into the lives of others.

She hadn't helped at all, and when she had the chance to help, the moment she needed to take a risk, step forward, maybe save a life, she had fled, disappearing into the privilege she'd been born into, the marriage to Frank—not really a love match at all or an uncontrollable passion, just an escape back into what she had been raised to do and be, and of course, she had failed at that too.

"No," she said quietly. "I don't want to wait. You're doing much more important things."

The muscles in her shoulders relaxed slightly as she spoke, and she loosened the hold on her purse. Then she realized what she had with her.

"I . . . um . . . I would like to make a donation," she said. "Do I do that with you?"

"Sure," the young man said, and slipped behind the nearest empty desk. He removed a receipt book from a drawer, and grabbed a pen.

She reached into her purse and removed the last envelope.

"Name?" he asked.

She licked her lips. She was on their rolls—had been, anyway, so that she could get *The Crisis*. She didn't want to give them a name again.

"Can I be anonymous?" she asked.

"Certainly," he said, as if he had expected it. Her cheeks grew warm. "How much?"

She opened the envelope and fanned the money so that everyone could see it. She didn't want anyone to take it for themselves.

"One hundred dollars," she said.

The nearby gasps were audible. He looked up at her, then at the money, and then back at the receipt book. His pen shook slightly as he wrote down the sum.

"Would you like to dedicate the donation?" he asked, as if he expected her to say no.

"Yes," she said. "Please dedicate it to Noreen Quarles."

He had her spell the last name, then he glanced at a nearby door. She could see shadowy figures behind the frosted glass. Probably that conference that Mr. White was attending.

The young man ripped off the receipt and folded it around the money, handing her the sheet behind the carbon paper that they apparently left in the receipt book for just this purpose.

"Thank you very much," the young man said.

She took the copy as if she had a real use for it. Then she nodded, and backed out of the room.

"At least take a newspaper or something," the young man said. "Or a notice, to see what we're working on."

He swept his arm toward a table littered with newspapers, some daily, some weekly, and extra copies of *The Crisis*. She hadn't seen that issue so she took it. She looked at the papers, but she didn't pick them up. Instead, her gaze caught a folded page from the New Orleans paper, *The Times Picayune*, from two days before, paperclipped to a legal pad.

DEATH SENTENCES FOR ATTACK GIVEN TO EIGHT NEGROES
Mistrial for Ninth Ordered in Assault Trial in Alabama

She couldn't help herself. She tapped the newspaper lightly.

"Is this the Alabama matter?" she asked.

"Yes," the young man said. "Have you heard about those boys? They were pulled off a box car two weeks ago, and they've already received a death sentence."

"Almost a lynching," someone said softly.

Lurleen looked up. She couldn't see who'd said it.

"We're trying to figure out who we can send to represent them on appeal," the young man said. He tapped the envelope she had given him. "This will help with travel expenses."

She nodded, feeling like she had done something, at least, however small. Then she let herself out of the office. She was halfway down the hall before she realized she had not said any good-byes.

She was in the elevator before she realized that giving the money left her with the same emptiness that handing out the five dollars had. She was helping, slightly, but only for a moment—travel expenses for some attorney, some representatives. Expenses, one-time, paid for and gone.

The walk back to the hotel seemed longer than the walk to the offices. She went through the glass doors on the Eighth Avenue entrance and stopped in the lobby, realizing that all the gold leaf, the ornate ceiling, the decorations, could feed a family for months.

Of course, Frank would have said that building this place had fed hundreds of families for years. Not to mention the jobs that would not exist right now if people like her did not stay in the expensive rooms at all.

She waited for an elevator, hovering around a table covered with brochures and timetables for everything from the subway to the trains. She grabbed a few, just so that she would have something to look at, so that the elevator operator wouldn't talk to her.

She needn't have worried. He nodded his hello as she gave him the floor, and then said little else. He didn't even look at her. When he let her out on her floor, he didn't even wish her a good day.

Someone else, someone entitled, would have had him written up for that. She expected he was merely as worn down by the day as she was. Always a crisis, always something going wrong. Always people dying for things that they hadn't done.

No one ever said, *He hadn't done it. He never did do it. He couldn't've done it.*

At least, not no one the people in charge listened to.

She frowned as she unlocked her door, something niggling at her. She closed the door, then picked up the old newspaper she'd grabbed on the train. It was a *New York Times* from a few weeks ago—before she had gone to Memphis.

She thumbed through it, remembering something she had seen. She found it in the middle of the paper, just before pages of ads.

JAIL HEAD ASKS TROOPS AS MOB SEEKS NEGROES
Riot Feared in Scottsboro, Ala., After Arrest of Nine,
Held for Attacking Girls

Lurleen leaned against the desk as she read the article, trying to see between the lines. The nine men were pulled off a box car, charged with attacking two girls. But there was something about a fight with white men, who left the box car at a different stop. The white men telegraphed ahead, and asked that the Negro men be arrested.

And then the mob.

She shuddered.

The sheriff had called for troops, preventing the lynching that the white men had so obviously desired, but these nine young men—still alive a few weeks later—had already been tried, convicted, and sentenced to death.

No wonder the NAACP wanted to appeal.

She knew, just from looking at the story, that this wasn't about rape. It was about sharing a box car, breathing the same air. About not acting unequal.

She glanced at the date. It had happened before she had gone to Memphis, before she saw that box car filled with men of different colors riding together, looking unhappy.

Before she had her uncharacteristic thought: *Oh, that's going to cause problems.* She'd had the thought because it already had caused problems.

Big problems.

She had, apparently, scanned and disregarded the story, because in the last few years, she had trained herself not to see stories like that, stories that would have led her to other places, other times.

She tossed the newspaper on the desk, then pulled off her hat and set it on its already customary place on the dresser. She peeled off her dress and hung it up, so that it wouldn't get creased.

Then she kicked off her shoes. She was going to have a nap before she went for dinner, although she couldn't bring herself to sleep.

Instead, she grabbed one of the railroad timetables, her hands knowing what her brain had yet to acknowledge.

The money helped. It did some good. But it couldn't stem the tide of misery. It wasn't even a stone in an already-breached dam.

She couldn't stop lynchings or those horrid, horrid deaths that had no name. The burning-alive deaths. The shotguns fired at point blank range.

She didn't have the courage for that. She really didn't have courage at all. She had been uncomfortable in the NAACP offices.

She hadn't belonged.

But she could investigate. She had already proven that. She had a knack for getting her own people to admit the horrors they had perpetrated. To *brag* about those horrors.

She had usually listened after the deaths. But those young men in Scottsboro, Alabama, they were still alive. Their story could be told and investigated, and maybe, someone else could save them. The legal defense people were already converging. They were "discussing that matter in Alabama," and if she knew anything about such discussions, then someone would go to the families, encourage them to fight and fight hard.

To fight, they would need evidence.

For evidence, they needed someone to talk to both sides—to admit to things that shouldn't even be discussed.

She would no longer call such investigations Good Works. They weren't Good Works. They were Necessary Evils—performed by a woman who had spent too much time with evil herself, a woman who couldn't properly stand up.

But she could lie for the sake of the truth.

She bent over the timetable, looking for a train out of New York, a train that would connect her to a train that would take her to Scottsboro, Alabama. Ironic that she had to come here to realize she needed to travel to her native land once again, that she needed to pretend for another few years, to capture what had really happened so that someone else—someone with actual courage, someone with a heart and a mission—could risk their own life to save other lives.

She would never be that person.

She would always hide in the shadows and send reports into the light.

It was the least—truly the least—she could do.

Not for Noreen, who had pointed a finger and lied.

But for the young man at the other end of that finger, holding a book and smiling at a little girl carrying a dolly, treating her kindly, like one human treated another—something so very rare in this world as to be memorable.

This would be for him, and all the people like him, who became names on a list at best, and postcards at worst.

She would do what she could for as long as she could.

Until the money ran out.

JONATHAN SANTLOFER *is the author of 5 novels including the best-selling* The Death Artist *and the Nero Award–winning* Anatomy of Fear. *He is the co-author, contributor, and illustrator of* The Dark End of the Street, *editor/contributor of* La Noire: The Collected Stories, The Marijuana Chronicles, *and the* New York Times *bestselling serial novel* Inherit the Dead. *His stories have been included in such publications as* Ellery Queen Magazine, The Strand, *and numerous collections. He is the recipient of 2 National Endowment for the Arts grants, has been a Visiting Artist at the American Academy in Rome, the Vermont Studio Center and serves on the board of Yaddo, the oldest arts community in the U.S. Santlofer has been profiled in the* New York Times, Publishers Weekly, Newsday, USA Today, *has been the subject of a* Sunday New York Times Magazine *"Questions For" column, and has been written about and reviewed extensively.*

Also a well-known artist, his work is included in such collections as the Metropolitan Museum of Art, Art Institute of Chicago, Newark Museum. A longtime Hopper fan, Santlofer's portrait of Edward Hopper was included in his 2002 exhibition of "Art about Art and Artists." He lives and works in NYC, where he is Director of Crime Fiction Academy at the Center for Fiction. He is currently at work on a new crime novel and a fully illustrated adventure novel for children.

Night Windows, 1928

NIGHT WINDOWS

BY JONATHAN SANTLOFER

T here she is again, pink bra, pink slip, in one window then the next, appearing then disappearing, a picture in a zoetrope, flickering, evanescent, maddening.

Yes, that's the word: *maddening*.

Then he thinks of another: *delicious*.

And another: *torture*.

He hadn't expected a replacement so soon. The last one, Laura or Lauren, her name hardly matters, gone now four or five months, not like he's not counting. They're all replaceable, one as good as the next. Though he liked the last one, her innocence—and taking it away. He tries to picture her but her features are already blurred, like she was a watercolor and he'd run a moist finger across her face, smearing her features, erasing her, creating her then destroying her. Exactly what he did. What he always does.

The woman in pink bends over, her rear end aimed right at him, and he would laugh but she might hear, might look across the alley and spot him, the man in the window opposite, the man in the dark, and he's not quite ready for that. The meeting has to be planned. And it will be. Soon.

The woman stands up, turns and leans on the window ledge, her blond hair backlit, and he thinks: *The gods have sent me a new one.*

That last one was lucky to have known him, a rube like her, easy to manipulate, almost too easy. He'd broken her in; just plain broken her.

So how did she have the strength to get away?

No matter. He was tired of her anyway, her whiny voice, her all too eager need to please.

This new one looks perfect, the way she glides past the windows oblivious to the fact that she is being watched.

This one will be easy.

He wipes sweat from his upper lip and stares at the three bay windows shining in the dark, his own private theater. He lets out a deep breath and a curtain in her window billows out, as if it is breathing along with him. *Ahhhh . . .*

The dark covers him, a veil; he can see her but she sees nothing.

He watches her bare feet on the ugly green rug, the same rug. This new one hasn't bothered to change it. He feels a tingle in his toes and a tug in his groin remembering his own bare feet on that rug, and the last one's ankle, cuffed to the old steel radiator.

Heat oozes in through the window he's opened for a better view, soggy warm air that dissolves around him into the apartment's central air conditioning, half his body cool, the other half sweating, as if he's in the middle of a weather pattern, cold front meeting warm, a storm brewing deep inside him. He reaches for the bottle, pours more Scotch into his tumbler, the ice mostly melted.

He spots the small metal fan behind her, rotating but not doing much good, he's sure of that, though he likes it, the way it blows her slip and her hair and it means her windows will remain open in this heat.

He brings the Scotch to his lips, the liquor sharp on his tongue but smooth in his throat, and he stares across the dark as if it's something physical, a runway that transports him directly into her apartment, can feel his eyes, like hands, on her body, soft then hard, harder till it hurts.

The woman moves away as if she feels the pain, the pink of her drawn into the back of the apartment, away from the window.

He waits.

Pictures the apartment he knows well, the drab interior, cramped bedroom, cracked tiles in the bathroom, tiny kitchen, the outmoded fixtures.

He can see the naked radiator in the living room, the apartment old and not yet renovated, an anomaly in this city. Of course he owns his brownstone, four stories, turn of the century, a backyard he never uses. He'd bought it during the economic downturn though it was expensive, now astronomical, even by his standards. Still, not the kind of place he ever imagined he'd be in, had always lived on the Upper East Side, in high-rise doormen buildings. But he's grown to like it here, the privacy.

He finishes his drink and pours another, impatient, Scotch spilling onto his hand in the dark.

What's she doing? What's taking so long?

He checks his watch; thin gold face on a thinner gold mesh band. Damn it, she's going to make him late for his business dinner.

Come on. Come on.

Is she taking a shower, a pee? He imagines both, wishes he were there to watch. Knows he will be soon.

He lights a cigar, no one around to tell him not to, not wife number one or two, so long gone they're not even bad memories, or that one from a couple of years ago who dared to say his cigars were a disgusting habit. Well, he showed her disgusting habits, didn't he?

A picture of his father—a big man smoking a cigar—sparks in his brain, the man's face florid with blood-filled rage, looming toward him with a belt or a fist or the smoldering tip of a cigar, though it's possible he's made it up or these images were supplied by his mother, who said his father had died when he was five, a lie he discovered years later though he never saw the man again.

A flash of pink, like a brushstroke of paint in her window, and he sits forward, head jutting like a turtle from its shell. Then she's gone but the pink of her lags in his mind, and he thinks of meat, tender veal, juicy pork, saliva gathering in his mouth like a dog.

He drags on his cigar, holds the smoke in until he's about to cough, then lets it explode, a gray cloud in front of his face. When it clears she's there again, farther back in the apartment, unhooking her bra beside a lamp that bathes her body in a soft gold light. He squints through the smoke trying to make out details, but cannot. She's an impressionist painting. Shimmering. Beautiful. Something he wants to put in a frame and hang on a nail, or in a cage, or strap to a wall.

Then she's gone again, and he thinks about the last one, young and pure, and how he stripped that away, watched the purity slake off her like old, dead skin.

He looks at his watch, he's got to get going, can't really be late for this dinner, a client from Dubai. But then the pink is back, clear and close to the window, the silky material of her slip sliding around her thighs in slow motion, something old-fashioned about it, a slip, and her figure too, rounder and curvier than the fashionably starving women he usually sees, picking at salads while their fish, always fish, goes cold, two-hundred-dollar meals wasted on women who do not eat, beards for dinners with businessmen from Dubai.

He stares at her and blinks as if taking pictures, wishes he'd kept his old 35mm Nikon with its telephoto lens, imagines himself Jimmy Stewart in *Rear Window*, and he's watching a murder—how great would that be?

The pink lady—his name for her—bends over, then she's up and practically twirling and for the first time he notices that farther back, half hidden in the shadows, is a mirror, something new, something he does not remember being there before, and for a moment he thinks she must surely see him reflected in it, and he pulls back, cigar smoke trailing him.

Of course it's impossible, he's too far away and let's face it, he's a vampire—*just try to catch my reflection!* He barks a laugh and if it were not for the street noise—buses, taxis, sirens—she might have heard him, might have averted everything that is to come.

And maybe she does. Because she stops twirling, comes to the window and looks out.

His breath catches in his throat and he pulls further back into the soupy darkness.

Is she looking for me, at *me?*

He can't tell where she's looking, her face dark, backlit, her hair a pale halo.

Then she's gone. He should get going too, and is about to get up when she's back, almost but not quite lost in the hazy interior light, opening her apartment door. Then the lights snap off and the windows go dark.

He could race to catch her as she leaves but he sits there, in the dark, smoking his cigar and sipping the last of his Scotch, forcing himself to wait. He likes this part, the part where they don't yet know him, but he knows them.

Three weeks and two days. A dozen more performances. The way he sees them, little plays, vignettes, the pink lady performing, just for him.

But enough. It's time. He can't put it off any longer without going crazy.

And it's easy. He sees when she comes and goes, lights on, lights off, sees her getting dressed for work and undressed when she comes home. Sees her go out on dates and come home alone. Always alone. And he likes that. He would never be interested in a tramp.

He's followed her twice to the same restaurant, watched her through plate glass, eating alone, using a book for a prop, looking lonely, shy—a good sign, something he can work with.

He checks the time. She will be home soon, and he is prepared, dressed as if for work, designer summer suit, hair in place but not slicked back like some Wall Street wolf, one thick lock, gray-streaked, casually arranged to fall across his self-tanned forehead. A splash of expensive English cologne, subtle and masculine, something to tickle the nose if she gets close, and he will make sure she does.

Lights flicker on in the triple-screen theater across the alley, hot, blinding, for a moment the world has gone phosphorescent. Then it cools and she is there, strutting across the living room in a business dress, plain, straight lines, dark blue. She disappears into the bedroom, and he waits. A few minutes later she is back in the living room, wearing a tank top and white jeans, then she is out the door.

And so is he.

On the street, nerve ends tingling though his heartbeat is low—it never goes above eighty—he catches his reflection in a storefront's glass, pleased, an attractive man, anyone can see that, and successful; he wears the attributes of wealth easily but impossible to miss.

He rounds the corner and there she is. Sky blue tank top, white pants, blond hair snatching the fading summer light as she comes out of her apartment building, as if out of a movie, *his* movie, the shape of her, details coming into focus, his skin crawling with anticipation, brain a low buzz as he follows her down the crowded city street and into the restaurant, where she is seated alone at a table for two, the place a faux French bistro, half empty. He snares the table beside hers, orders a glass of Malbec, and watches her over his menu, as if she is performing on the edge of it, a mini-stage he has created just for her.

She orders white wine, Chardonnay, takes a sip and he notices it's the same color as her hair. When she orders the niçoise salad he waits until the waiter, a young man with oily hair and an equally oily French accent, stops at his table, then says with a nod in her direction, his voice loud enough so she will hear, "I'll have the same as she's having," and when she looks over he smiles and she smiles back, and that's it, the hook in her cheek, the rod in his hand and he is starting to reel her in.

"Have you eaten here before?" he asks.

"What?" she says, looking up from her book. "Oh. Yes. A couple of times."

"So you like it."

She's a little older than he thought, early thirties, and the restaurant's dim light softens her features so that he wonders, worries, if perhaps she's even older. He likes them at least a decade younger than he is, though not too young, he's no pervert.

"You live in the neighborhood?" he asks.

Another nod. He can see she is checking him out, wary, not sure if she wants to converse with this somewhat older man, handsome and distinguished, but still, a stranger.

He eases up on his imaginary reel, turns away, takes out his phone, pretends to check email, the whole time watching her as she reads her book.

Thank God her lips do not move.

He likes them shy and naïve, easy to manipulate, but not stupid. Never stupid. What's the fun in that? Where's the challenge?

That last one, Laura or Lauren, wasn't exactly a genius, but no dummy either. Just easily duped, and younger, early twenties, and a virgin. The shock of learning that, the delight. He always takes something but that, well, that was an added gift.

When the salads arrive, he nods in her direction and says, "You're not from New York, are you?"

"Salina," she says. "I'm sure you've never heard of it."

"Kansas," he says, and she looks surprised, but smiles.

"Kim Novak. *Vertigo.*"

"Excuse me."

"The Hitchcock film. Kim Novak, her character, I mean, is from Salina."

"Oh," she says.

"You've never seen it?"

"No."

"A great movie," he says, thinking how Jimmy Stewart remakes Kim Novak's character, as if bringing her back from the dead. The opposite of what he likes to do. "There's a Hitchcock festival at Film Forum right now. You should go. No, I should take you."

She looks surprised, eyebrows arched, but not displeased.

"Sorry, I don't mean to be—well, maybe you're married, or involved. I shouldn't have—" He adds the look, shy, slightly self-conscious, that he's learned from watching movies.

"I'm not involved—or married—I'm new to the city, and to be honest it scares me, a little."

"Nothing to be scared of," he says, rearranging his features from shy to friendly, to compassionate.

"I have to say it's not easy meeting people."

"Hey," he says with a big smile. "Why don't you join me," and before she can say no—and frankly she doesn't look like she wants to—he sidles over to her table, carrying his salad, signaling the waiter, who moves his wineglass, and then he is across from her trying to see her as real, not just the pink lady in the night window, though the image burns in his brain.

After another glass of wine she's telling him her life story—from Salina high school prom queen to secretarial school in Topeka, to a job for an accounting firm where she was "bored to death, all those accountants," she says and pulls a face.

"Well, you won't be *bored to death* here," he says, "and I'm no accountant."

He orders more wine, and after another glass she is telling him how she's thirty-two, divorced, here to start a new life, and he keeps her talking, offering little, just that he works for himself, "in finance, nothing special, but it pays the bills."

She laughs. Then eyes him and says, "How come a good looking man like you is single?"

"I was married, *once*," he says and adds, "I wouldn't mind trying again," tugging at the hook, seeing it cut into flesh, a trickle of blood down her cheek, red not pink.

Then he's walking her home.

A beautiful night, not the usual Manhattan summer, breezy, low humidity, the warm air like a light mask over the mask he's already wearing.

"This is me," she says at the entrance to her building.

An awkward moment, but he won't fill the silence, wants to see how she will.

"Well . . ." she says, and extends her hand.

He takes it in both of his, holds it a moment. "A real pleasure," he says. "So what do you think?"

"About?"

"Film Forum. Hitchcock."

"Oh," she says. "When?"

"The festival is every night for two weeks. How's tomorrow?"

"Oh," she says again, chewing her soft lower lip. "I guess. What's playing?"

"Double feature. *Vertigo* and . . . *Psycho.*"

"I've always been afraid to see *Psycho.*"

"Don't worry," he says. "I'll protect you."

He watches her disappear into her building then rushes back to his apartment in time to see her undressing in her window, white jeans pushed down, tank top up and off, and she stands there a moment, in the middle of her living room, and he wonders if she feels him watching her, the way she suddenly crosses her arms across her breasts.

"I loved them both," she says, as they head out of Film Forum onto the Greenwich Village street, the night hotter, the air wetter. "Take my picture, right here," she says and hands him her cell phone.

He snaps a shot of her in front of the *Psycho* movie poster, and she giggles like a teenager, takes the cell back and holds it out, snapping the two of them.

"I hate having my picture taken," he says, and it's true, he never allows it. He considers grabbing her phone and smashing it against the wall. "Erase it, will you?"

"Oh, well, sure," she says, pushing buttons on her phone. "Sorry, I didn't mean to—"

"Forget it," he says, forcing a smile but he can feel her discomfort, needs to fix it.

"So, *Psycho*, what did you think?"

"Oh, *so* scary."

"But great. Even after multiple—" He stops to find the right word, was about to say *orgasms.* "—viewings." He is as pent up as a champagne bottle. Sitting through two movies with the girl beside him, the smell of her perfume, her shrieking and grabbing his arm during the shower scene and later when the detective gets stabbed and later still when the mother's corpse is discovered. By then he was close to losing it, seated there for so long, controlling himself while Norman Bates had all the fun.

A taxi ride home this time, the interior frigid, the driver on his phone the whole way, jabbering.

"I'm glad to be out of there," he says, as he slams the cab door.

"Me too, but too bad I can't store up the cold."

"How come?"

"No air conditioning, and I've been too lazy to buy a window unit, though I suppose I should."

"Summer's almost over. Why bother?" Thinking how he wants her windows open, that fan whirring and blowing her hair, her slip.

"My place is cool. Why don't you come over?"

She looks down at the pavement. "I don't think so."

"Your place then?" he asks, and adds a laugh.

"I hardly know you," she says.

"Really? I feel as if I know *you*." He tries to catch her eyes but she's still looking down. He touches her chin, tilts her face up, a studied, movie gesture, says, "It's okay. Another time, when you *know* me better, when you trust me."

"Oh, but I do. It's not that." She shifts her weight from one foot to the other, flats on her feet tonight, open-toed, nails painted pink. It's clear, she loves the color. He does too.

"I understand, but I have to say that I like you, I do. And it's rare that I find a woman I really like."

"Why?" she asks.

"The women I usually meet are so . . . New York. Starving themselves to death and no fun. But who's fun when they're *starving*?"

She laughs, opens her arms in a gesture that says *look at me*. "Clearly, I'm not starving."

"Thank God," he says, taking in her curves, then leans in, a chaste peck on the cheek though he wants to bite it, tear the flesh with his teeth. "I'll call you."

"Good," she says, turns and dashes into her apartment building.

He watches her go, knows the hook is already in, no matter how fast she runs.

He lets a week pass, as difficult for him as he imagines it is for her, though he has the triplex playing outside his window, the pink lady in her bra and slip, pink lady in panties, pink lady naked. The delayed time is like pulled taffy, sticky and sweet.

Finally he calls, watching her through the window.

"Oh," she says, standing in her living room, cell phone to her ear. "Nice to hear from you," though she sounds cool and distant.

"I was busy with work, and had to travel."

"No cell phone service? Where were you?"

The hook is in deeper than he imagined.

"Just very busy," he says. "Sorry."

"It's okay," she says, softening, trying to unbutton her blouse with one hand while holding the phone in the other.

He sees it all, knows she has just come home, watched her lights go on only minutes ago, now slipping off the blouse as she talks, the whole thing like a pantomime, her voice on the phone not really attached to the woman he is watching.

"You free tonight?" he asks.

"I'm supposed to meet a coworker for drinks."

"That's too bad. I guess I deserve that. Last minute and all."

A pause. "You know, let me call my coworker. I'm sure I can see him another night."

"Him?" The word falls out unintentionally. "Just kidding. Who am I to be jealous?"

"Are you? Jealous, I mean?"

"A little."

"My ex was never jealous."

"Okay then, I'm *very* jealous."

She laughs. "Give me an hour. I need to shower and change."

He watches her put the cell phone down, step out of her skirt, walk to the windows, look out, then tug down the shades, one at a time.

Did she know he was watching?

Did she see someone else watching?

Damn.

He squeezes the glass of Scotch so hard it shatters, blood leeching from his palm, dropping small rosebuds onto his perfect wooden floor, spreading like water lilies.

In his all-white bathroom he runs the wound under cold water, watches his blood swirl in the sink and pictures the *Psycho* scene, blood in the bathtub spiralling down the drain though he knows Hitchcock used Hershey's syrup, a convincing double for blood in black-and-white, though hardly sufficient in life.

Nothing serious he decides, no arteries cut though it throbs and takes three Band-Aid changes to stanch the bleeding. An auspicious beginning to the evening, he thinks: blood, pain.

"What happened to your hand?"

"It's nothing," he says.

They sit opposite one another in the French bistro, crowded tonight, noisy. He intentionally speaks in whispers so that she has to lean forward to hear him, her face only inches from his.

They order salads again though he wants meat, rare, pink, wants to taste blood in his mouth, but better to put it off, wait for the real thing.

The dinner drags, interminable small talk, when all he can think about is getting her back to her apartment.

He fingers the handcuffs in one pocket, a Swiss Army knife in the other.

This time she invites him in. The place is almost exactly as it was a couple of months ago, the way the last one had it, she hasn't changed a thing. He wants to ask her why, but how can he?

"Your hand," she says.

He sees blood has seeped through the Band-Aid.

"Come with me." She leads him into the bathroom, plucks the Band-Aid off in one fast tug and he tries not to wince. "That's quite a gash," she says.

"Chinatown," he says.

"What?"

"That's exactly what Faye Dunaway says to Jack Nicholson in *Chinatown*."

She looks puzzled.

"One of the greatest films, ever."

"You're quite a movie buff."

"I've watched it dozens of times. And the ending . . ." He shakes his head, pictures Faye Dunaway, eyeball blown out of her head.

"Bad?"

"Sometimes bad endings are inescapable," he says, looking her up and down.

"Wow," she says, "that's heavy."

"You should see it some time," he says, careful not to wince again as she applies a fresh Band-Aid, smoothing it down, causing him to shiver.

"Need a drink?" she asks, leading him into the familiar kitchenette, pouring brandy into two glasses, handing him one.

He drinks it down in a gulp.

She refills his glass though she hasn't touched hers.

"The brandy was here when I moved in," she says.

He almost says *Right, I remember,* picturing the last one who lived here, but catches himself. He gets an arm around her waist, tugs her to him, kisses her, soft then hard, harder, forcing his tongue past her half open teeth.

She presses her hand to his chest, pushes him back. "Wait."

He expels a breath, about to explode. "How long?"

"I'm not very experienced."

"But you were married, weren't you?"

"That doesn't make me *experienced,*" she says, and they both laugh.

Then she kisses him back, a long kiss, pulls away again and asks, "Do you have protection?"

He pats his pocket.

"You came prepared? That makes me feel way too predicable."

"I'm always prepared," he says.

In the bedroom he watches her undress. She's wearing the pink slip and the bra. He almost gasps when he sees them, up close, lace trim he couldn't see from a distance.

He thought she'd be shy, like the others, that he'd take the lead the way he always does, but she's already on the bed, naked. "Aren't you joining me?" she asks, sounding almost irritated.

"Sure," he says, feeling for the handcuffs in his pocket, but before he can get them she's pulled him onto the bed, tugging his pants down, her hands on him, her mouth practically devouring him, and he can't control her, can't control himself and he forgets the cuffs and the idea of blood, his head spinning, practically delirious, so that she has to stop him and remind him to put on the condom and then it's over and he's embarrassed at his loss of control, can't believe it, after all of his planning.

The girl's already out of bed, shimmying into her slip. She nods at his withering cock, the condom hanging off it, and hands him a tissue.

He's flushed with embarrassment.

How did she turn it around?

"The bathroom?" he asks, as if he doesn't know where it is.

"Through there. Oh, and don't flush that thing or it will stuff up the toilet."

He stares at himself in the familiar bathroom mirror, all this build-up and nothing, no cuffed girl, no ignored safe word, no screams, no begging. He wants to go back in, show her who's boss, force her into the cuffs, but that's not his style. He's a gentleman; he needs them to comply, at first, or it's no fun. He crumples the tissue with the used condom and tosses it into the trash along with his hopes for the evening.

Maybe this one was a mistake.

She's fully dressed and playing with the handcuffs when he comes back in the room.

"Look what I found," she singsongs.

He can feel his mouth open, but he struggles for words. "It's just—a toy."

"You weren't planning to use them on *me*, were you?"

He manages to say "Would you like that?"

"Maybe next time," she says and hands them back to him.

"Your finger," he says, noting a spot of blood.

"I snagged it on my zipper. It's nothing." She sucks on it. "I'm going out for some milk, can't drink my morning coffee without it." She shifts her weight from one foot to another, impatient.

He stands there, naked, shivering, though the room is hot, pictures himself at eight or nine, refuses to remember that he was almost fourteen, in his mother's bedroom after wetting his bed and the way she'd wash him then bring him under her covers to *spoon*, her soft body wrapped around his, engulfing him, smothering him, the smell of her perfume, suffocating.

He hurries into his clothes.

On the street, he just wants to get away, but it's she who says goodbye first, gives him a quick kiss, then turns and hurries down the street leaving him there feeling like a fool.

A day passes. Two. He can't concentrate, can't think about anything but his failure to act and the way the girl took charge, controlled him. He never lets it happen like that, can't bear the idea that he's wasted weeks and didn't go through with it, didn't reduce her to whimpering and begging. That *he* is the one who has been reduced.

He has to correct this.

The shades are drawn in her windows but he knows when she comes home and he is ready this time.

He sits in the armchair, drink at his side, cigar burning, waiting.

The shades go up and there she is, the way he first spotted her, in her pink bra and slip.

He tugs the cell phone from his pocket and is about to call her when she leans out the window—and waves.

What?

He pulls back, a reflex, drops his phone, which clatters along the hard wood floor. When he picks it up the screen is cracked.

"Fuck!"

The girl waves again, calls out "Come over," at least he thinks so though he can't believe it, her words drowning in the city's early evening drone.

Had she known he was watching all along?

He stands in the middle of his dark room, clutching his broken cell phone trying to make sense of it. Then he dares a few steps closer to the window and sees she is waving to someone else, someone just . . . below him? *But who?*

He has to find out.

He squashes the cigar out, downs the rest of his Scotch.

Just outside her apartment building, he hovers, his brain hammering, body practically vibrating. But there's no one there.

Maybe they are already inside.

He presses the bell to her apartment and she buzzes him in, no words exchanged.

He takes the stairs to the fifth floor two at a time, out of breath, and is about to knock on her door—he wants to pound on it, scream her name, smack her, finally do all the things that he has wanted, planned to do to her—then notices the door is slightly ajar, and he hears voices from inside.

He pushes the door open, takes a few tentative steps in, murderous thoughts careening through his brain—he will kill her and whomever she is with.

The foyer is empty. Voices coming from the living room, canned, electric.

The television set.

A news show. Blue light cast into the living room, which slowly comes into focus. Throw pillows on the floor. An upended chair. Rug bunched up as if there has been a struggle. His normally quiescent heart beats faster.

Spots on the tan linoleum floor, a trail that he follows into the bedroom where they become streaks. A pool of blood on the crumpled white sheets beside her bed. More blood on the naked mattress. He spies half of her pink bra beside the bloodstained sheets, the other half across the room, along with her familiar pink slip, which is torn and clotted with blood.

He swallows hard, the taste of cigar gone acrid and foul in his dry mouth, his body pulsing to the sound of sirens that he did not hear a moment ago, but they are close.

Blood is pumping into his neck, his face, he can feel it bloom in his cheeks, hot. He spins in one direction than the other, spies the curtains in her bedroom window billowing and makes a dash for the fire escape. *But why?* He's done nothing.

He's halfway out the window when the police burst into the room, guns drawn, shouting for him to stop.

Why are they here? How did they know?

The interrogation room is airless but frigid. How long has he been here? He has lost track of time. They have given him three or four cups of black coffee and his bladder is aching but when he asks to use the bathroom they act as if they haven't heard him.

One detective after another asking the same questions, making the same inane statements.

Did you know the girl?

Where is she now?

What have you done with her?

It's hours before he gets his one phone call.

His lawyer, Rich Lowenthal, whom he has known since college, never a friend, he has none really, but someone he trusts, stares at him, sighs, laces his hands across pinstripes straining at his belly.

"What have you told them?"

"Nothing."

"Good." Lowenthal leans in closer, whispers, "But you can tell me. The girl, who is she? What was she—to you?"

"She was—" He thinks a minute. "Nothing. I hardly knew her. We'd gone out a couple of times, that's all."

Lowenthal sits back. "You don't have to tell me, I'll defend you no matter what, but—"

"There's nothing to tell."

And there isn't, is there? He didn't do anything, except watch her. He's committed no crime. Unless stripping young women of everything, reducing them to nothing but sniveling needy wretches is a crime, and he doesn't think so. They all agreed, at first, before they were broken, too broken to fight back. More than one of them professed love, didn't they?

He tries to picture the girls and two or three come to mind, an image of the last one, Laura or Lauren, the one before this girl, flashes through his mind—sobbing, begging him to stop, to love her—then fades.

"You two have a fight that got out of control?" Lowenthal asks. "You can tell me."

"You sound like the cops."

Lowenthal sighs. "They say they've got stuff."

"*Stuff?*" For a moment he thinks his lawyer is a moron, like the rest of them, like everyone.

"Your fingerprints, for one, are all over the apartment."

"Well, sure, I've been there before, once—" *No, more than once.* Many times with the last one, but with this one, only once. "Once," he says again.

"Okay. Fine. But they found a used condom in the trash. It's with their tech team. Tell me it is not going to have *your* semen in it."

He swallows hard. "So what if we had sex. It's not like I killed her!"

"Easy there, buddy. No one says you did. And there's no body, not yet, so that's in your favor."

He feels his face flush, a rash inching up his neck. "This is insane. I didn't *do* anything!"

Lowenthal sucks his lip. "They say there are pictures of you on her cell phone."

"Are there? So what?"

"And she's written things."

"What—*things?*"

"They wouldn't tell me, not exactly, but enough. The rest they're saving for the DA. Apparently she made notes in her phone that say she was afraid for her life, afraid of *you*, that she found out you'd been watching her from your window and—"

"But I—"

"Your windows face hers, right?"

"Yes, but—"

"She's written that you watched her, stalked her, fooled her for a while before you handcuffed her, started threatening to kill her."

"I never—It wasn't like that."

Though it was, wasn't it? With the *others*. But not with her. He never got past watching her.

Lowenthal sighs, says, "If I'd known, I would have stopped them from searching your apartment. They've found handcuffs. And a knife. And they say there's blood on the knife. Also with the lab."

He stares at his lawyer until the man's features blur and he sees her, the pink lady, sucking on her cut finger. *I snagged it on my zipper.*

"She's from Salina," he says. "Kansas."

"And?"

"You have to find her."

"In Kansas?"

"I don't know? Maybe. I—I think she set me up."

"Why?"

He has no idea. He's not even sure it's true. "Somebody else had to have been there, in her apartment. She was waving to someone from her window. I saw her."

"When was this?"

"Just before, before I came over and found . . ."

"So you *were* watching her?"

One of the detectives comes back into the room holding a plastic evidence bag. Inside it, his Swiss Army knife.

She pictures the pink bra and slip, not sure why she chose them except they seemed sweet and innocent and good for the part. She remembers tearing the bra in half, rending the slip, dripping them with blood. She will never tell her sister about that, about any of it. She's not sure Lauren could take it, or would even have wanted her to do it. Dear sweet Lauren, who is broken, medicated. Her little sister, whom she adores, and would do anything to protect. Too late for protecting her, but revenge, there's always time for revenge.

She feels Lauren's sharp shoulder blades when she hugs her, pulls back to see her sister's pretty eyes, glazed.

"How many pills have you taken today, honey?"

"Pills?" Lauren shakes her head in slow motion. It has been two months since she got out of the hospital, and she seems no better, though the scars on her arms are fading, along with the ones on her belly and legs, the cuts *he* made, though the ones inside, the psychological ones, will take longer to heal.

"I don't remember," Lauren says.

"You can't take that many pills, honey. It's dangerous."

Lauren's glazed eyes land on her sister's bandaged wrist. "What . . . happened?"

"Oh, this? No big thing. A scratch, is all." She touches the bandage, feels the wound throb beneath her fingertips, remembers how she slid the razor across her wrist, couldn't believe how much blood there was, though she'd hoped there would be, close to fainting by the time she'd stopped dabbing it on the sheets and mattress, and how much gauze she'd needed to wrap it. Nothing like the tiny prick she'd made on her thumb with his knife, and the way she'd smeared her blood along the blade before closing it and putting it back in his pocket.

"Where did you . . . go?" Lauren asks.

"I had some business to take care of, but I'm back now. And Maria took good care of you, didn't she?" She smiles at the Mexican girl she's hired to take care of her sister while she was gone, the same girl who helped her buy a house, who will go with them when they leave.

"I have packed all of Miss Lauren's things," Maria says.

"Where . . . are we going?" Lauren asks, her words slurred by drugs.

"Somewhere safe," she says.

For a moment Lauren's eyes focus and blaze, her hands splay out in front of her as if fighting an invisible attacker. "No! No! Stop!"

She takes hold of Lauren's hands gently. "It's okay, honey. You're safe. Everything's been taken care of."

Lauren quiets, leans into her big sister, who has always looked out for her.

The big sister who knows they will soon be coming to talk to Lauren, who had lived in that apartment, whose name is on a lease somewhere.

But her name, her name is nowhere.

So let them come. They will be gone by then, in the house in Puerto Morelos, bought under neither one's name, waiting for them. It is a small sacrifice to make for her sister, and she has always liked Mexico.

"Everything will be okay," she says, stroking Lauren's hair.

She's knows it's hard to convict without a body, without a real girl they can find and identify. But she also knows that juries have convicted on less, and either way he will be under investigation for a very long time, that he will be watched.

JUSTIN SCOTT *is the author of thirty-four thrillers, mysteries and sea stories including* The Man Who Loved The Normandie, Rampage, *and* The Shipkiller, *which the International Thriller Writers lists in* Thrillers: 100 Must-Reads.

*He writes the Ben Abbott detective series set in small-town Connecticut (*HardScape, StoneDust, FrostLine, McMansion, *and* Mausoleum*), and collaborates with Clive Cussler on the Isaac Bell detective adventure series.*

The Mystery Writers of America nominated him for Edgar Allan Poe awards for Best First Novel and Best Short Story. He is a member of the Authors League, The Players, and the Adams Round Table.

*Paul Garrison is his main pen name, under which he writes modern sea stories (*Fire and Ice, Red Sky at Morning, Buried at Sea, Sea Hunter, *and* The Ripple Effect*) and thrillers based on a Robert Ludlum character (*The Janson Command, The Janson Option*).*

Born in Manhattan, Scott grew up on Long Island's Great South Bay in a family of professional writers. His father, A. Leslie Scott, wrote Westerns and poetry. His mother, Lily K. Scott, wrote novels and short stories for slicks and pulps. His sister, Alison Scott Skelton, is a novelist, as was her late husband, C. L. Skelton. Scott holds bachelor's and master's degrees in history, and before becoming a writer, drove boats and trucks, built Fire Island beach houses, edited an electronic engineering journal, and tended bar in a Hell's Kitchen saloon.

Scott lives in Connecticut with his wife, filmmaker Amber Edwards.

A Woman in the Sun, 1961

A WOMAN IN THE SUN

BY JUSTIN SCOTT

C ould she change his mind? Four steps to the open window, lean out
and call, "Don't."

Or walk to the window and call, "Go ahead, do it. Good luck."

Or stand here and do nothing.

He had left her his last cigarette. She had talked him into leaving the
gun and he had kept his word. It was still on the night table, wrapped
in one of her stockings. She had the time of the cigarette to make up her
mind. More time, if she didn't smoke it. Let it smoulder.

She glanced at herself in the cheval mirror.

A naked woman smoked a cigarette in the morning sun. She stood
beside a single bed. Her high-heels were under it. She was too tall for the
bed. Her feet had pushed the blanket loose, stuck out and got cold. He
was taller and had spent some of the night sitting up in the armchair.

"You stand like a dancer," he told her.

"No, I don't. I'm a tennis player. Where do you think I got these legs?"

Strong as a man's, muscled like a man's.

That got a grin out of him, and the cloud drifted from his face for a moment.

"Amateur or pro?"

She could have said, Where do you think I got these breasts, up-turned like a girl's. Years of sharpening her game had saved them from gravity, cinched for day and night practice since she budded at twelve. Or she could have said, "Pro," and left it at that. But it turned into a night for talking.

"When you lose every match in the season, you're not a pro."

"Did you win before your losing streak?"

"Yes, I did."

"So what's different? You're too young to be getting old. What's happened?"

Good question.

She played so little this season she lost her tan and her hair was darker, a natural color she hadn't seen in years. "I miss the sun. I miss being outdoors . . . I played yesterday, first time in a month." A test. Amazing after so long off, her timing was still dead-on, footwork like lightning, and she hit harder than ever. The skills were there. But still not the heart to win. "My coach died," she said. "My father."

She leaned forward and caught the mirror at an angle that reflected the night table, the gun on it, and her other stocking tossed over the lampshade. One last night to remember, he had asked in the bar, like a soldier shipping out to war.

"And next time I walk in here, you'll be bragging to the bartender."

"Dead men don't talk."

"Yeah, until you change your mind."

"I am not changing my mind."

She believed him and got the idea in her head to change it for him.

She couldn't blame the booze. She had sipped from an endless Seven and Seven, a glass that seemed to last all night. They talked. He nursed a beer in the silences. The bartender poured him a second at one point. He barely touched it.

"What if your last night is so memorable you want to do it again?"

"We'll have all night. I'm not dying in the dark."

"I mean again the next night."

"I'm just looking for a good-bye to remember."

"Or painting an elaborate scheme to get me into bed. Walk out the next morning, don't follow through, and leave me wondering why did I fall for it."

"I will leave you knowing you did me a great kindness that I will remember for eternity."

For some reason that made her laugh. He laughed too, and the cloud lifted and they stepped out into the warm night and kissed in the parking lot.

"I told you I'd get a smile out of you."

"I said that, not you."

"You said it, I thought it."

"Last chance to laugh."

"Laughs don't count. They're less than a smile. You can't help a laugh. You have to want to smile."

She asked, "Isn't suicide a sin?"

"Only for Catholics."

"I can't remember what it is for Protestants."

"Character flaw."

She liked that enough to leave her car and climb on his motorcycle.

He had been vague about whose house this was. It hadn't mattered. They had the place to themselves.

She heard the screen door bang. He wasn't on her cigarette clock.

"Tell me again why you want to kill yourself."

"I already told you, it's nobody's business."

"When did you get the idea?" She had no clue how the question had formed in her head but a change in his expression told her she had asked the right one. He thought for a while.

"Right when I sold my car and bought the bike."

"Before or during?"

Again he thought. "During. I asked why am I doing this and the answer came up, because I'm ready to die."

"Did you ask yourself why?"

"Sure," he said quickly, then shook his head. "No. That's not true. I didn't ask. I just knew it."

"Knew what?" she asked, sharper than she intended.

"Knew it was right—listen, there's no big story here."

"I don't believe you. You're making this up. When did you first get in the idea? First time."

"I was in country."

"In country? What do you mean? What country?"

"It's an expression. It means out in the boondocks. Up river. In the jungle. Do you know where Viet Nam is?"

"It used to be French Indochina. I went out with a French player who grew up there. His father was a diplomat."

"Okay, that's where I was in country when I got the idea."

"Did you ask why?"

"Didn't have to. It was such a relief . . . Do you remember, I told you I was a helicopter mechanic?"

"Yeah."

"They dropped me in country to fix a machine that went down in the jungle. In a grove of bamboo. I kept thinking, bamboo is what they torture people with."

"Who?"

"I knew a guy they captured."

"Who are your talking about?"

"Viet Minh. The rebels. Viet Cong. Scared the hell out of me. I'm thinking if they find me before I can fix this thing and fly it out of here, they'll torture me."

"Were you all alone?"

"All by my lonesome. We were thin on the ground. They couldn't spare more than one."

"Which they?"

"United States Marines."

"You were expected to fix the helicopter and fly it out of there with no protection?"

"Navy Colt. That one." He nodded at the gun on the night table. "I was scared, paralyzed. Jumping at every sound—of which there are many in the jungle. Then suddenly it hit me."

"What?"

"This great feeling: *I don't have to be here. I can get away anytime I want.*"

"How could you get away?"

"The gun. The gun was for me."

"But you're not there, now."

"It became a habit."

She turned to the mirror again. She looked annoyed with herself. Wondered why. I don't want to be sour. What did I do? What do I do next? The mirror had reflected both of them in the lamplight. He'd knelt beside the bed and laid her legs on his shoulders.

He said, "Unless you want to come with me."

"I don't think so."

He lit his last cigarette, dragged deeply, and gave her the rest, the tip dry as bone.

Out the bedroom door, down the hall.

He pushed through the screen door.

His bike was shimmering in the sun. Had anything changed? Woman with troubles? Guy with troubles picks up a woman with troubles? He had hoped to spend the night with a woman. Got what he hoped for. A good-bye. A very fine good bye. Troubles aside, a fine, fine good-bye.

Great pickup line. Helluva pickup line.

Have to use it again if he came back in another life.

She had talked him into leaving the gun and he had kept his word. It was still on the night table.

She had the time of the cigarette to make up her mind. If she didn't smoke it, if she just let it smoulder, she'd have more time. She heard the screen door bang.

She stepped through the pool of sunlight. At the window, the sun was blinding. She saw him in silhouette, black against the light. He was climbing onto his motorcycle. He didn't need the gun, had never planned to use it. The bike was foolproof. He couldn't accidently miss. Eighty miles an hour into a tree, eternity guaranteed.

If she didn't speak before he started the engine he wouldn't hear her.

He stood up on the kick-starter.

"Do you really want me to come with you?" she called.

"Only if you want to."

"All right," she said. "I'll give it a try."

She stepped into her heels, swung her strong legs over the window sill, and jumped lightly to the sand.

He watched her walking toward him, a smile forming, liking what he saw, liking how she looked, liking her nerve.

"You could catch a cold dressed like that."

"The sun's warm."

LAWRENCE BLOCK *has written a surfeit of novels and short stories, along with half a dozen books for writers. Over the years, he has somehow contrived to edit a dozen anthologies, most recently* Dark City Lights. *Edward Hopper has been a favorite painter of his for decades, and is name-checked three or four times in his fiction, particularly in the books about Keller, the Urban Lonely Guy of assassins. The premise for* In Sunlight or in Shadow, *like so many ideas, came to him while he was trying to think of something else, and he found it irresistible.*

Automat, 1927

Oil on canvas, 36 × 28 ⅛ in. (91.4 × 71.4 cm). Des Moines Art Center, Permanent
Collections; Purchased with funds from the Edmundson Art Foundation, Inc., 1958.2.
Photo Credit: Rich Sanders, Des Moines, IA.

AUTUMN AT THE AUTOMAT

BY LAWRENCE BLOCK

T he hat made a difference.

If you chose your clothes carefully, if you dressed a little more styl-
ishly than the venue demanded, you could feel good about yourself.
When you walked into the Forty-second Street cafeteria, the hat and coat
announced that you were a lady. Perhaps you preferred their coffee to what
they served at Longchamps. Or maybe it was the bean soup, as good as
you could get at Delmonico's.

Certainly it wasn't abject need that led you to the cashier's window at
Horn & Hardart. No one watching you dip into an alligator handbag for
a dollar bill could think so for a minute.

The nickels came back, four groups of five. No need to count them,
because the cashier did this and nothing else all day long, taking dollars,
dispensing nickels. This was the Automat, and the poor girl was the next
thing to an Automaton.

You took your nickels and assembled your meal. You chose a dish, put your nickels in the slot, turned the handle, opened the little window, and retrieved your prize. A single nickel got you a cup of coffee. Three more bought a bowl of the legendary bean soup, and another secured a little plate holding a seeded roll and a pat of butter.

You carried your tray to the counter, moving very deliberately, positioning yourself in front of the compartmented metal tray of silverware.

The moment you'd walked through the door you knew which table you wanted. Of course someone could have taken it, but no one did. Now, after a long moment, you carried your tray to it.

She ate slowly, savoring each spoonful of the bean soup, glad she'd decided against making do with a cup for the sake of saving a nickel. Not that she hadn't considered it. A nickel was nothing much, but if she saved a nickel twice a day, why, that came to three dollars a month. More, really. Thirty-six dollars and fifty cents a year, and that *was* something.

Ah, but she couldn't scrimp. Well, she could in fact, she had to, but not when it came to nourishing herself. What was that expression Alfred had used?

Kishke gelt. Belly money, money saved by cheating one's stomach. She could hear him speak the words, could see the curl of his lip.

Better, surely, to spend the extra nickel.

Not for fear of Alfred's contempt. He was beyond knowing or caring what she ate or what it cost her.

Unless, as she alternately hoped and feared, it didn't all stop with the end of life. Suppose that fine mind, that keen intelligence, that wry humor, suppose it had survived on some plane of existence even when all the rest of him had gone into the ground.

She didn't really believe it, but sometimes it pleased her to entertain the notion. She'd even talk to him, sometimes aloud but more often in the privacy of her mind. There was little she hadn't been able to share with him in life, and now his death had washed away what few conversational inhibitions she'd had. She could tell him anything now, and when it pleased her she could invent answers for him and fancy she heard them.

Sometimes they came so swiftly, and with such unsparing candor, that she had to wonder at their source. Was she making them up? Or was he no less a presence in her life for having left it?

Perhaps he hovered just out of sight, a disembodied guardian angel. Watching over her, taking care of her.

And no sooner did she have the thought than she heard the reply. *Watching is as far as it goes, Liebchen. When it comes to taking care, you're on your own.*

She broke the roll in two, spread butter on it with the little knife. Put the buttered roll on the plate, took up the spoon, took a spoonful of soup. Then another, and then a bite of the roll.

She ate slowly, using the time to scan the room. Just over half the tables were occupied. Two women here, two men there. A man and woman who looked to be married, and another pair, at once animated but awkward with each other, who she guessed were on a first or second date.

She might have amused herself by making up a story about them, but let her attention pass them by.

The other tables held solitary diners, more men than women, and most of them with newspapers. Better to be here than outside, as the city slipped deeper into autumn and the wind blew off the Hudson. Drink a cup of coffee, read the *News* or the *Mirror,* pass the time . . .

The manager wore a suit.

So did most of the male patrons, but his looked to be of better quality, and more recently pressed. His shirt was white, his necktie of a muted color she couldn't identify from across the room.

She watched him out of the corner of her eye.

Alfred had taught her to do this. Your eyes looked straight in front of you, and you didn't move them around to study the object of your interest. Instead you used your mind, telling it to pay attention to something on the periphery of your vision.

It took practice, but she'd had plenty of that. She remembered a lesson in Penn Station, across from the Left Luggage window. While she kept her eyes trained on the man checking his suitcase, Alfred had quizzed her on passengers queuing for the Philadelphia train. She described them in turn and glowed when he praised her.

The manager, she noted now, had a small, thin-lipped mouth. His wing-tip shoes were brown, and buffed to a high polish. And, even as she observed him without looking at him, he studied his patrons in quite the opposite manner, his gaze moving deliberately, aggressively, from one table to the next. It seemed to her that some of her fellow diners could feel it when he stared at them, shifting uncomfortably without consciously knowing why.

She had prepared herself, but when his eyes found her she couldn't keep from drawing a breath, barely resisting the impulse to swing her eyes toward his. Her face darkened, she could feel it change expression, and when she reached for her coffee cup she could feel the tremor in her hand.

There he stood, beside the door to the kitchen, his hands clasped behind his back, his visage stern. There he stood, observing her directly while she observed him as she'd been taught.

There he was. With just a little effort, she managed to take a sip of coffee without spilling any of it. Then she returned the cup to the saucer and took another breath.

And what did she suppose he had seen?

She thought of a half-remembered poem, one they'd read in English class. Something about wishing for the power to see oneself as one was seen by others. But what was the poem and who was its author?

What the restaurant manager would have seen, she thought, was a small and unobtrusive woman of a certain age, wearing good clothes that were themselves of a certain age. A decent hat that had largely lost its shape, an Arnold Constable coat, worn at the cuffs, with one of its original bone buttons replaced with another that didn't quite match.

Good shoes, plain black pumps. Her alligator bag. Both well crafted of good leather, both purchased from good Fifth Avenue shops.

And both showing their age.

As indeed was she, like everything she owned.

What would he have seen? The very picture of shabby gentility, she thought, and while she could not quite embrace the label, neither could she take issue with it. If her garments were shabby, they nevertheless announced unequivocally that their owner was genteel.

A man at the table immediately to her right—dark suit, gray fedora, napkin tucked into his collar to shield his tie—was alternating between sips of his coffee and forkfuls of his dessert, which looked to be apple crisp. She'd given no thought to dessert, and now a glimpse of it ignited the desire. She couldn't remember the last time she'd had their apple crisp, but she remembered how it tasted, a perfect balance of tart and sweet, the crisp part all sugary and crunchy.

They didn't always have apple crisp, which argued for her having a portion now, while it was available. It wouldn't cost her more than three nickels, four at the most, and she still had fifteen of the twenty nickels the cashier had supplied. All she had to do was walk to the dessert section at the far right and claim her prize.

No.

No, because her cup of coffee was almost gone, and she'd want a fresh cup to accompany her dessert. And that would only cost a single nickel more, and she could afford that even as she could afford the dessert itself, but even so the answer was—

No.

The word again, in Alfred's voice this time.

You are stalling, Knuddelmaus. It's not the pleasure of the sweet that lures you. It's the desire to postpone that which you fear.

She had to smile. If some corner of her own imagination was supplying Alfred's dialogue, it was doing so with great skill. *Knuddelmaus* had been one of his pet names for her, but he had used it infrequently, and it hadn't crossed her conscious mind in ages. Yet there it was, in his voice, bracketed with English words full of the flavor of the Ku'damm.

You know me too well, she said, speaking the words only in her mind. And she waited for what he might say next, but nothing more came. He was done for now.

Well, he'd said what he had to say. And he was right, wasn't he?

Robert Burns, she thought. A Scotsman, writing in dialect sure to baffle high school students, and she'd lost the rest of the poem but the one couplet had come back to her:

O wad some Power the giftie gie us
To see oursels as ithers see us!

But really, she wondered, would anyone in her right mind really want such a power?

The man with the gray fedora put down his fork and freed his napkin from his collar, using it to wipe the crumbs of his apple crisp from his lips. He picked up his coffee cup, found it empty, and moved to push back his chair.

But then he changed his mind and returned to his newspaper.

She fancied she could read his mind. The restaurant was not full, and no one was waiting for his table. He'd given them quite enough money—for his chicken pot pie and his coffee and his apple crisp—to keep his table as long as he wanted it. They didn't rush you here, they seemed to recognize that they were selling not just food but shelter as well, and it was warm here and cold outside, and it's not as though anyone were waiting for him in his little room.

Or for her in hers. She lived a ten-minute walk away, in a residential hotel on East Twenty-eighth Street. Her room was tiny, but still a good value at five dollars a week, twenty dollars a month. She'd long ago positioned a doily on the nightstand to hide the cigarette burn that was a legacy of a previous tenant, and hung framed illustrations from magazines to cover the worst water stains on the walls. There was a carpet on the floor, sound if threadbare, and downstairs the lobby furniture might have seen better days, but didn't that make it a good match for the residents?

Shabby genteel.

Two tables away, a woman about her age spooned sugar into her half-finished cup of coffee.

Free nourishment, she thought. The sugar bowl was on the table and you could make your coffee as sweet as you wished. The manager, who watched everything, no doubt registered every spoonful, but didn't seem to object.

When she'd first begun drinking coffee, she took plenty of cream and sugar. Alfred had changed that, teaching her to take it black and unsweetened, and now that was the only way she could drink it.

Not that the man had lacked a sweet tooth. He'd had a favorite place in Yorkville with pastries he proclaimed the equal of Vienna's Café Demel, and paired his Punschkrapfen or Linzer torte with strong black coffee.

You must have the contrast, Liebchen. The bitter with the sweet. One taste strengthens the other. At the table as in the world.

His words were strongly accented now. *Vun taste strengsens ze uzzer.* When she'd met him he was new in the country, but even then his English held just a trace of Middle Europe, and within a year or two he'd polished away the last of it. He'd allowed it to return only when it was just the two of them, as if she alone was permitted to hear where he'd come from.

And it was when he talked about the past, about times in Berlin and Vienna, that it was strongest.

She took a last sip of coffee. It wasn't the equal to the strong dark brew he'd taught her to prefer, but it was certainly more than acceptable.

Did she want another cup?

Without shifting her gaze, she allowed herself another visual scan of the room, saw the manager look at her and then away, studied the woman whom she'd seen adding sugar to her coffee.

A woman dressed much as she was dressed, with a decent hat and a well-cut dove gray coat, neither of them new. A woman whose hair was graying and whose forehead showed worry lines, but whose mouth was still full-lipped and generous.

Now the woman was looking at her, studying her without knowing she was being studied in return.

Pick an ally, Schatzi. They come in handy.

She let her eyes move to meet the woman's, noted her embarrassment at the contact, and eased it with a smile. The woman smiled back, then turned her attention to her coffee cup. And, contact established, she picked up her own cup. It was empty, but no one could know that, and she took a little sip of nothing at all.

You are stalling, Knuddelmaus.

Well, yes, she was. It was warm in here and cold out there, but it would only grow colder as afternoon edged into evening. It wasn't the wind or the air temperature that made her reluctant to leave her table.

It was the fourth of the month, and her rent had been due on the first. She'd been late before, and knew that nobody would say anything until she was a week overdue. So there'd be a reminder in three days, a gentle advisory delivered with a gentle smile, directing her attention to what was surely an oversight.

She didn't know what the next step would be, or when it would come. So far that single reminder had achieved the desired effect, and she'd found the money and paid the monthly rental a day after it had been requested.

That time, she'd pawned a bracelet. Three stones, carnelian and lapis and citrine, half-round oval cabochons set in yellow gold. Thinking of it now, she looked down at her bare wrist.

It had been a gift of Alfred's, but that had been true of every piece of jewelry she'd owned. The bracelet was evidently her favorite, as it had been the last to make the trip to the pawnshop. She'd told herself she'd redeem it when the opportunity presented itself. She went on believing this until the day she sold the pawn ticket.

And by then she'd grown accustomed to no longer owning the bracelet, so the pain was muted.

We get used to things, Liebchen. A man can get used to hanging.

Could anyone speak those lines convincingly other than with the inflection of a Berliner?

And you are still stalling.

She put her handbag on the table, then was taken by a fit of coughing. She put her napkin to her lips, took a breath, coughed again.

She didn't look, but knew people were glancing in her direction.

She took a breath, managed not to cough. She was still holding her napkin, and now she picked up each of her utensils in turn, the soup spoon, the coffee spoon, the fork, the butter knife. She wiped them all thoroughly and placed each of them in her handbag. And fastened the clasp.

Now she did look around, and let something show on her face.

She got to her feet. Not for the first time, she felt a touch of dizziness upon standing. She put a hand on the table for support, and the dizziness subsided, as it always did. She drew a breath, turned, and walked toward the door.

She moved at a measured pace, deliberately, neither hurrying nor slowing. This Automat, unlike the one closer to her hotel, had a brass-trimmed revolving door, and she paused to let a new patron enter the restaurant. She thought about the desk clerk at her hotel, and the twenty dollars. Her purse held a five-dollar bill and two singles, along with those fifteen nickels, so she could pay a week's rent and have a few days to find the rest, and—

"Oh, I don't think so. Stop right there, ma'am."

She extended a foot toward the revolving door, and now a hand fastened on her upper arm. She spun around, and there he was, the thin-lipped manager.

"Bold as brass," he said. "By God, you're not the first person to walk off with the odd spoon, but you took the lot, didn't you? And polished them while you were at it."

"How dare you!"

"I'll just take that," he said, and took hold of her handbag.

"No!"

Now there were three hands gripping the alligator bag, one of his and two of her own. "How dare you!" she said again, louder this time, knowing that everyone in the restaurant was looking at the two of them. Well, let them look.

"You're not going anywhere," he told her. "By God, I was just going to take back what you stole, but you've got an attitude that's as bad as your thieving." He called over his shoulder: "Jimmy, call the precinct, tell the guy on the desk to send over a couple of boys." His eyes glinted—oh, he was enjoying this—and his words washed over her as he told her he would make an example of her, that a night or two in jail would give her more of a sense of private property.

"Now," he said, "are you gonna open that bag, or do we wait for the cops?"

There were two policemen, one a good ten years older than the other, though both looked young to her. And it was clear that neither of them wanted to be there, enlisted to punish a woman for stealing tableware from a cafeteria.

It was the elder of the two who told her, almost apologetically, that she'd have to open the bag.

"Certainly," she said, and worked the clasp, and took out the knife and the fork and both spoons. The policemen looked on with no change in expression, but the manager knew what he was seeing, and her heart quickened at the look on his face.

"I like the food at this restaurant," she said, "and the people who dine here are decent, and the chairs are comfortable enough. But as for your spoons and forks, I don't care for the way they feel in my hands or in my mouth. I prefer my own. These were my mother's, they're hallmarked sterling silver, you can see her monogram—"

The apology came in a rush, and found her unrelenting. It would be the manager's pleasure to give her a due bill entitling her to thus and so many meals absolutely without charge, and—

"I'm sure nothing could induce me to come here ever again."

Well, he was terribly sorry, and fortunately no actual harm had been done, so—

"You've humiliated me in front of a room full of people. You laid hands on me, you grabbed my arm, you tried to grab my purse." She glanced around. "Did you see what this man did?"

Several patrons nodded, including the woman who'd spooned all that sugar into her coffee.

More words of apology, but she cut right through them. "My nephew is an attorney. I think I should call him."

Something changed in the manager's face. "Why don't we go to my office," he suggested. "I'm sure we can work this out."

When she got back to her hotel, the first thing she did was pay her rent, the month that was overdue and the next two in advance.

Upstairs in her room, she took the knife and fork and spoons and returned them to her dresser drawer. They were part of a set, all monogrammed with a capital J, but they had not been her mother's.

Nor were they sterling. Had they been, she'd have contrived to sell them. But they were decent silver plate, and while she did not customarily carry them around with her, they served admirably when she warmed up a can of baked beans on her hotplate.

And they'd served admirably today.

In his office, the manager had tried to buy his way out with a hundred dollars, and doubled it quickly when it was apparent he'd insulted her. A deep breath followed by a firm shake of her head had coaxed another hundred out of him, and she weighed that, hovering on the brink of accepting it, only to sigh and wonder if she wouldn't be best advised to call her nephew after all.

His offer jumped from three hundred to five hundred, and she had the sense he might well go higher, but Alfred had impressed upon her the folly of wringing every nickel out of a situation. So she didn't jump at it, but thought for a long moment and gave in gracefully.

He had her sign something. She didn't hesitate, jotting down a name she'd used before, and he counted out the appointed sum in twenty-dollar bills.

Twenty-five of them.

Or ten thousand nickels, Liebchen. If you want to give the cashier a heart attack.

"But it went well," she told Alfred, speaking the words aloud in the little room. "I pulled it off, didn't I?"

The answer to that was clear enough not to require his stating it. She hung her hat on the peg, her coat in the closet. She sat on the edge of the bed and counted her money, then tucked away all but one of the twenties where no one would think to look for them.

Alfred had schooled her in hiding money, even as he'd taught her how to get hold of it.

"I couldn't be sure it would work," she said. "It came to me one day. I had a fork with one bent tine, and I thought how low-quality their cutlery was, and I could imagine a woman, oh, one who'd come down a peg or two over time, bringing her own silverware in her purse. And then I forgot about her, and then she came back to me, and—"

And one thing led to another. And it had worked splendidly, and the nervousness she'd felt had been appropriate to the role she'd been playing.

Now, seeing the incident from a distance, viewing it with Alfred's critical perspective, she could see ways to refine her performance, to make more certain the taking of the bait and the sinking of the hook.

Could she do it again? She wouldn't need to, not for quite a while. Her rent was paid through the end of the year, and the money she'd tucked away would keep her for that long and longer.

Of course she couldn't return to that particular Automat. There were others, including a perfectly nice one very near to her hotel, but did the chain's managers keep one another up to date? The man she'd dealt with, the man with the thin lips and the mean little eyes, had hardly covered himself with glory in their encounter, and you'd think he'd want to keep it to himself. But one never knew, and the less one left to chance—

Perhaps, for at least a while, she'd be well advised to take her custom elsewhere. There were many places nearby where the shabby genteel could dine decently at low cost. Childs, for example, had several restaurants, with a nice one nearby on Thirty-fourth Street, in the shadow of the Third Avenue El.

Or Schrafft's. The prices were a little higher there, and they drew a better class of customer, but she'd fit in well enough. And if one of them had the right sort of manager, she'd know what to do when her funds got low.

One had to adapt. She was too old to slip on a just-mopped floor at Gimbel's, too frail to stumble on an escalator, and there were all those routines Alfred had taught her, gambits you couldn't bring off without a partner.

Schrafft's, she decided. And she'd begin by scouting the one on West Twenty-third, in the heart of the Ladies' Mile.

Would they have apple crisp? She hoped so.

PERMISSIONS

All works by Edward Hopper (1882–1967) and oil on canvas unless otherwise noted. We gratefully acknowledge all those who gave permission for material to appear in this book. We have made every effort to trace and contact copyright holders. If an error or omission is brought to our notice we will be pleased to remedy the situation in future editions of this book. For further information, please contact the publisher.

Megan Abbott, "Girlie Show"
The Girlie Show, 1941 (p. 2)
32 × 38 in. (81.3 × 96.5 cm). Private collection/Bridgeman Images

Jill D. Block, "The Story of Caroline"
Summer Evening, 1947 (p. 22)
30 × 42 in. (76.2 × 106.7 cm). Private collection © Artepics/Alamy Stock Photo

Robert Olen Butler, "Soir Bleu"
Soir Bleu, 1914 (p. 40)
36 ⅛ × 71 ¹⁵/₁₆ in. (91.8 × 182.7 cm). Whitney Museum of American Art, New York; Josephine N. Hopper Bequest 70.1208 © Heirs of Josephine N. Hopper, licensed by Whitney Museum of American Art. Digital Image © Whitney Museum, NY

Lee Child, "The Truth About What Happened"
Hotel Lobby, 1943 (p. 52)
32 ¼ × 40 ¾ in. (81.9 × 103.5 cm). Indianapolis Museum of Art, William Ray Adams Memorial Collection, 47.4 © Edward Hopper

Nicholas Christopher, "Rooms by the Sea"
Rooms by the Sea, 1951 (p. 62)
29 ¼ × 40 in. (74.3 × 101.6 cm). Yale University Art Gallery, Bequest of Stephen Carlton Clark, B.A. 1903

Michael Connelly, "Nighthawks"
Nighthawks, 1942 (p. 80)
33 ⅛ × 60 in. (84.1 × 152.4 cm). Friends of American Art Collection, 1942.51, The Art Institute of Chicago

Jeffery Deaver, "Incident of 10 November"
Hotel by a Railroad, 1952 (p. 92)
31 ¼ × 40 ⅛ in. (79.4 × 101.9 cm). Hirshhorn Museum and Sculpture Garden, Smithsonian Institution; Gift of the Joseph H. Hirshhorn Foundation, 1966. Photography by Lee Stalsworth

Craig Ferguson, "Taking Care of Business"
South Truro Church, 1930 (p. 106)
29 × 43 in. (73.7 × 109.2 cm). Private collection

PERMISSIONS

Stephen King, "The Music Room"
Room in New York, 1932 (p. 118)
37 × 44 ½ in. (94 × 113 cm). Sheldon Museum of Art, University of Nebraska-Lincoln, Anna R. and Frank M. Hall Charitable Trust, H-166.1936. Photo © Sheldon Museum of Art

Joe R. Lansdale, "The Projectionist"
New York Movie, 1939 (p. 126)
32 ¼ × 40 ⅛ in. (81.9 × 101.9 cm). Given anonymously. The Museum of Modern Art, New York, NY. Digital Image © The Museum of Modern Art/Licensed by SCALA / Art Resource, NY

Gail Levin, "The Preacher Collects"
City Roofs, 1932 (p. 156)
29 × 36 in. (73.7 × 91.4 cm). Private collection

Warren Moore, "Office at Night"
Office at Night, 1940 (p. 168)
22 ³⁄₁₆ × 25 ⅛ in. (56.4 × 63.8 cm). Collection Walker Art Center, Minneapolis; Gift of the T.B. Walker Foundation, Gilbert M. Walker Fund, 1948

Joyce Carol Oates, "The Woman in the Window"
Eleven A.M., 1926 (p. 184)
28 ⅛ × 36 ⅛ in. (71.3 × 91.6 cm). Hirshhorn Museum and Sculpture Garden, Smithsonian Institution; Gift of the Joseph H. Hirshhorn Foundation, 1966. Photography by Cathy Carver

Kris Nelscott, "Still Life 1931"
Hotel Room, 1931 (p. 208)
60 × 65 ¼ in. (152.4 × 165.7 cm). Madrid, Museo Thyssen-Bornemisza. Inv. N.: 1977110. © 2016 Museo Thyssen-Bornemisza/Scala, Florence

Jonathan Santlofer, "Night Windows"
Night Windows, 1928 (p. 234)
29 × 34 in. (73.7 × 86.4 cm). Gift of John Hay Whitney. The Museum of Modern Art, New York. Digital Image © The Museum of Modern Art/Licensed by SCALA / Art Resource, NY

Justin Scott, A Woman in the Sun
A Woman in the Sun, 1961 (p. 256)
Oil on linen, 40 ⅛ × 60 ³⁄₁₆ in. (101.9 × 152.9 cm). Whitney Museum of American Art, New York; 50th Anniversary Gift of Mr. and Mrs. Albert Hackett in honor of Edith and Lloyd Goodrich 84.31 © Heirs of Josephine N. Hopper, licensed by Whitney Museum of American Art. Digital Image © Whitney Museum, NY

Lawrence Block, "Autumn at the Automat"
Automat, 1927 (p. 264)
36 × 28 ⅛ in. (91.4 × 71.4 cm). Des Moines Art Center, Permanent Collections; Purchased with funds from the Edmundson Art Foundation, Inc., 1958.2. Photo Credit: Rich Sanders, Des Moines, IA.